SADDLE UP
FOR MURDER

The Carson Stables Mystery series
by Leigh Hearon

Reining in Murder

Saddle Up for Murder

SADDLE UP
FOR MURDER

Leigh
Hearon

KENSINGTON BOOKS
http://www.kensingtonbooks.com

KENSINGTON BOOKS are published by

Kensington Publishing Corp.
119 West 40th Street
New York, NY 10018

All Kensington titles, imprints and distributed lines are available at special quantity discounts for bulk purchases for sales promotion, premiums, fund-raising, educational or institutional use. Special book excerpts or customized printings can also be created to fit specific needs. For details, write or phone the office of the Kensington Special Sales Manager. Kensington Publishing Corp., 119 West 40th Street, New York, NY 10018. Attn.: Special Sales Department. Phone: 1-800-221-2647.

Kensington and the K logo Reg. U.S. Pat. & TM Off.

ISBN-13: 978-1-4967-0035-3
ISBN-10: 1-4967-0035-X
First Kensington Mass Market Edition: November 2016

eISBN-13: 978-1-4967-0036-0
eISBN-10: 1-4967-0036-8
First Kensington Electronic Edition: November 2016

10 9 8 7 6 5 4 3 2 1

Printed in the United States of America

For Alan

PROLOGUE

TUESDAY, APRIL 26

Ashley Lawton dug into her jacket pocket and pulled out a key, a single strand of green yarn fluttering from the top. She turned to the woman beside her and said proudly, "Mrs. Carr lets me have my own. It's not strictly company policy, but she can't move around very well and it takes her a long time to get to the door."

Her companion nodded appreciatively. She was a willowy brunette dressed in an old-fashioned jumper. Ashley acknowledged her friend's tacit approval with a quick return nod and inserted the key into the lock in front of her. The knob turned, and she leaned inside, calling out, "Mrs. Carr? It's Ashley. I've brought a friend."

They stepped into a small vestibule and a tropical climate. Spring may have arrived on the Olympic Peninsula, but Mrs. Carr's comfort apparently required a higher temperature. Ashley rushed to the thermostat on the wall and peered at the setting.

"She must have forgotten to turn it down." Ashley gave a small, embarrassed laugh. "She gets cold a lot."

"How old did you say she was?" Ashley's friend was still standing by the door, hesitant to venture farther.

"She'll be ninety-six on her next birthday. And still has every one of her brain cells. She's amazing."

"Wow. I want to meet her."

"Right this way." Ashley walked through a hopelessly cluttered living room, picking up dog-eared magazines and crocheted blankets along the way and throwing them onto a sagging love seat. She navigated as someone who knew the house and the habits of its occupant.

"Mrs. Carr? I'm coming into your bedroom. It's ten o'clock. Time for your pills."

The two women walked down a hallway crowded with old family photos long faded from the passage of time.

Ashley pushed open the bedroom door. "Mrs. Carr?" Her friend stood on tiptoe to look over her.

Mrs. Carr's form was barely discernable in the large four-poster bed that took up most of the bedroom. The bed was piled high with comforters in a rainbow of colors. A reasonable person might wonder whether the woman was there at all.

"That's odd. Usually she's sitting up by now." Ashley walked quickly over to the side of the bed and lifted one comforter, then another. Mrs. Carr was now visible, at least from the neck up. But there was no vitality left in her face. Her wide-open eyes had sunk deep into the sockets, and the pallor of her skin was pasty white. Ashley tugged at the comforter, and a clawlike hand emerged, grasping the edge of the cloth, seeming to resist any attempt to take away her last bit of warmth.

"She's dead." Ashley's voice registered astonishment.

Behind her, her friend slid to the floor in a dead faint.

CHAPTER 1

MONDAY, MAY 2

A piercing shrick brought Annie Carson out of her reverie. Not to mention her rear firmly back down on her saddle.

She'd been standing in her stirrups to get the maximum view of her sheep pasture. It was a panoramic view   her mount was a 16-hand thoroughbred, which already put her more than five feet off the ground. The sight of seventy-five ewes and as many lambs in the grassy lea reminded Annie of a Constable painting she'd once seen in a museum. Even the billowing clouds overhead looked painted.

Now she wheeled Trooper around and nudged him forward. The horse took off at a hard canter, turning abruptly in response to Annie's rein onto the trailhead of an old logging road. She pulled the horse up short a few seconds later.

"Hannah! Thank god you're safe!"

"Shhhh!"

If Annie thought it odd that an eight-year-old who'd just issued an earsplitting scream was now telling her to be quiet, she didn't say so. Instead, she calmly walked her horse closer to Hannah's. Bess, fortunately, was not making any noise. She was munching grass, very quietly.

"What's going on?" Annie kept her voice neutral.

"I saw someone in the woods! A man! I think he had a gun."

Annie scanned the thick trees in front of her. It was early May, and the Pacific Northwest was in the full flower of spring. She saw nothing but a suffusion of ferns and undergrowth forming a luxuriant pillow against densely packed Douglas fir.

"What was the man doing?"

"Hiding! He was behind a tree. Then I saw him run to another one. I didn't scream until I saw his weapon."

Hannah's father ran a security business that included transporting Loomis trucks filled with cash from local businesses. She was well acquainted with different caliber handguns and shotguns.

"What kind of weapon?"

"I'm not sure. I think it was a pistol. But I screamed, and then he ran away back there." Hannah pointed with her left arm into the woods.

"Why did you scream? Were you afraid?"

"Just a little. But I thought if I screamed, he'd go away. If he started to shoot at me, I figured I'd just gallop away. Maybe."

Annie was sure Hannah had every intention of galloping away. The problem was Bess, Annie's twenty-five-year-old Morgan who thought indulging in anything beyond a stately walk did not befit her dignified age.

"What did Bess do when you screamed?"

"Grazed."

So much for Hannah's fast getaway from the bad guy.

But Annie was more concerned about Hannah's near encounter than she let on to her little companion.

The sound of shifting leaves caught both riders unawares. They started and whipped around in their saddles. Hannah clapped her hands over her mouth to make sure another scream wasn't forthcoming. From the dark forest floor, a fawn emerged, almost perfectly camouflaged against the lush, green backdrop. Walking carefully on its long and spindly legs, it wended its way through the thicket and out of sight. Hannah and Annie remained motionless on their saddles.

"A fawn!" breathed Hannah. "A baby deer! I thought I was going to jump out of my saddle, Annie, but I didn't! Even Bess jumped. A little."

"That's because you're nice and relaxed in your seat, Hannah," Annie replied. "So when something like this happens, it's easy to stay balanced."

Annie was a stickler who told all of her riding students not to grip the horse's ribs with their knees. It didn't help their equilibrium, and it impacted their horse's ability to move freely.

Hannah looked thoughtfully at Annie and nodded. "Do you think the fawn will find its mother?"

"I'm sure it will. The fawn isn't going to move far just because a couple of horses are passing through. I wouldn't be surprised if we saw a deer clearing in the next hundred feet."

"Let's go find it!"

"Nice try, kiddo. Fawns only want to be found by their mommies. Besides, hot chocolate awaits us."

This was the traditional ending to Hannah's riding lesson, and afterward Annie had driven the little girl to her doorstep. Usually, she let Hannah walk back to her home through a well-worn path; after all, the Clare household was only a quarter mile away. But now Annie recalled recent news stories of young children who'd been abducted just a short distance from their own homes, and she had no intention of taking unnecessary chances.

Taking care of her own safety was just as important. When Annie had opened Carson Stables, her training facility for equines, every man she'd encountered had flat out told her that a single woman who weighed a mere 125 pounds would never be able to handle the workload, let alone adequately protect herself from things that went bump in the night, both animal and human.

"Don't expect me to come to your rescue every time you hear a scary noise in the woods," Suwana County Sheriff Dan Stetson had grumbled after she'd dismissed his advice for the tenth time.

Annie had merely laughed. "I won't," was her breezy reply.

That conversation had occurred fifteen years ago. In the intervening time, she'd proven Dan and everyone else wrong. Not one of her detractors knew how hard she worked to make sure no harm came to her or her animals. She'd learned that the best way to keep danger from coming to her doorstep was to meet it head-on.

After dropping off Hannah, she parked her F-250 near the stables and called for Trooper, now contently munching on a flake of orchard grass in the paddock. It was time to find out exactly who had been lurking off the old logging road. If the man Hannah had seen was simply taking a shortcut through her property, he'd be long gone by now. She certainly hoped so.

As usual, the thoroughbred was up for another trail ride. She slipped a hackamore over his nose and, using a rail post, hopped on his back, deciding to eschew his saddle on this trip. At forty-three, Annie was less enthused about playing leapfrog over a horse's back to mount as she'd been in her twenties, but the joy of riding on a horse, sans saddle, still held a certain thrill. The connection with the animal was undeniable. After whistling for Wolf, her Blue Heeler, she cantered the short mile back to the sheep pasture and entered the now-familiar logging trail.

What she found in the interior brush was not a deer clearing, but rather one made by a human, or humans. True, the rough campsite was on the edge of Annie's property, but it looked as if it had been recently used, and for all she knew would be occupied again that evening. The folded army bedroll and cigarette butts littering a small fire pit were enough to confirm that no one had broken camp yet. The only item that was incongruous to the site was a small stuffed animal scrunched partway under a blanket. Annie slid off Trooper to take a closer look, and discovered it to be a very worn, and therefore presumably very much loved, toy lamb. Annie looked it over carefully, then back at the campsite. There was nothing else to intimate a child had been sleeping or living here—just a person who enjoyed inhaling carbon monoxide. She positioned the lamb in the vee of a nearby tree. She figured it wouldn't hurt for whomever was staying here to know that their secluded home had been busted. And for some unknown reason, she felt like keeping the inanimate toy safe. Maybe it was the remnant of a homeless person's former life that he or she carried with them.

Maybe Dan knows who might be living here. Annie snorted as soon as the thought came into her head. Fat chance. The county abounded with homeless people, and the only transients the sheriff knew were the ones who landed in the county jail. However, there was no sign of a man in the vicinity, armed or otherwise.

Annie clambered onto Trooper's back, turned her

reins toward the horse trail paralleling the sheep pasture, and headed for home. She waved to Trotter, her donkey of indeterminate age, still fully capable of keeping any would-be predator out of the electrified barriers that encased him, her ewes, and their offspring. When summer ended and the sheep returned to Johan Thompson's farm where they wintered, Trotter would rejoin the rest of Annie's horses. The rotation would begin again in the spring, just before birthing season. Annie kept her sheep for their prized wool, not their taste. She had nothing against meat but preferred that anything she ingested had not first been fed and sheltered by her. It was a specious rationale, but Annie didn't spend too much time worrying about it.

When the barn and tack room loomed ahead and her four horses nickered to her from across the pasture, Annie put the makeshift campsite out of her mind. She leaned forward slightly, Trooper's cue to canter. Normally, Annie wouldn't let anyone canter a horse back to the barn—it was a bad habit and hard to break—but Trooper, bless his equine soul, was a perfect gentleman and knew exactly how far he could go and when to stop.

Annie quickly ushered the horses into the paddock, which adjoined the row of stalls inside the stable. Everyone was ready for dinner and a warm stall, and each horse knew his or her place, although Rover, a once-starved horse Annie had rescued, predictably veered toward Trooper's stall, which held a flake more of Timothy hay than his own. It took one quick sideways look from the thoroughbred to convince Rover he'd made a mistake.

Watching each equine politely enter its stall, she thought smugly, *My horses behave better than most children.* Annie was more than satisfied with playing big sister to Hannah and other youngsters who loved horses. She was less than thrilled at playing the same role to her real half sister, Lavender, who'd trekked out from Florida earlier this year and temporarily found refuge in Annie's home. Lavender had left their father's home after learning he intended to marry a woman younger than she was. Annie couldn't have cared less about her father's marital exploits; he'd divorced her own mother more than twenty years before, and she hadn't had contact with him in years. But Lavender, despite being a full-fledged adult—at least in age, if not maturity—had always relied upon their father's financial support. Annie had discovered that her half sister now expected her to provide the same level of care and feeding she'd enjoyed in Florida. There were so many things in her own universe to explore, she explained to Annie, she simply didn't have time for a paying job. Annie noticed that Lavender still had plenty of time to criticize the way she lived, however. Fortunately, the situation had remedied itself, and Lavender now lived a safe three miles away. Annie had made sure Lavender returned her extra house key.

Before turning off the stable light, she stepped inside each stall and quickly ran her hands down each horse to make sure all was well. Normally, she would have lingered by them, inhaling and loving the smell of their manes and quietly grooming them as they munched their dinners.

But tonight she had a phone date with Marcus Colbert, the man who had given her Trooper. A few months earlier he'd mysteriously disappeared after his wife, Hilda, was murdered, and he resurfaced—by way of a cryptic postcard—only after the case was solved. The entire world had been convinced that Marcus was on the run from the crime of killing his wife, but Annie's faith in Marcus's innocence had never wavered and she'd been proven right when the real killer was apprehended. Tonight, she would speak to him for the first time in almost two months. His personal assistant in San Jose had set up the phone appointment last week and had promised that Marcus would answer all her questions. And she had a bucketful.

CHAPTER 2

Walking toward her farmhouse, Annie saw a white van slowly round the curve in her driveway. It wasn't UPS, and she couldn't remember ordering anything from State Line Tack. She quickened her step, and Wolf, who'd been by her side, raced toward the vehicle.

"Wolf! Stay!"

The dog knew better than to rush into oncoming cars. But he loved surprise visitors. Maybe he thought it was a delivery from the makers of gourmet pet food.

Instead it was the delivery van from Port Chester's most chichi grocery, the one that sold French cheeses that cost more than a T-bone. Annie assumed the driver was lost and wondered how she could convince him that he'd really come to the right address.

As it turned out, he had, and after confirming that she was, indeed, Annie Carson, she watched in astonishment as the driver unloaded three cartons of food, carried them into her kitchen, and then gave detailed instructions on how to heat and serve the meal.

"The tomato and pepper gazpacho soup with sherry doesn't need any help," he explained to Annie, who was now sitting down, her mouth unattractively open. "It's served chilled, and should still be the right temperature now—it's been refrigerated the entire way over. But the rib roast with Madeira sauce will need to be gently heated."

He saw Annie glance at her microwave. "And *not* in that," he said severely. "Put the dish in your oven at 300 degrees for about twenty-five minutes. And keep the foil tent on."

Annie gave him a quizzical look. "Really?"

"Really. The sauce is to die for. You don't want it to evaporate in *that* machine. Besides, microwaves zap all the nutrition out of your food and create carcinogens while they're doing it."

He and Lavender would get on like a house on fire, Annie thought. Her half sister loved to regale total strangers about the unhealthful attributes of the food they loved most. It was highly annoying. But Annie decided not to argue with her server. There was too much good food being unloaded, and she didn't want it to stop.

Kenneth, as Annie now knew him, went on to discuss which cheese was to be eaten now and which after dinner.

"Although you must have a sweet tooth, because your client doubled up on dessert."

"My client?"

"Marcus Colbert. He said you had an important phone conversation to be discussed over dinner."

What a guy. "And, ah, what dessert did my client decide to pair with the cheese?"

"Well, it doesn't really fit, but who cares. Double-dark chocolate cake with bourbon-whipped crème fraîche."

Annie couldn't help her hedonistic groan.

Kenneth took his time about leaving. He carefully placed the roast into Annie's antiquated electric oven, clearly distrustful of her ability to follow through on his orders. He placed the cheeses on one of Annie's few china plates and tossed the arugula salad for her. In fact, he was the epitome of a perfect waiter until he saw the label on the wine Marcus had selected.

"Saint Émilion Grand Cru! My god, look at the year! And the château!" Kenneth looked over at Annie with undisguised envy. "What kind of business do the two of you have together, if you don't mind me asking?"

"Thoroughbred horses." This was technically true. Annie was in charge of finding homes for Marcus's dead wife's twenty-three horses.

Kenneth seemed impressed, and finally took his leave.

Annie was sprawled in a living room chair, a glass of wine in one hand while she stuffed gloriously runny cheese into her mouth. The reason behind Marcus's extravagant dinner had finally come to her. On the back of the mysterious postcard she'd received over a month ago, he'd written, "I'll tell you everything over dinner. And this time, I promise not to be a no-show." Well, Marcus had certainly fulfilled that promise in consummate style. Annie knew the entire message by heart.

Her cell phone suddenly lit up, flashing the time and a California number on caller ID. Eight o'clock—Marcus was right on schedule. She hurriedly swallowed and took a large bolt from her wineglass, probably not in a way that Kenneth would approve of, she realized. She picked up the phone.

"Annie Carson."

"Marcus Colbert."

There was a long silence. Then Annie remembered her manners. "Your dinner arrived, and it's wonderful. Delicious." She paused. "Thank you."

A low chuckle followed. Marcus's voice was so sexy that even his quiet laughter made her body tingle.

"I wish you were here to enjoy it with me." This was two glasses of wine speaking, but Annie didn't care.

"I do, too."

Another long pause followed.

Then Annie blurted out the question she'd asked herself nearly every day since late February. *"Where have you been?"*

This time, the response on the other end was a long sigh.

"Annie, if you only knew how much I've wanted to confide in you all this time."

"And how much I've wanted you to. Marcus, I need to know everything. Where were you the day you disappeared?"

"Straight to the point, as usual, Annie. I love that about you." She could feel Marcus readjust himself in whatever he was sitting. "I was with my wife's killer."

Annie shuddered, recalling the traumatic events of just a few months before. Until now, she'd avoided thinking about them or even saying the killer's name. Their encounter was just too painful to relive. She took a deep breath.

"I thought as much. You know we never got to question him. He's dead."

"Yes, I know. And I learned that you were almost one of his victims, as well."

Annie gave an impatient *tsk-tsk*. "That never would have happened."

"Well, it almost happened to me. In fact, I was just damn lucky that he thought he'd finished me off and left me for dead."

"Marcus. Please—why did you disappear?"

"It wasn't my idea," Marcus replied drily. "I'd been developing my own suspicions and decided to confront him myself. Bad move. Apparently I'm no longer the heavyweight boxing champion I was in my youth. He went after me with a sharp little horse tool—"

"It's called a hoof pick," Annie interjected. "For cleaning horses' hooves."

"Or killing meddling widowers," Marcus replied. "He nicked me pretty good. The blood flow from my neck was horrendous. But that's not what did me in. It was when I tried to take him down. I twisted my back something awful and something snapped. I think I passed out from the pain of that injury rather than from my neck wound."

Annie felt faint. She took a deep breath and then a deep swallow of very good wine.

"What happened next?"

"I woke up in a forest. The Olympic National Forest, I learned later. At the time, all I knew was that I was in the middle of nowhere, surrounded by ferns and tall trees, and was wetter, colder, and hungrier than I'd ever been in my life. Plus I hurt all over. My head ached. And my guess is that I looked very much the part of a serial killer, which is what I realized I was still accused of being.

"I wanted to just lie down and go to sleep, but I knew that would literally be the death of me. So I tried to clean myself up as best I could and crawl out and find some semblance of civilization. My back was still killing me. I doubt I managed more than a few miles a day."

"What did you eat?"

"I didn't. I was in the forest for what seemed to be forever. All I could do was drink from a few random creeks I came across. If I hadn't had water, I wouldn't have survived."

What ultimately had saved Marcus was his stumbling onto a Native American reservation on the outskirts of the national park.

"I wandered into a village with half a dozen huts and collapsed on the doorstep of the first one I saw," he said with a rueful laugh. "It was not one of my finer entrances, but frankly at that point I didn't care if I lived or died, or who knew about my past. Of course, my identification had been confiscated when I was dumped, as well as my cash, so I figured making friends wasn't going to be easy."

But Marcus discovered that it was considerably easier than he'd envisioned. He was taken to the home of a Native woman, who, he said, tended to him as professionally as a doctor in any hospital. And once he'd told his finders that he did not want to be found, they immediately agreed. No one, it seemed, wanted an unnecessary visit from either the tribal police or federal agents.

"I stayed in the elder's home for almost a month," Marcus went on. "When my neck and back had healed and I'd put on weight again, I figured my new friends had been hospitable long enough. So I made a collect phone call to my attorney, Jim Fenton, and learned you'd already single-handedly solved the case and exonerated me."

"Well, Wolf helped."

"Yes, and I heard Dan Stetson also played a minor role."

"True enough." It was still hard to think of her old friend the sheriff as the one who shot Hilda's killer and saved her life.

"Believe me, I thanked Dan plenty when Jim and I met with him the next day."

"You *WHAT?*"

"Well, I was grateful to him, Annie. He did come to your rescue."

"You've *talked* with Dan?"

"Well, of course I have, Annie. Several times. And he's been tolerably nice toward the guy he once thought was responsible for every recent homicide on his turf."

Annie was so angry that she barely took in what Marcus was now telling her.

"So after he officially had all charges dismissed against me and the court file sealed, Dan said I was free to contact you. That was about a week ago. The media are going to learn that I'm alive pretty soon. Annie? Are you there?"

Annie counted to ten. She inhaled and exhaled through her toes. It wasn't helping.

"Marcus, I'm thrilled to talk to you and get the whole story. I just wish that that jackass Dan would have thought to tell me that you were all right as soon as he knew."

"I guess he had his reasons. But listen, Annie, let's not argue over something that really doesn't matter now. Let's talk about the future, and when we're going to see each other."

This was far more pleasurable territory. By the time she clicked off her cell, Annie and Marcus had agreed that he would fly up to the Olympic Peninsula as soon as his crushing work load permitted to go over, as Marcus put it, "everything." That encompassed a great number of possibilities.

Annie went to bed feeling happier than she had in a very long time. She would soon see Marcus. And, if she had her way, she'd soon have Dan Stetson's rear in a sling.

CHAPTER 3

The next morning, Annie cleaned her stalls with such vigor that half the "horse apples" tossed toward her wheelbarrow flew high overhead, landing on fresh cedar shavings already laid down in the next stall. Cursing, she jabbed the errant items back onto her fork and tried to calm down. She'd been thinking of the perfect verbal zinger for Dan Stetson and still hadn't come up with one that was lethal enough. Sweat was trickling down her back, and her face was red. Twelve hours after her conversation with Marcus, she was still steaming, in more ways than one.

She was returning the mucking wheelbarrow to its reserved place on the tack room wall when her landline phone rang with an old-fashioned trill. She knew only people who couldn't reach her any other way resorted to this number. Cell reception was fairly intermittent in the horse barn; sometimes calls came through, but often they did not. Annie liked it that way. She grabbed the phone and barked out her greeting.

"Annie speaking."

"Annie, it's Dan. I need you on an animal rescue today. I'll swing by in about twenty minutes. Have that gooseneck hitched and ready to go."

"Where are we going?" The knowledge that an animal needed her help had brushed aside every other thought from her mind.

"Across the bridge and far away. Apparently, we're the rescue team of last resort."

"I'll be ready." Annie already was hunting for her truck keys in her jacket pocket.

"Oh, and Marcus is back. Thought you might like to know."

A zinger came flying out of her mouth.

"Old news, Dan. We had our first dinner date last night." It was only a slight exaggeration, her Bad Angel assured her.

But Dan had already hung up the phone. She was playing to an empty hall.

Annie fumed as she set up the three-stall gooseneck trailer to her F-250. She'd kept her emotions in check while feeding the horses. But now that the herd had left the paddock for the great outdoors, she gave full vent to her fury at Sheriff Dan Stetson. *How dare he keep Marcus's rescue from her?* He, of all people, knew just how much Marcus's disappearance had disturbed her, and as much as she tried, she could not think of a single reason why he would be compelled to keep this information from her. Well, any single reason that made sense. The only explanation she could think for his failure to notify her the second Marcus had surfaced was he wanted her to think that Marcus was dead. He certainly couldn't pin Hilda Colbert's death on the man anymore.

Then she recalled a recent conversation with Tony Elizalde, Dan's right-hand deputy, and was glad Dan hadn't heard her sarcastic remark.

"He's about as down in the dumps as I've seen him," Tony had told her when she'd run into him at the local post office. "You'd think he'd be riding high after solving three homicides inside of a month. But Dory's playing hardball. She's asking for half of his pension, the house, and, if you can believe it, *maintenance.* What's the matter, can't *Wally* afford to take care of her now?"

Wally was an old high school classmate who now owned beachfront property in San Diego. Dan's wife, Dory, had discovered him on Facebook last winter, and the ensuing affair grew hotter than a California wildfire. She'd texted Dan with the news that she wanted a divorce while boarding a plane to join her new paramour. Annie had hoped that the fling would soon blow over, but it appeared that Dory was standing firm in her resolve to get on with her new life. She'd hired the one barracuda divorce attorney in Port Chester while Dan was still reeling from the idea of divorce after twenty-five years of marriage. He still hadn't hired his own counsel, despite everyone's urging to do so.

Annie checked the brake lights on the trailer once more and sighed. Poor Dan. No wonder he didn't want anyone else to be happy. She'd give him a break, she decided. No snide remarks about keeping Marcus's reappearance a secret. After all, her Good Angel reminded her, she hadn't told Dan about the postcard she'd received a month ago. She trudged up to her farmhouse, poured coffee into the tallest traveling carafe she could find, and called for Wolf. He came bounding in the open kitchen door, looking exceptionally pleased with himself. Annie sniffed the air. No doubt about it—Wolf had been rolling in something that had recently died. Well, Wolf could ride with Dan. He needed the company.

Dan's reaction to the pungent odor Wolf had donned that morning was much more vocal.

"What in the Sam Hill has that mutt been rolling in?" he bellowed at Annie, holding one massive hand across his nose and beating the air with his other equally beefy arm. The odor was so strong that he'd forgotten to tip his hat to her, she noticed. This attempt at male chivalry was his trademark hello to every female who crossed his path.

"Haven't the foggiest. Maybe he put on the fragrance just for you."

Some local residents might have thought twice about poking fun at the head law enforcement officer of Suwana County. Annie was not one of them; she'd simply known Dan too long. They'd grown up together, gone to school together, and in one ill-fated moment decided to attend the senior prom together. Dan had been dating Dory even then, but as Annie recalled, Dory had given Dan the bum's rush at the eleventh hour. It seemed now she was showing her stripes early. If only Dan had taken notice then.

While they'd each created their own professional pathway—Annie was a horse trainer, Dan was a cop—they were occasionally thrown together by one common interest: keeping animals out of the hands of stupid and neglectful humans. Twenty years earlier, they'd formed the Suwana County Rescue Brigade and now were the go-to agency for animal control, animal shelters, and any other entity that learned of an endangered animal that needed saving.

To Annie's regret, Dan parked and locked his patrol vehicle and announced that she was driving. Wolf was relegated to his crate in the truck bed, where Annie hoped the fumes would dissipate by the journey's end.

"What's the scoop?" Annie asked once they were on the highway leading to Worden Canal Bridge, the span that linked the Olympic Peninsula with the adjoining county. She was willing herself not to bring up Marcus.

"We're buying a mule."

"Say *what*?"

"You heard me right."

"I thought we were in the animal rescue business."

"We are. We're doing this as a favor to Bruscheau."

Now this would be a first, Annie thought. Jim Bruscheau was the sheriff of Harrison County, where they currently were heading. He and Dan had maintained a simmering feud for years. Harrison County was far more populated and hence had more taxpayers' dollars at its disposal. It also had more crime, but, as Sheriff Bruscheau once publicly pointed out to Dan, more cases were solved on his watch because his operation "had equipment that was purchased later than the 1950s." If Deputy Elizalde hadn't grabbed Dan's arm at that point, Annie was certain Dan would have landed a punch, and she had no doubt it would have hurt.

"Since when did you owe Jim Bruscheau anything?"

"Never. But he called me up this morning and asked for my help, and you never know when I'll want a favor in return."

"Seems to me you'd have been happy to tell him where to shove it."

"Now, Annie, we all have to get along in law enforcement. You know that."

She gave a mocking laugh. "What does he have that you want, Dan? Let's cut to the chase."

"I have no idea what you're talking about."

"Well, then, let's talk about the mule."

The mule, Dan explained, belonged to a family that lived in a double-wide on a five-acre lot in rural Harrison County. The double-wide was about to be repossessed. The parents were under investigation by CPS. Chances were good that the kids would enter foster care sometime soon. The father, Dan intimated, was about to be charged with numerous felony counts of domestic violence. The wife already had been ordered into inpatient rehab.

"There ought to be a test for parenting," Annie said gloomily.

"Yup," Dan replied. "But you know our elected officials would never stand for it. They'd claim it interfered with citizens' 'free will' or something."

Annie chose not to respond. She and Dan were polar opposites when it came to politics, and she knew from experience that any attempt to alter Dan's way of looking at the world was futile. She opted for more neutral ground.

"Why's he still living with the family?"

"He won't be much longer. The kids are having a Mac Meal with the guardian ad litem right now. As soon as we pull out of the driveway, I'm to alert Jim. The punch-happy dad'll be in custody a few minutes later."

"I can't believe the mule is the only animal on the place."

"'Course not. There's a couple of pit bulls, a handful of cats, and I believe a parakeet."

"Swell. And remind me again why Sheriff Bruscheau is making this our problem?"

"The miscreant father is his brother."

Annie sat in stunned silence for a moment. Dan continued.

"Jim's recused himself from the criminal investigation, of course. He and his wife plan on taking in the three girls, and the smaller animals will go with them. But the wife drew the line at the mule."

"Probably the most well behaved of the lot."

"Now, Annie, that's not fair."

"Yes, it is. I've had years of comparing children to four-footed animals, and the animals always come out on top."

"Well, Jim wanted to keep this as quiet as possible, so he asked me, rather than the Harrison County animal rescue team, to pick up the mule. Apparently the kids are crazy about the animal. Jim's hoping Susan will soften over time; he lives on fifteen acres himself and could easily build a stable for it. If not, then we'll find a good home for the nag on our side of the water."

"How much are we paying? And who's footing the bill?"

"Jim authorized me to go as high as two thousand dollars. It'll come out of his pocket."

"That must be one good-looking mule."

An hour later, Annie cautiously pulled onto a nondescript dirt road in the poorest rural area of Harrison County. She couldn't help but notice the signs declaring that trespassers would be shot and that vicious dogs freely roamed the area. Annie gave Dan an uneasy sideways glance.

"Does Mr. Bruscheau know we're coming? The bad brother, I mean. Or, perhaps I should say, the less bad of the two."

"Nope." Dan didn't sound terribly enthusiastic himself. He unconsciously put his hand on the Glock hitched to his belt.

"Great. You do the talking and I'll take the mule."

"Deal."

They silently drove along a long, bumpy road, made more difficult to traverse by fallen branches from a recent windstorm and sloping tree limbs that should have been trimmed back years ago.

"Slow down." Dan leaned forward. "Jim said to look for the driveway with the Christmas tree lights on the mailbox."

"Of course." Annie, who hadn't bothered to put up a wreath at her own home since her mother died, was baffled by the number of local residents who thought Christmas lights should be displayed all year round.

"There it is." Dan pointed to a mailbox on the left-hand side, festooned with tiny bulbs.

"I don't suppose you checked to see if this guy has a concealed weapons permit."

"As a matter of fact, I did. He doesn't. But that's only because he's got a bunch of DUIs and an assault conviction. Couldn't get one if he tried. But I won't be surprised if he displays a shotgun or two. Maybe even an illegal assault weapon."

"How reassuring."

Annie glanced back at Wolf in his crate. He'd come to her rescue not long ago, and she had no doubt he would again, if the need arose. He was standing up now, tongue out and panting, intuiting that his mistress was finally arriving at her destination, where he was sure fun abounded. Annie wished she could be as delusional as her dog.

A dingy double-wide appeared in her vision; judging by its dilapidated condition, she was sure it contained mold and other noxious substances. She hoped there wasn't a meth lab in one of the nearby shacks, ready to blow if someone lit a match. A muddy pasture, ringed with barbed wire and posts of various lengths, stretched from a sunken backyard patio to the rim of the ever-present forest. Loud, aggressive barking permeated the air. Annie immediately decided to keep Wolf in his crate.

"Let's get this over with." Dan heaved himself out of the truck and stood up straight, arching his back. *Male posturing, pure and simple,* Annie thought with amusement, but she was glad he was along and fully armed. Her own Winchester was in her truck's gun rack, but she had no desire to provoke what undoubtedly would be a stressful encounter with the owner.

He appeared now, opening a sagging screen door. Predictably, he had a shotgun slung through one arm.

"Larry Bruscheau?" Dan strode toward the trailer with a sheaf of papers in his hand.

"You've found me." A sideways stream of tobacco juice hit the ground.

"I hear you've got a mule for sale."

"Where'd you hear that? And who the hell are you?"

"I'm Dan Stetson, sheriff over in Suwana County. Your brother told me you were looking to sell the animal. I'm interested in acquiring it."

"Well, you heard wrong. None of my animals is for sale."

This is going to be tough, Annie thought. She certainly didn't envy Dan his job.

The incessant, angry barking of the pit bulls within the double-wide continued unabated. Meanwhile, Wolf was vociferously announcing his displeasure at being locked up in his crate. Their combined conversation was not helping the atmosphere.

"Well, Mr. Bruscheau, we can handle this one of two ways—the hard way or the easy way. The hard way is that I serve you with these papers from the county giving me the right to take your mule because too many neighbors have complained about the way you don't take care of it. That means you get fined, possibly charged with animal neglect, and never see that mule again. The easy way is to sell the mule to me, and when you've proven to me that you're capable of taking care of the nag in a proper environment, I might sell it back to you. I might even give you a deal. What do you say?"

"It ain't a nag. It's a mule. And that makes it a hell of a lot smarter than you are."

A loud whinny, ending in a long hee-haw that Annie's donkey, Trotter, would have envied, echoed off the falling-down lean-to that Annie imagined passed as a shelter. She wanted to leave this unpleasant tête-à-tête and check out the mule, but she knew that if she took one step forward, she'd be technically trespassing and probably in the crosshairs of the man's shotgun.

"Mr. Bruscheau, we have to make a decision here. And I'd like to do it without any further fuss. So put down your shotgun and let's talk like reasonable men."

"What's reasonable to me is that you get off my property."

"I'm going to ask you one more time, Mr. Bruscheau. Put down your shotgun and let's decide what we're going to do."

Mr. Bruscheau glanced down at his shotgun and ratcheted back the loader.

"Put the shotgun down! *Now!*"

Dan had raised and pointed his Glock at the man faster than Annie had ever seen the sheriff move. Cold sweat ran down her back. This was serious. She now wished she'd gotten her Winchester out of her truck. Her feet seemed rooted to the ground, unable to move.

Larry Bruscheau gazed at Dan for what seemed an interminable time. Finally, he gave a short shrug of his shoulders and placed the shotgun on the ground. Dan was up in front of him in two strides and kicked the shotgun away. Annie ran over and picked it up. It was a .30-.30 Winchester, just like hers, oiled and ready for action.

"Turn around! Get on the ground!" Dan caught him by the back ruff of his shirt and slung him to the ground. Larry emitted a short *hunff.* Annie suspected the wind had just been knocked out of him.

She'd never been present when Dan made an arrest, and she wordlessly watched him frisk the man, find and pocket a small handgun from his boot, and handcuff him to one of the barbed wire fences. If he tried to get away now, Annie was sure he'd get cut. She was impressed at Dan's ability to subdue and control Larry so quickly. All she could subdue and control were horses— although she generally was a lot nicer about it.

"One second, Annie." Dan trotted back to her F-250 and made a call from inside the cab. She had no doubt he was calling Sheriff Bruscheau, to let him know that he'd just corralled the subject and had read him his rights.

"Well, Mr. Bruscheau," he said, walking up to the man, who now crouched on the ground, his left arm hanging to the rail, "I guess we're going to do this the hard way."

CHAPTER 4

Thirty minutes later, Dan and Annie were back on the road, now with an 800-pound mule in their tow. Annie could see why the three young girls in the family doted on the animal. True to her breed, she was intelligent and even-tempered. She'd loaded without balking and did not wish her previous owner a single hee-haw good-bye, although in truth her signature song was somewhere between a neigh and a donkey's bray. *It was lovely,* Annie thought.

Larry was of absolutely no help—not that he could be much, attached to a barbed wire fence. But he obviously thought exercising his right to remain silent extended to Annie. Her queries of when the mule had been last vaccinated and had had its hooves trimmed were met with stony silence. It didn't matter. One look at the mule's hooves made it clear that the last time a farrier had paid a call was long ago; its toe ends curled up off the ground and were chipped in several places.

Any hoof trimming, she suspected, had been done by her owners, randomly, and with no particular skill.

She'd discovered the mule's name only by espying a worn halter hanging on a nail in the sagging lean-to. The name "Molly" had been childishly scrawled with a black felt marker on front, and the headpiece was adorned with faded ribbons. This meant the mule was the offspring of a mare and a jack, or male donkey. It also meant it was unlikely that Molly had ever given birth to another mule, and judging by her teeth, any gestation cycles now were few and far between. The price Sheriff Bruscheau was willing to pay for the animal was far more than what a reasonable person would consider fair value; for the first time, Annie thought Dan's competitor might have a heart after all. As expected, he was not present when Harrison County vehicles swooped in seconds after Molly was safely parked in Annie's trailer.

A mile from the Worden Canal Bridge, a flashing highway sign blinked a discouraging digital message: BRIDGE CLOSED FOR MARINE CROSSING. Annie sighed, eased her truck into the long line of cars in front of her, and turned off the engine. Depending on the agility of the ship's navigator, bridge closures could last as long as an hour.

Dan took the unexpected break to call the Sheriff's Office to describe his daring exploits in loud and expressive terms to Esther, the sole 911 operator in Suwana County and Dan's personal girl Friday. Esther, who'd just turned seventy-three, apparently was a very good listener. Annie, unimpressed, climbed out of the cab to check on Molly. The mule seemed unconcerned about the unexpected delay, and more intent to demolish the bag of hay Annie had put inside the trailer. Returning to the truck, she discovered that Dan had rolled down the passenger window and was still on an exuberant roll with Esther. She decided to remain outside. Using her own phone, she punched in the number for Jessica Flynn, the vet who tended to Annie's herd, as well as most of Suwana County's equine population. Jessica regularly donated her services to rescue animals when needed, and Annie knew that Molly was going to need more than a bit of babying before she was ready to adopt out.

"Don't tell me. You've rescued another wee bairn," was Jessica's opening line.

"How'd you know?" Annie was intrigued.

"I can hear Dan's healthy vocal cords in the background. And the only time the two of you hang out is when you're coming to the aid of four-legged animals."

"So true, so true. Well, I've got a new one for you—a Molly mule, aptly named Molly. I'd say she's twenty if she's a day, and in remarkably good shape, except for her hooves. But she'll need a full going over, and frankly I don't know if she's ever been vaccinated in her life."

"How's her personality?"

"Sweet as can be. Fortunately, three girls were her caretakers, not their bio dad, who's meaner than a junkyard dog and not half as pretty."

"Wonderful. I love mules. I had one growing up, and it was the best friend I ever had."

"Well, your new best friend is on her way. We should hit your place in a couple of hours. By the way, where are you?"

Annie knew that one never knew which quadrant of the county a large-animal vet might be roaming at any given time. Their commutes were long, were seldom the same, and commenced as soon as the phone rang with an emergency call.

"Believe it or not, I'm at the clinic, and expect to be

here all day, knock on wood. So come on by. I'll make fresh coffee and get a stall ready."

Dan had finally ended his call, and Annie judged it was safe to reenter the cab. Gazing ahead, she could see no sign of movement, either from the waiting cars to cross the bridge or from the vessel in the water.

"So what's new in the land of law enforcement?" Annie immediately regretted her opening gambit. The last thing she wanted to hear was Dan talk about his recent conversations with Marcus and his attorney. Dan knew very well that Annie had a full-blown schoolgirl crush on the man, and she just couldn't stand that he knew it. But Dan was smart enough to avoid the topic as well.

"Not much," he admitted. "We have a quasi-mysterious death of an old woman that we're trying to figure out. When Hank first reported it, we assumed it was just a case of her dying in her sleep, something we should all hope for. God knows she was old enough to die—ninety-five, according to her death certificate."

Hank, Annie knew, was the county coroner. "So what makes it mysterious?"

"The old lady was prescribed a million meds, and when we took an inventory, half of them were missing. The crucial half—the ones for her heart, and the super-duper ones for pain."

"So you're thinking suicide?"

"Maybe. Her adult son says no way—he talked to his mom the night before and everything was hunky-dory. 'Course, he wasn't too happy to hear that an autopsy is now in order."

"I suppose not. Well, who's this in-home nursing service? Maybe someone on the staff stole the pills. It happens."

"Don't I know it." Dan sighed. "Those drugs are just too tempting for a lot of kids, and that's who mainly goes in to care for these folks. Plenty of time to peruse the bathroom cabinets while Grandma is taking her afternoon power nap. Don't worry, we'll be talking to every kid who cared for the old lady."

"*Kids?* They hire kids to take care of senior citizens?"

"You know what I mean, Annie. 'Young people.' People considerably younger than you and me."

Well, that was a depressing thought. Annie regarded herself as someone who had yet to hit the prime of life.

"Speak for yourself, Dan Stetson. I am still in the first blush of youth and, thanks to hanging out with horses, will never age."

"Good luck with that, Annie. Personally, as long as this old lady's death doesn't turn into another god-awful homicide like the ones we just had, I'll be a happy man. Even if I am old and decrepit."

At long last the line of cars began to move, and by three o'clock Annie was pulling her rig into the parking lot of Jessica's clinic. Jessica was delighted to make Molly's acquaintance, and it seemed the feeling was mutual. Annie and Dan stayed long enough to be assured that nothing appeared significantly off-kilter with the mule and that she would get Jessica's full attention over the next few days. The sun was just going down as Annie drove into the driveway leading to her stables. It had been a long day.

Wolf was deliriously happy to be sprung from his crate. Annie had naively assumed he'd be out helping her urge neglected horses into the trailer. Instead, the poor guy had spent most of the day cooped up, she thought guiltily. The Blue Heeler raced off and out of sight. By now, the odor of rotting things on his fur had been somewhat dispelled by the outside air, but a whiff was still present, and Annie realized, a nanosecond too late, that he might be heading back to the source for another good roll.

"Back in a flash," Annie yelled at Dan as she raced after her dog. He'd gone around the hay barn and appeared to be heading into the back pasture that now lay fallow. Annie was keeping this section of her property temporarily devoid of horses so that the spring rains would replenish the grass. Unless she installed an intricate water system, this was necessary to ensure her herd had sufficient pasture to munch on all summer long. And even if she'd been allowed to use all that water for this purpose, it was far too expensive to even contemplate as a solution.

"Wolf! Wolf!" Annie called out, and hoped her dog wouldn't embarrass her in front of Dan and fail to respond. She was relieved to see his head pop up in the field and his body come to attention.

"Good boy! Come, Wolf! It's dinner time!" Whether or not Wolf understood the words, they usually were enough to get him to come running. But today he remained at attention.

"Damn," grumbled Annie, and started to jog toward him. The smell of this morning's roll increased as she came closer to him.

Then she stopped, horrified. On the ground, near Wolf's feet, was a small lamb. It had been badly mangled and was in a state of severe decay. *Could it be one of hers?* Annie instinctively clutched her arms around her chest, then breathed out. *No. It could not be.*

This lamb was too young. All of hers had been birthed at least three weeks ago and were accounted for. This one appeared to be only a day or two old when it met its death, although that had clearly been several days ago. It should have been joined to the hip with its mother, who probably was going nuts right now, thought Annie, baaing and baaing for the lamb that would never come home. Annie felt tears spring into her eyes. She gazed down at Wolf, who seemed oblivious to the cruelty of Mother Nature. She knew that Wolf would never have killed this animal; on the contrary, he, as well as her donkey, Trotter, knew that keeping her lambs and ewes safe was their primary job. But he couldn't be faulted for giving in to his atavistic side and smearing the smell of a dead animal on him.

"Damn!" Annie said again. Seeing a small animal dead because of an unknown tragic encounter with a predator was always heartbreaking, and Annie, despite her tough exterior, was no more immune to the intense grief that seeing such a death produced. She sighed and took Wolf by his collar.

"Come on. Let's go find a shovel. And let's see if your buddy Dan will be a gentleman and help."

Dan was and did. Annie rewarded him afterward with one of her coveted glasses of Glenlivet. Once they were inside the house, Annie noticed that the phone message light was blinking, but Annie had no intention of sharing her friends with the sheriff. He knew more about her than he needed to, anyway. Besides, it might be Marcus who'd called.

The eerie sound of baying coyotes penetrated the air when Dan opened Annie's kitchen door to leave. Wolf sprang from his posture of repose by the woodstove to full alert and growled.

"Easy there," Dan told the dog. "They're a mile away. Go back to sleep."

Annie looked at Wolf, who was ignoring Dan's advice.

"Yeah, but it sounds as if they're coming from the area where Wolf found the lamb. Who lives over there who might have lost one?"

Dan shrugged. "No one comes to mind. It's just a big, old empty space that bumps up to the highway. Finding one lamb out there doesn't really make a lot of sense."

Annie waited impatiently until his patrol vehicle had gone slowly up her driveway and exited onto the county road. She then leapt for the phone and jabbed the message button.

"Hi, Annie. It's Marcus. I just missed hearing your voice. Call me when you have a chance."

Annie gave Wolf a chew bone and firmly put the poor little lamb out of her mind as she quietly punched in Marcus's number.

CHAPTER 5

Today, Annie decided, would be devoted to *her* animals. Starting with a bath for Wolf.

This was done in her mudroom, which had hot and cold running water and a large mat on the floor for just such purposes. Annie had yet to take a shower after feeding her horses and cleaning their stalls, but she saw no reason to take one now, since Wolf was doing a fine job of making sure she was wet all over.

"This isn't your first rodeo, buddy," Annie grumbled to the squirming Blue Heeler, as she vigorously scrubbed the parts of his fur that seemed most odiferous. Wolf looked up at her with big brown eyes that implied she was inflicting severe pain on his torso, while Max, Annie's black-and-white cat, meticulously cleaned himself in the corner. The cat was in Wolf's direct line of sight. One would have thought he was there to remind Wolf that *some* animals didn't need help keeping themselves clean.

"There!" Annie said with satisfaction, as she tossed a very hairy terry towel in the direction of the washer. "Now don't you look handsome?"

Finally free of his mistress's clutches, Wolf responded with an immense shake of his entire body, splattering Annie and Max in the process. Max ran for cover. Annie merely laughed and got to her feet.

"Time for all smart dogs to take naps by the wood-stove," she instructed Wolf, who trotted into the house, looked in vain for food in his dog bowl, and settled down by the stove with a sigh. Sasha, Annie's young Belgian Tervuren, padded out from the bedroom and joined Wolf. She had already experienced two baths in her short life-time and had wisely decided to hide under the bed that morning until the danger had passed.

A knock on the back door caused Annie to involuntarily yelp. She wasn't used to visitors to her home, especially those who were uninvited. Her ranch was a quarter mile from the nearest neighbor, and that was as the crow flies. Her relative isolation was deliberate; her favorite friends, now out in the pasture, were all the company she generally needed or desired.

Peering through the screen door, she realized her visitor probably was the *only* person she would be happy to see without warning, barring Ed McMahon with an oversized check. Annie undid the dead bolt and opened the door.

"Martha! What a nice surprise!"

The petite octogenarian in front of her smiled back at Annie and held out her hands, which contained a covered plate.

"I'm so glad I found you at home, Annie. I didn't want to leave these on the doorstep. I was afraid they might be eaten by something other than yourself."

Annie peeked underneath the tea towel. Pecan shortbread. Annie loved pecan shortbread, and Martha Sanderson knew it.

"You are too kind," she said, meaning it. "Come on in. But be forewarned, I've just given Wolf a bath."

"If a bath was required, I'm glad I came now instead of sooner."

"Good point," Annie replied. "He *was* pretty rank. And it was so sad—he found a newborn lamb that had been taken by a predator."

"Oh, Annie, that's terrible. I don't dare tell Lavender. She'd burst into tears just knowing it happened."

Oh, yes, let's protect Lavender, Annie thought sourly. *God forbid that she face reality head on.* Lavender was good at freely dispensing advice to others on how to live but firmly shut the door on reality whenever life became too uncomfortable for herself. Ignoring a bevy of traffic tickets back in Florida was the reason her half sister was still taking the bus. She gave silent thanks that Martha had agreed to let Lavender live at her home after three weeks of sharing her own.

"Ah, how is Lavender?" she asked cautiously.

"Well, dear, that's one of the reasons I stopped by."

Looking at Annie's panicked face, Martha put her thin, veined hand on Annie's arm.

"No, nothing's wrong with Lavender. Not really. She's had a bit of a shock recently—an event she perhaps wasn't quite prepared for—but I really came by to share the *good* news—that Lavender has found employment. I thought you might want to come over for dinner to help us celebrate."

"Lavender has a *job?*"

"Why, yes, dear. She started work about a week ago, and for the most part seems to be enjoying it."

"Who hired her?" Annie's tone suggested that no business owner in his or her right mind would want to engage her half sister for any task that required a modicum of good sense.

"I'll let Lavender tell you all about it," Martha said demurely. "It's her achievement, and she has every right to show off a bit."

Annie made a noncommittal sound in her throat, but Martha politely ignored it.

"How about this Friday? And bring the dogs. I'll make a special meat loaf for them."

Martha was always spoiling her dogs.

"Oh, of course, Martha, I'd love to come." Annie's childhood upbringing kicked in, and she realized she was being petty over Lavender's small success. "But please promise me that Wolf and Sasha won't be the only ones eating meat."

Martha laughed. It was always such a treat to hear her laugh; it literally tinkled its way out of Martha's throat and wafted on the air around her.

"Of course. And Annie, do try to be supportive. You have no idea how much your younger sister looks up to you."

"Humph." This time, Annie's remark was audible, but she smiled as she said it.

The next animal to receive Annie's attention was the newest boarder on the ranch, and Annie's latest training project. Layla was a stunning, jet-black Tennessee Walker who needed, in her owner Sarah's words, "a major tune-up." The Walker had been started at three, and had developed beautifully on the ground and under saddle. By age five, Layla was leading the pack on trail rides with her natural, exquisitely elongated gait, and clearly enjoying herself. According to Sarah, theirs was a match made in heaven.

Then the world caved in. Sarah was diagnosed with breast cancer and life irrevocably changed, both for rider and horse. As soon as she'd recovered from surgery but before she'd finished chemo, Sarah was ready to get back in the saddle. The boarding facility with which Sarah had reluctantly left Layla had promised her that her beloved mare would be faithfully exercised. She discovered that Layla had been ridden, all right, but by a person Sarah now called "the bully," who'd jerked on Layla's mouth and dug his spurs into her sides for the slightest reason or for no reason at all. Consequently, the Walker was now terrified of having anyone on her back; the mare was constantly fearful of doing the wrong thing.

"And it's all my fault," Sarah tearfully told Annie when she dropped off Layla at her stables. "If only I'd taken the time to actually *watch* the bully while he so-called 'exercised' her, I would have seen what was happening and yanked his butt off my horse. But every time I called the facility's owner, she assured me that Layla was doing just fine and loving all the attention. And I *believed* her."

"It's not your fault," Annie replied. "How were you to know the exerciser was a jerk-and-spur? You were doing what you had to do—get well. Remember, I took you to chemo a time or two last year. You had about as much strength as a kitten. But now you're back, loaded for bear, and fully capable of stomping on the cowboy's head next time you see him. Until that time, let's work on getting Layla back on track."

Sarah had laughed at Annie's bluntness, but at least she'd stopped crying.

Annie knew that the memories Layla had stored up from her year away from her human companion would never be erased. Fortunately, the Walker had not acted out during this time. She hadn't bit anyone, kicked a human, or shown any kind of violent behavior. This was excellent news, because if Layla had, she would never be 100% trustworthy again, even though she could be rehabilitated. It wouldn't be her fault; she would only be remembering what idiot humans had done to her previously and responding with equine PTSD.

In the month that Layla had boarded at Carson Stables, Annie had worked with her only a half dozen times; the return of her ewes and the lambing season that quickly followed had taken up most of her time. But Layla had been out with Annie's herd, and Annie knew that her mares were teaching the Walker when she could not. And when she had found time with the mare, what she saw looked very promising. Layla was essentially a forgiving horse, and smart enough to know that one bad human does not all humans make. She trusted Annie, and that was half the battle.

Today, Annie decided to work on Layla's mouth, which had become granite-like under the rough rein of her previous rider.

She was in the round pen, teaching the Walker to yield through the not hard but consistent backward pull of her reins when her peripheral vision caught the sight of another unexpected visitor to her ranch. This one Annie was certain she did not know.

Well, it was time to see how Layla reacted around strangers, she decided. She bent down, opened the round pen gate, and gently asked the mare to walk outside. She was pleased to see Layla respond to just the slightest touch of her heels to her side. In a week or two, she hoped she wouldn't even have to do that, and could simply use her energy as the cue to "walk."

The young woman approaching them was reed slender, perhaps nineteen or twenty years old. She was dressed entirely in Western garb—clean and pressed Levi's jeans, a plaid button-snapped blouse, and traditional cowboy boots. Her long, blond hair swirled around her shoulders. Despite her smart appearance, the young woman did not come across at all confident to Annie. She admiringly looked around Annie's expanse of tack room, hay barn, and stables, but the expression on her face reflected her uncertainty as to whether she'd get a warm welcome.

When she saw Annie advance on horseback, she stood still and waited calmly for them to join her. Annie's brain clicked into gear: *The kid must know something about horses to wait for our approach.*

"Can I help you?" Annie said once Layla was within a few feet of the young woman. "Are you out of gas?"

"No," was the nervous reply. "Actually, I'm looking for work. I'm Ashley Lawton. We met a few years ago at one of the horse club meetings in Port Chester. You probably don't remember me. You told us about your rescue brigade."

Something in Annie's memory stirred. "You were part of the Port Chester Equestrian Drill Team, right? You were about to perform at the State Fair."

"That's right." The young woman's face lit up. She seemed happy that Annie had remembered the event, at least, if not every attendee. Then she averted her head in sudden shyness. Annie looked directly at her, and noticed that her visitor had difficulty making eye contact again. Finally, the young woman spoke, tentatively.

"You have a beautiful place."

"Thanks."

Silence ensued. Normally, Annie would have tried to truncate the conversation at this point, but there was something so appealing about the waif that she decided to play it out a bit longer.

"What kind of work are you looking for, Ashley?"

"Anything to do with horses," she responded eagerly. "I grew up with them. Had one until I graduated from high school, but then he got sold."

"That's too bad."

"Yeah, well, I didn't know he was sold until my dad told me." A note of bitterness had crept into the young woman's tone. Evidently she disapproved of her father's decision. "He said Jumper was a 4-H project and that part of my life was done."

"How horrible. But you said you grew up around horses. That seems like a strange thing for a father to do."

"Oh, we didn't have horses ourselves. I just used to ride a neighbor's horse. Started when I was seven years old. Then I got jobs working at local stables to pay for my own horse and save for college."

Well, she's certainly got the right work ethic, Annie thought.

"I can do anything—muck stalls, feed, exercise, do turnout. And I'm a pretty good vet assistant, too."

"Do you have a vet tech degree?"

"Well, no. Not yet, anyway. That's what I was saving up for. Still am. But I need to work to get there."

"I hear you. Well, who have you worked for recently?"

"Um, for a while I was working for an in-home nursing service. You know, the kind where you go into people's homes and care for them so they don't have to go into old folks homes?"

Dan just mentioned one, remembered Annie. "How'd you like that?"

"Oh, it was fine. . . . Actually, a lot of it was really rewarding. Old people are so sweet and they're so grateful for your help. But after a while, well, it just got too heavy on the soul."

Too heavy on the soul. Now, that wasn't an expression you'd expect to hear out of the mouth of a millennial.

"Do you have references?"

"Oh, yes." The woman pulled a piece of paper out of her jeans pocket and handed it to Annie. "These are the names and phone numbers of all the stables I've worked at for the past five years. They'll all vouch for me."

Annie leaned down and took the paper, torn from a lined notebook and containing neatly printed information from a ballpoint pen. Apparently not everyone owns a laptop, she realized. She recognized most of the names on the sheet. They were all good horsewomen whom Annie respected.

"Where are you living now? Is it far from here?"

"On the Squill River. In a cabin with my boyfriend." She shifted her weight from one foot to the other, and then looked up at Annie, squinting a little from the unexpected sun that had emerged from the clouds. She was so patently hopeful that Annie would give her a job.

Annie smiled. "Well, Ashley, I'm sure your references check out fine. But here's the deal. I'm pretty much a one-woman show around here. I train one or two horses at a time, and the rest of my workday I'm tending to my sheep. I don't really need any extra help. But you might try contacting Samantha Higgins in Arndrop, on the other side of the water. She's got a much bigger operation than I do, and I know she's always looking for good, reliable help."

"But I don't have a car." The woman looked down, so clearly disappointed that Annie's heart momentarily ached for her.

"Listen. Give me your cell number. If I hear of anything, I'll give you a call."

"Thanks." The word came out without a shred of enthusiasm. Annie wordlessly handed back the reference sheet. The young woman scrawled a number on it and then handed it back to Annie. But her facial expression had changed. Instead of the downtrodden, shy look, Ashley's face now showed a touch of defiance and determination.

In a clear, even voice, she told Annie, "If you're trying to get a backup on that horse, you might try talking to her feet, maybe disengage her hindquarter first. Her mouth looks pretty hard. She might respond better. I think she knows what you want." Then she turned, and said in the same listless voice as before, "Well, have a nice day."

"You too, Ashley." Annie sat still on Layla as she watched the woman trudge up her driveway. Then she shifted to the left, and Layla picked up her feet and turned with her, heading back to the round pen. *No doubt about it, the horse is more responsive every time I ride her. At least, going forward.*

They reached the round pen and Annie bent down to open the gate, belatedly realizing the latch was a good eight inches behind her. It was time to test Layla's yield to pressure once more. But what had Ashley suggested? *Talk to the feet. Of course.* She tightened up one rein and asked Layla to bring her head toward her leg. As soon as the horse moved, she gently toggled a few backward pulls with both reins. As if on cue, the Walker quickly backed up two pretty steps.

Hot damn, the kid was right. Annie was struck by Ashley's intuitive sense of how to solve a problem that had stymied her that morning. And, truth be told, she was tired of mucking six stalls every day. Besides, she was now on Marcus's payroll, in her new job of finding homes for his deceased wife's horses. She could afford to have a little help right now.

She turned around in the saddle and called out, "Ashley? Wait up a sec."

But Ashley seemingly had disappeared into thin air.

CHAPTER 6

The next morning, Annie cursed herself for not hiring Ashley the previous day. She'd overslept—something she *never* did—and it was all Marcus's fault. He had phoned again last night and the conversation had lasted far beyond Annie's usual bedtime. His calls, as delightful as they might be, made her do things like roll over at six AM and turn off the alarm in her sleep. It was unthinkable. As soon as her chores were done at the stables, she intended to find the phone number Ashley had given her, call her up, and tell her if she wanted a job, she had one. Immediately.

For all of her adult life, Annie had eschewed outside help with her horses. The primary reason was that deep down she thought only she could best do the job. But the secondary reason was that she really didn't want to share her horses with anyone else—at least, not on a daily basis. Her life had not been particularly easy. Her father had left the family when she was eleven, and her mother had died of cancer when she was in her early twenties. She had no siblings; Lavender, the progeny of her father's second marriage, didn't count in her book. Aside from her own short-lived marriage after college, she'd had no real or long-standing relationship with a man. The reality was that her closest relationships were with her horse companions.

But horses could be fickle. Introduce a new person to the herd and all of a sudden a horse who never let Annie comb her tail without swishing it out of her hands—that would be Baby, her youngest, and a Saddlebred—would suddenly let a youngster pull on and swing from its tail without batting one of its pretty eyelashes. As Annie recalled, that's how she'd met Hannah, the eight-year-old who lived nearby and was certifiably horse crazy. Hannah had never tried such a dangerous stunt again in Annie's presence, and had become a very good young rider. She also had a way of melting the most persnickety or world-weary horse's heart.

Now, leaning on her muckrake, Annie thought seriously about her existing circle of friends. Aside from her horses, whom was she truly close to? She had lots of acquaintances—she had regular contact with horsemen and women in the tri-county area, and her relationships with Dan and the deputies she knew through rescue missions were usually tolerable. But there really wasn't anyone to whom she could tell her innermost hopes, dreams, and fears—except her horses. Which is why opening up—just a crack, but it was a crack—to Marcus now was making her deliriously happy and angry with herself at the same time. How could she risk a human relationship if she was letting down her horses?

But talking to Marcus was so much fun. She smiled, remembering their conversation the previous night, when Annie had described Ashley's unexpected visit.

"Tell me how you start your day, Annie," he'd urged. "You've never told me."

"It's not that exciting."

"Let me be the judge of that," he'd replied, and Annie had plunged in.

"Well, I roll out of bed around six, feed the dogs and cat, get in my mucking gear—"

"What's that?"

"Clothes only my horses see me in. Old jeans, flannel shirts, mucking boots . . ."

"No designer labels, I take it?"

"'Fraid not." Annie had laughed at the idea. "Then I feed my horses, turn them out, muck their stalls, make their mashes for the evening, that kind of thing. Next, I drive up to the sheep pasture and feed the ewes and Trotter—he's there for the summer—and then go home. And take a shower. Believe me, by then I need it."

There had been a long pause. Then Marcus had asked, warily, "Are you telling me every single animal on your ranch is fed breakfast before you?"

Annie had been taken aback. She'd never thought about it before.

"I guess so."

"Hire this woman," Marcus had promptly replied.

Annie sighed. She should have, but since she hadn't—yet—her long workday stretched out before her, and it was time to start whittling away at her chores. She stored the wheelbarrow in its usual place and grabbed the dolly next to it. Her hay supply was running low in the tack room. It was time to replenish it from the hay barn in back.

Annie was proud of her hay barn, which she'd built two years ago after an exceptionally good shearing season. She'd hired local builders and overseen every beam they'd erected and every nail they'd hammered. The structure was tall and sturdy, impervious to mercurial weather patterns, including sideways rain and the occasional snowstorm. The concrete floor was large enough to hold four tons of Eastern Washington Timothy and the same amount of local orchard grass. The sliding doors were well oiled and hitched back securely. Air outlets in the ceiling ensured no fire would erupt during the few hot summer months the Peninsula granted its residents. Two LCD lights in protective coverings made the barn easy to navigate in the dark in winter months, when twilight started at four-thirty and darkness would swathe the entire farm by six. It was a thing of beauty, Annie thought whenever she gazed upon it, and just to make sure it would always appear so, she'd paid a high school kid to apply a clear coat of stain a few months after it had been built.

She strode toward it now, pride of ownership foremost on her mind. Wondering how much hay she could reasonably stack on the dolly and still push it, she slid open the doors, flipped on the overhead lights—and screamed.

Hanging still, only a few feet off the ground, was Ashley Lawton. Her head leaned to one side, and Annie could see thin, angry red marks creased into her neck from the hay twine that had served as her noose. Her face was bluish, and her tongue protruded from her mouth. She was wearing the same clothes she'd had on when Annie had encountered her just the day before—only now, instead of clean and pressed, they were rumpled, with stains of mud and grit on every side.

Annie realized she was shaking. She carefully put the dolly to one side and stood still, etching every frame of the scene into her brain. She cautiously looked up. The twine, normally used to secure hundred-pound bales of hay, extended to a low beam by the left door. It was the only one she could have used; the ceiling beams framing the barn were far too high and could be accessed only by an extended ladder, which was not kept here. She wondered how it could have happened. Why it happened. *When* it happened. And throughout her swirl of thoughts, Annie kept wondering, *Really? You hang a few feet off the floor and you kill yourself? That's all it takes?*

Feeling a bit steadier, she walked quietly around the hay barn, searching for anything that Ashley might have left behind. She found nothing—no note, no handbag, not a single scrap of anything that gave a clue to the scene before her. She'd worn her ranch gloves when she entered the barn—bucking hay without them could be murder on one's hands—and now was glad she had, as she knew fingerprints on the door handles would be taken. Murder. Had she thought about murder? Was this death a homicide? Annie once again felt dizzy and plunked down on the nearest hay bale. Hell, maybe the hay bale was evidence. Maybe she should just leave. In her daze, she got up, dusted off her rear, and exited the barn, now securing the doors with a lock. It was time to call the experts.

"Stop finding dead bodies" was Dan's terse greeting when he arrived at her stables.

"Sure thing, Dan. I'll remember to do that."

Annie looked at Dan with what she hoped was cool disdain.

By now, Annie had taken a quick shower—the thought that hot water might be erasing key evidence had been trumped by the odor amassed from mucking six stalls. She also had consumed a much needed cup of coffee.

The last time Annie had discovered a dead body, it

had been in a home in the nearby community of Shelby, and there was no question that it had been a homicide. She'd watched Suwana County deputies in action that day as they staked out the crime scene, collected evidence, and generally took over the home. Now her own property had been desecrated and was being similarly ransacked by cops.

There was one thing more that troubled Annie, although she tried to shove it to the back of her mind. If she hadn't been so busy flirting with Marcus on the phone last night, she might have taken the time to call Ashley to offer her a job. Maybe she could have saved her. Or not. She dreaded hearing from Dan or the coroner the time that Ashley had died.

Annie and Dan were standing in front of the stables, where Dan had parked his patrol vehicle. In the distance, she watched Deputy Elizalde snake his way inside the barely cracked barn doors with gloved hands as several other deputies began to wrap "accident scene" tape around the barn perimeter. She was glad he had a face mask on.

"Do you have any idea who's hanging there?" Dan jabbed one angry finger toward the hay barn.

"I told Esther. Ashley Lawton. She walked onto my ranch yesterday and asked for a job. I told her I didn't have any but would let her know if I heard of anything. She gave me a list of references and her cell number. Then she left. Ironically, I was thinking just this morning of calling her and offering her at least part-time employment."

I wish I'd called her last night. Annie could not push the thought out of her head.

Dan sighed. "I guess I wasn't making myself clear. Remember that case I told you about while we were waiting for the bridge to open? About the old lady who allegedly died in her sleep?"

"Yeah." A few neurons fired up in Annie's brain. "Ashley said she'd recently worked for an outfit like the one taking care of the lady who died."

"Not 'like one.' *The* one. Ashley Lawton was the primary home care aide assigned to take care of the old lady, one Eloise Carr, and the one who found her deceased. After we discovered the missing pills in the home, we ran a background and discovered Ashley has—had—a pending case in Suwana County Superior Court for drug possession without a prescription. Predictably, her employer canned her. You may have been about to hire little missy, but I was about to haul her in for questioning."

Annie was stunned. She'd talked to Ashley for all of five minutes, but she found it hard to believe that this shy but earnest young woman was guilty of stealing pills.

"But she seemed so nice!" She instantly felt like Sarah, bemoaning her failure to see through the boarding facility owner's assurances that her Tennessee Walker was doing just fine. "Besides," Annie went on, "she probably has—had—a lawyer by now. What makes you so sure you'd have been able to talk to her, anyway?"

"Damn public defenders. Always there when you least want them," Dan grumbled, conceding the point. "But you're not the only one who was taken in. Ronald, Mrs. Carr's son, was pretty shocked when he heard about Ashley's criminal history. Said he never would have suspected Ashley of doing such a thing to his mother. Claimed he'd often seen the two of them interacting when he visited. According to his mom, Ashley was more like a granddaughter than a caretaker. Just goes to show."

"Show what, Dan?" Annie's tone was sharp. "Both of

them are dead, so now we'll never know whether Ashley was innocent or not."

"Maybe, maybe not. It so happens that Ashley was training a new home aide the morning she discovered Mrs. Carr dead in her bed. Her apprentice went with her to the Carr residence and saw everything."

"Well, bully for you, Dan. I hope you find out the truth."

"You tell me. The aide-in-training was your sister, Lavender. Is she even capable of telling the truth?"

Annie didn't have an answer.

CHAPTER 7

Dan had mercifully left Annie alone after giving her the news about Lavender. She thought of calling Martha and letting her know, but then recalled their conversation yesterday and intuited that the "bit of a shock" Martha had alluded to was Lavender finding Eloise Carr dead in her home. She refused to think about Lavender's possible involvement with any drug thefts. Lavender was so squeaky clean that she probably didn't take Aleve for menstrual cramps but chewed some kind of plant bark instead.

However, Lavender's reputation for truthfulness was not entirely spotless, as Annie had learned during the few short weeks she had shared her home with her half sister. True, most of Lavender's lies had been those of omission—for example, her failure to tell their shared bio father that she was taking his Aston Martin on the road without a valid driver's license. Or assuring Annie she was skilled in paranormal animal communication, and had deep connections with local Native American elders, who probably ran when they saw her coming. Yet deep down, Annie knew that Lavender's deceptions were deployed only to cover up her own insecurities and lack of confidence. These reasons hardly compensated for her half-truths, but they were somewhat understandable. Somewhat.

The horses were far out in the pasture now, enjoying new, delicious spring grass and, judging by their absence, had zero interest in what was taking place back at the stables. Annie wished she could be as blasé as her herd. She walked over to Leif, the local volunteer fireman who had the distinct honor of driving the prized fire truck housed in Oyster Bay to every local accident and disaster. Leif also sheared her sheep twice a year. Privately, Annie thought Leif was a better shearer than EMT, but she kept her opinion to herself.

Leif and the fire truck had arrived five minutes before the sheriff this morning. This was hardly surprising; Annie knew that Leif kept his police and fire radio on 24/7 and he was four miles closer to her place. He was standing by the barn now, trying to get information but, judging by the lack of interest around him, not getting very far.

"Hey, Leif." Annie walked up and stretched out her hand.

"Annie! Can you believe it? We're working on another case together."

Her sarcastic nature, Annie's way of trying to control her temper, emerged again.

"Hardly, Leif. I just happened to find a dead woman swinging from the barn rafters this morning. Not an everyday occurrence, so I thought I'd share it on the airways so all my neighbors could take a look, too. Have you had the pleasure yet?"

Leif, immune to Annie's gallows humor, ignored her rude rejoinder and answered honestly.

"Not yet. They're still doing their thing in there and won't let me have so much as a glance. I could be here three more hours until they cut her down and let me haul her over to Hank." He sounded so crestfallen, Annie laughed.

"Most people don't relish the job of transporting stiffs."

"Annie, that's not fair! I'm just trying to do my civic duty *and* earn a living. I'm happy to help out, you know I am, but I got to pay the bills, too. And the garage pays me only when I'm there."

He had a point. Like many Peninsula residents, Leif cobbled together several professions in order to survive. Fall and spring, he'd be working on every sheep operation within a fifty-mile radius. During the winter, he was a dependable grease monkey at the Oyster Bay garage. Annie wasn't sure what Leif did during the summer. He probably went out on his sailboat and drank beer. And why not? Summers on the Peninsula were too precious to waste working inside all the time.

"Have you learned anything?" she asked Leif.

"Only that she's a twenty-year-old local female and probably died from asphyxiation, possibly also cerebral hypoxia. That's typically what happens from a short drop."

Bile filled Annie's mouth.

"How do you know all this?" *Leif probably took books about causes of death to bed with him*, Annie thought.

"Oh, I just try to keep up on things that might pertain to my job," he said modestly. "You know I'm taking the police officer exam next month."

"I had no idea, Leif." Annie was honestly surprised. "But good for you. I get that Ashley was strangled by the

twine. But cerebral hypo . . . whatever you said. I'm assuming that means her neck was broken? That's what I always thought happened when a person hanged."
Annie's knowledge of death by hanging was limited to what she'd seen in old Westerns.

"Ashley? You know her name?" Leif asked eagerly.

Why not? It'll be in the online edition of the Port Chester Gazette *tonight, if not already,* Annie thought. The printed version wouldn't be out for another week; the local newspaper came out only on Wednesdays.

"Ashley Lawton," Annie clarified. "She actually came here yesterday afternoon, looking for work at the stables. Not sure why she chose to hang herself here."

"Whoa. That's deep."

Annie thought "deep" didn't cover the half of it. She felt immense guilt over Ashley's death, and wished, for the hundredth time, she'd offered the young woman a job when she'd asked for one. At the same time, she felt a small surge of anger for Ashley's decision to kill herself on her ranch. She had a feeling that the memory of encountering Ashley's body would never quite go away.

"Obviously, I didn't have work for her. But to stage her body so I'd find it . . . it just seems harsh. Or, to be honest, it doesn't fit with what little I know of the woman."

"Well, I'm real sorry, Annie. I mean, how were you supposed to know how depressed she was? Did you know her very well?"

"Not at all. Apparently, she'd heard me speak at a horse club meeting a few years back and remembered me. But her face didn't ring a bell with me."

"Weird. Well, as I was about to tell you, she probably didn't break her neck at all—rope's too short. That's why it's called a short drop. She might've lost consciousness first. Happens if the noose tightens and blocks the jugular vein and carotid arteries. Without a lot of blood flow to the brain, she'd be out of it, and probably wouldn't even know she was being strangled."

"Well, let's hope so," Annie said fervently.

"No kidding. The other scenario isn't as pretty. If she was conscious, it might have taken her ten, twenty minutes to actually die. I'd hate to be awake for that."

Annie felt a bit sick.

"Although, if the rope had been longer, she might've broke her neck, and death would be virtually instantaneous," Leif prattled on.

"*LEIF!*" Dan Stetson's stentorian voice bellowed out, and the sheriff angrily strode toward them.

"Leif, you don't know what the Sam Hill you're talking about. You haven't seen the body, you don't know the victim, and you sure as hell don't know forensic science. So quite scaring Ms. Carson here and get back to your job."

Leif looked sheepishly at Dan.

"Sorry, Sheriff. Annie was just asking if I knew anything about what happened when people hung themselves. . . ."

"I find that highly unlikely. More likely you were just shooting off your mouth to make yourself look smart. If you want to pass that exam next month, I suggest you go back to your truck and pick up your law enforcement manual. You won't be the first to flunk just because you think you already know everything."

Leif slunk away, avoiding Annie's eyes.

But Annie wasn't looking at Leif. She wasn't looking at anyone. She was looking inside her own mind, going over the scene she'd memorized of Ashley hanging motionless and silent in her cavernous barn. Something Leif had said was troubling her.

"Sorry, Annie." Dan put one of his massive paws on

Annie's arm. "Leif just gets carried away sometimes with his own so-called book smarts."

She shook it off. "Dan," she said urgently. "Let's go someplace private where we can talk." She motioned to the tack room, off the stables. It was as peaceful a place as any on her ranch right now. Once inside, she dusted off a chair and motioned for Dan to sit down. She sat on the only other chair in the room. Annie didn't often have human visitors here.

Dan's cell phone squealed. He gave a short curse and jabbed a button on the screen with one of his large fingers.

"Stetson."

He listened intently for a minute, gave a curt "Thanks," and put the phone away.

"What was that?"

Dan sighed. "I'm telling you this because Ashley's death occurred on your property, understand? It is not for public consumption, which includes Leif, and most important Lavender. No one is to know what I'm about to tell you. Understood?"

Annie nodded meekly. Dan had been a lot more circumspect about sharing information about ongoing cases with her since the last homicide. She was grateful to get any tidbit at all.

"The autopsy results are in on Eloise Carr. Coroner suspects a drug overdose. He's sending off for a tox report now."

"So . . . suicide or homicide?"

"We don't know yet. But it's looking more like the latter, based on what we found today. That's why I need you to tell me everything you remember when you walked into the barn this morning."

Annie looked directly at Dan. She took a deep breath.

"I needed to stock more hay in the tack room. The barn doors weren't locked; they never are."

"They were when we got here."

"That was to make sure no one went in without me knowing it. Normally, they're always unlocked. When I need hay when it's dark out, I don't want to fiddle with any locks. Besides, no one steals hay."

"You'd be surprised. But go on."

"I had a dolly with me for transport, but I put it to one side so I could use both hands to open the doors. Then I flipped on the light switch on the left. I immediately saw Ashley's body. It was absolutely still. She was just hanging there. There was no question that she was dead, probably for quite a few hours, so I didn't bother checking for a pulse."

Which was the last thing I wanted to do, anyway, she thought.

"I won't deny that I was upset, but I knew you'd be asking me questions later, so I tried to take in the scene as best as I could before calling 911. I didn't touch anything—honest—beyond the barn door handles and a hay bale I sat on for about ten seconds. Besides, I had gloves on the whole time I was in the barn."

Dan slowly nodded.

"I looked for a suicide note, or anything she might have left behind. Nothing. Absolutely nothing. And that's what's bothering me now. I've just assumed that Ashley committed suicide. But, Dan, now it just doesn't make sense. Sure, her feet were just three feet off the ground, but no one can jump three feet in the air, grab a noose, and put it around their neck. Can they? I mean, wouldn't you expect to find a bale of hay nearby, or something that she would have used to get her neck into the noose?"

"You nailed it, Annie." Dan's voice was grim. "I just wanted to make sure you hadn't moved anything that would have fit the other scenario. Tony's tried to do exactly what you've described—he can't do it, and he's one of our fittest officers. The absence of a stool, plus scratch marks on both her hands and neck, make it pretty clear that Ashley Lawton was murdered. And fighting for her life to the bitter end."

CHAPTER 8

THURSDAY EVENING, MAY 5

By five o'clock, everyone had finally packed up their gear and left. Dan and Tony were the last to go, and their final act of the day was to silently transfer ten bales of Timothy from the hay barn to Annie's tack room. They did it without asking. Annie was impressed.

The barn had lost all semblance of a neat and tidy receptacle for sweet-smelling hay. The "accident scene" tape that had been tacked up upon arrival had been replaced with tape proclaiming CRIME SCENE: DO NOT CROSS. It would remain there, Dan reminded Annie, until the Suwana County Sheriff's Office told her otherwise. This did not impress Annie.

"I have no intention of entering that structure until Lavender's given it a good smudging," she told the sheriff. She was joking, of course. Her half sister had once smudged her own home, and it had taken weeks to get the cornmeal out of the corner crevices. She could well imagine the rat infestation if she repeated the Native American ceremony in her barn.

"Nothing personal, Annie, just standard police procedure," Dan replied. "We just want to make sure that no one goes in until we're sure we didn't leave some key piece of evidence behind."

"Speaking of keys," Tony interrupted, "we found a couple on the body. I don't suppose either looks familiar to you?" He pulled on a pair of latex gloves as he spoke, then reached into a thick paper evidence bag, pulling out a plastic bag that held the items. One looked like an ordinary door key, with wispy green yarn tied to the top. The other was more mysterious. It had a black plastic covering and unusual markings. Annie peered at both.

"Nope," she said. "Never seen them before."

Tony nodded, and sealed the bag with tape.

"And, just for the record, what size shoes do you wear?"

"Jeez, Tony! We're getting a bit personal, aren't we?"

"We found traces of a couple of different shoe prints inside. As well as fingerprints. We've got your prints on file from the last case, but it would help us eliminate you from our long list of suspects if you'd tell us this detail."

This was Tony being droll.

"Eight and a half. Anything else?"

"Who else has been in your hay barn recently?"

"Aside from half the deputies from the Sheriff's Office today? No one. 'Cept me, of course." Although she said nothing, Annie felt uneasy about the realization that unknown people had been traipsing through her farm structure. Obviously, Ashley had been there. But others? As in Ashley's killer? It was downright creepy.

"So what do you think at this juncture? Should I be concerned that the killer might return?"

Dan and Tony looked at each other. Dan cleared his throat.

"I think the chances are pretty close to nil. But it wouldn't hurt for you to take that .30-.30 out of your truck and lug it into your house."

For once, Annie decided to take the sheriff's advice.

At ten o'clock that night, she was aiming the shotgun straight into her sheep pasture.

Watching the deputies, EMTs, and paramedics swarm around her farm all day had exhausted Annie. After she'd fed the horses, she'd obediently unbolted her Winchester from the gun rack in her Ford and taken it inside, where she'd cleaned and loaded it. One restorative glass of Glenlivet after that had done her in. She'd tumbled into bed without having eaten dinner, still fully clothed. A few hours later, Trotter's frantic hee-hawing brought her instantly to her senses. Grabbing her parka and her shotgun, she'd raced to her truck, heaved it into reverse, and barreled down the back road to her sheep pasture. Out of the corner of her eye, she saw her horses in the paddock, ears forward, uneasily at attention. She noticed Wolf beside her in the cab only when she pulled up to the pasture gate.

She jumped out, Wolf instantly following her, and trained her eyes on the dark landscape in front of her. Trotter was still braying, although not as urgently. A cluster of sheep huddled around the donkey, plaintively baaing. The ones who couldn't get close enough to their savior were jumbled in the rain shelter in the pasture. From her vantage point, they looked like one indistinct mass of white. Wolf bounded away; she had no doubt he was in hot pursuit of a predator's scent. She brought the Winchester to her shoulder and slowly scanned the interior, and then the perimeter of the fence line. She saw and heard nothing except the sonorous drip of dew falling from heavy leaves to the mossy earth.

Finally, she put down the gun, opened the pasture gate—still firmly locked—and walked inside, threading her way through the mass of ewes and lambs. She reached into her parka, then pulled out a dusty carrot and a couple of horse treats and handed them to the sheep's protector.

"Good job, Trotter. Good job." Trotter stopped braying long enough to eat his reward.

Once Annie was sure that the predator was truly gone, she called for Wolf, who took a full minute to reappear. He came jogging out from the forest, near the area where Annie had found the makeshift campsite a few days before. Hell's bells! How could she have forgotten to tell Dan and Tony about that? For all she knew, it might be the hideout for Ashley's killer. He might be there now.

Scrambling back into her truck and calling for Wolf, she placed the shotgun by her side and maneuvered the vehicle down the old logging road. If someone was on her property, she was damn well going to know about it. As she rounded the corner leading to the site, she dimmed her headlights. Anyone who was in the vicinity undoubtedly was already aware of her presence, but she wanted to give them as little help as possible. All was quiet and immensely dark in the area where she'd first seen the fire pit and frayed army bedroll. She reached into her glove compartment, pulled out a flashlight, and turned it on. The batteries were dead. And the replacement batteries were back in her home. She breathed softly for a minute, straining to hear any noise outside.

Again, the forest was silent. Well, either her visitor was a trained sniper who knew how to keep every muscle tightly coiled, or no one was there. She didn't feel like taking any more time to find out. She put the truck in reverse and eased back along the logging road, hoping that the ring of a weapon firing wouldn't pierce the night air as she did so. When she found a small clearing, she made a neat three-point turn and headed back to the farm. The house was dark; she hadn't taken the time to switch on her outside light. What a crack detective she was turning out to be.

But the motion detector light by the paddock area was shining brightly. This was hardly alarming, as Annie closed her stall doors only while the horses were eating their dinners. This was merely to ensure that everyone ate the right supplements and there was no fussing over whose dinner mash was bigger or who got more hay. The rest of the time, the horses could come and go from their stalls as they pleased. If someone wanted to take a constitutional in the paddock at three o'clock in the morning, they were free to do so, but under the light of several motion detector bulbs strategically placed in the stall beams.

She parked her truck by the light. A chorus of low nickers greeted Annie as she approached the paddock. Murmuring to her horses, she ducked into the tack room and grabbed a flashlight that still had juice. Outside, she could see the forms of all her horses along the back fencing. No one appeared upset, so Annie merely rubbed the necks of Baby and Sam, who happened to be closest to her, and headed back up to her home. She swept the walkway with the flashlight as she trudged up the hill. Once inside, she heaved a long shudder of stored anxiety. Wolf was the only one who seemed refreshed from the outing; he looked at her, tail wagging, as if to thank her for enlivening his usual boring evening with a late-night truck ride and romp through the forest.

Glancing at her phone, she noticed the red message light was flashing. Marcus. She'd forgotten all about their now-ritual nightly chat. Well, it probably was for the best. She'd endured more than her share of horrors today, but all she needed now, she told herself, was a good night's sleep. Then her life could start again.

Her cell phone buzzed from the inside of her parka, where it had lain all day. Pulling it out, she recognized the California area code. She reluctantly punched the accept button.

"Annie, it's Marcus. I've been trying to reach you all day. Are you all right?"

He was the first person to ask. She burst into tears.

CHAPTER 9

FRIDAY, MAY 6

"You have *got* to stop taking foolish chances."

"Excuse me, Dan? Do I not have a right to protect my property from unwanted squatters?"

"You do. Try calling 911 next time."

"Well, I would have, if I'd seen the guy. But my flashlight was dead."

"That is *exactly* what I'm talking about! Let us do the investigating, not you!"

"What, and have a couple of your big lugs thrashing around the forest? Compared to my skills at stealth and sneakiness?"

"What stealth? I thought you drove your rig down here."

"Well, I'm not entirely stupid."

"Not entirely."

Dan and Annie glared at each other while Tony and two other deputies resolutely sifted through the detritus left in the now-deserted campsite. According to Tony, whoever had been staying here probably had vacated before Annie made her late-night drive-by. The fire had long been extinguished, he said, and Annie couldn't imagine anyone huddling out here without its warmth.

"Maybe," Tony said when Annie suggested this theory. "But we've uncovered two empty fifths of Old Crow, so liquid warmth was in ample supply."

That was less than reassuring.

Fortunately, Dan had not berated her for failing to tell him about the transient's site the day before. He'd saved all his criticism for her decision to check out the space, alone, in the dead of night, even if she did have her shotgun and faithful hound by her.

"Would the two of you quit bickering for one second? I found something." Kim Williams strode toward them, holding an evidence bag in her latex-gloved hand. It was an unusually warm day for May, almost seventy degrees under a near-cloudless sky, and a thin line of perspiration creased Kim's upper lip. Her uniform could not hide the well-toned muscles of her arms and legs. She should have been a bodybuilder, Annie thought, instead of a lowly deputy who had to take Dan's orders.

Dan peered inside the bag and sniffed.

"Well, that's consistent with what I saw last night."

"What?" Annie said the word crossly. She was unduly irritated that she was being left out of the look-what-I-found game.

Kim closed the bag carefully. "It's remnants of meth, Annie. I hate to tell you this, but I think that fire was used as a makeshift chemical lab, not for keeping warm. We found empty Sudafed packets back there"—she nodded to the dense forest beyond—"and an empty blowtorch just off the road."

"Great. My innocent little lambs were within spitting

distance of crazed druggies who could have blown up the place. Did they leave their business card, by any chance?"

"Not in so many words. But we'll test the bedroll and the blowtorch for DNA and fingerprints. And anything else we find."

"Is the place contaminated? Do I need to don a hazmat suit just to feed my sheep?"

"This was a small-time operation, in the open air. My guess is whoever stayed here was making enough for personal consumption but not enough to sell on the street. We'll clean up the place thoroughly before we leave. You and the sheep shouldn't suffer any ill effects."

"Well, thank god for that. What do you make of the lamb?"

Annie was referring to the dirty little toy lamb that she'd discovered on her first trip here. It was still wedged in the tree where Annie had left it when the Sheriff's Office had arrived this morning. It now resided in yet another brown paper evidence bag.

"Hard to say. One of the camp occupants could have been a female, maybe Ashley. We'll be testing the stuffed animal, too."

As Kim walked away, Annie turned to Dan. "What did you mean, the meth was 'consistent with what I saw last night'?"

"Well, that's a bit of a story." Dan walked over to the bed of Annie's truck, where he refilled his Styrofoam cup with more steaming coffee from the thermos Annie had brought with her. He took a sip and leaned back on the bumper. As always, Annie felt a bit jealous whenever she saw Dan drink black coffee. She needed the caffeine but couldn't stomach it unless it was fully loaded with milk and sugar, and preferably cream.

"I met Ashley's mother last night," he said grimly. "Interesting encounter. You'd think the mom might be a bit broken up about the tragic death of her twenty-year-old daughter. Not this lady. 'Course, she was stoned out of her mind. The news might just now be sinking in. Couldn't tell me a thing about her daughter—where she had last worked, where she lived, who her friends were, or even the name of her boyfriend. All she wanted to know was whether she could sue you, since you provided the barn in which Ashley died."

Annie squawked. "Sue me? Is she out of her mind?"

"Pretty much, most of the time, it seems. She lives in that trailer park just outside of Greenburg proper. You know, by the Arco gas station."

Annie knew the place. It was a dump. She'd never known a single person who lived there, and now she decided she didn't want to.

"Does Ashley have any siblings? Maybe they'd care about their sister's death. By the way, what did you tell Ashley's mother? Suicide or homicide?"

"Suicide. That's the official version for now, which we're not trying to publicize, either. Makes it easier to catch someone in a lie if they think they're off the hook for murder."

That made sense.

"Any other kids?"

"Older brother, in the navy. Mom said she'd let him know. I'll be calling his commanding officer this afternoon, just to make sure the message gets through."

"So was Ashley's mom high on meth?"

"No, I think her substance of choice is the more mellow kind."

"Well, it is legal now, you know."

"And you don't know what a headache that's turning out to be."

"Oh, bite me. People can't smoke and drive any more than they can drink and drive. They can't even have more than a joint in the glove box, as I recall."

"Doesn't stop people from ruining their brains by keeping it in a constant haze, so much that they don't even remember their daughter's address."

Annie fell silent. Dan's zero tolerance for any kind of drug use was well known to her. Annie wasn't a recreational drug user—not when she was custodian and provider for more than a hundred sheep, seven horses, one donkey, two dogs, and a cat. But the truth was, even if she'd lived in an apartment and had only potted plants to tend to, she wouldn't have imbibed. It simply wasn't part of her nature. Still, she was a bit more open-minded about other people's usage. Annie was rather partial to Glenlivet, herself. Then again, she didn't have to enforce the law.

"So where did you get the meth connection?"

"My next stop—Ashley's home on the Squill River, the address on file with the nursing service. Kim went with me."

Good plan, Annie thought. Kim would make excellent backup. She was suddenly curious about Ashley's private life. She'd glimpsed so little the day she'd met her, but what she'd seen reflected a perfectly nice young woman who loved horses. Annie still couldn't believe that she'd been brutally murdered. Every time she thought about Ashley's death, guilt flooded her body and she felt incredible sadness seep through her. If it had happened anywhere other than on her property, perhaps her feelings might not have been so intense. But it had.

"So tell all."

"Got lucky. We found Ashley's boyfriend at home. Name's Pete Corbett. He's Eddie Trueblood all over again."

Annie knew he was referring to the son of one of
Suwana County's first and finest families, who'd squan-
dered his life away. She sighed. What was it with children who had everything from birth? It was as if they'd
been born with a gene that guaranteed they'd make a
mess out of their lives.

"What's Pete's background?"

"Oh, a half-dozen juvie cases, mostly alcohol- and
drug-related. One theft of a car, but it was his father's,
who refused to press charges. He's never spent more
than a day in jail, but judging by his tats, you'd think
he'd spent ten years in prison. Very impressive. He was
higher than a kite when I came to the door, and practically
bouncing off the walls the entire time we talked. Broke
down when I told him about Ashley, but that doesn't mean
much—could just be killer's remorse. Claims he's never
been near your place. Said he was having dinner with
Mom and Dad the night before you found Ashley. Can't
think of a reason why Ashley would want to kill herself.
In fact, he kept referring to her as his 'fiancée,' even
though Ashley filed a restraining order against his ass
six months ago."

"Really? What'd she say?"

"The usual. She came home, he was high, she tried
to leave, and he wouldn't let her. Photos a friend took
on her phone showed a lot of ugly bruises on Ashley's
arms and legs, as well as a black eye. Only problem was
that no one called us, and Ashley was a no-show at the
hearing ten days later. So Pete was never formally charged
with domestic assault."

"I thought the state didn't let that happen anymore."

Annie was referring to the prosecutor's office policy
of going forward with domestic violence cases even if
the victim didn't want to, changed their mind, or allegedly recanted.

"We do our best to nail the miscreants, but unless law enforcement is called in close to when the incident occurs, there's not much we can do."

"So what *are* you going to do?"

"Pete's agreed to come in for a formal taped interview this afternoon. Unless he agrees to being put on the box and passes, we'll put surveillance on him 24/7."

"The box," Annie knew, referred to a polygraph test, which Kim was trained to give. She just hoped that Pete's parents wouldn't have him "lawyered up," as Dan irreverently described it, before the time the interview was to take place.

Annie always felt a bit of trepidation when she visited Martha Sanderson's tiny home, just a few miles away from her own. Martha was so . . . well . . . proper, in an old-fashioned way, and Annie was never sure her own manners measured up. Then there was her houseguest, Lavender Carson. While infinitely grateful that Lavender bunked with Martha instead of her, she knew that her half sister had an unerring ability to say or do things that threw Annie into an instant fury. The last thing Annie wanted to do tonight was cause any contretemps between them. It would be so upsetting to the lady whom both of them loved. Their fondness for Martha was one of the few things the sisters had in common.

At least Lavender's pink hair was gone, if not her hippy-dippy clothes, Annie thought, as her half sister opened the door, beaming a beatific smile that even her lambs couldn't match.

"Sister! We're so happy you could come tonight."

Annie managed a grimace that she hoped looked

friendly. She held out a bottle of wine. It was white Zinfandel, the best the gas station down the road had to offer. Marcus's gift of Saint-Émilion Grand Cru was long gone.

"How have you been, Lavender?" *As if I don't already know.*

"So many things to tell you, sister! Please, come in."

Lavender extended her arm as if she were ushering in the Queen of England. Annie sighed and stepped inside Martha's parlor. Fresh flowers adorned every spare space, which was rare—every table displayed a tableau of tiny Dresden china dolls and other precious items. Lacy coverlets draped over a russet-colored love seat and two wingback chairs. In the corner stood an antique pedal organ, with sheet music for an old hymn on the music rack. Annie felt as if she had entered a petite fairy kingdom whenever she was in this room.

Martha appeared around the corner, wearing an apron dusted with flour. Wolf and Sasha, who'd been standing politely at Annie's side, now rushed to her, showing their obvious preference in humans. Martha was the source of never-ending treats. Annie was far more parsimonious.

"Perfect timing, Annie. We're just about to sit down. And what a nice wine you've brought us. Why don't you open it, Lavender, and then we'll sit down at the table."

The evening went better than the dinner guest expected. Lavender fully disclosed her small part in discovering Eloise Carr's body, but aside from her far too dramatic description of her subsequent faint, she had little to say on the subject.

"I mean, it's not as if I *knew* Mrs. Carr," she said carelessly. "Ashley said she was really nice, and I'm sure she was. But I never met her. Ashley was the one who was upset. After all, she'd helped take care of her for two years."

It was obvious Lavender did not read the local newspaper and so did not yet know about Ashley's demise. Annie's Bad Angel encouraged her to delve further.

"So, how's Ashley doing now?" Annie tried to sound indifferent.

"All right, I guess," was Lavender's doubtful reply. "I haven't seen her since that morning. And we'd only met that day. I got assigned to another caregiver for training after that. I imagine Ashley wanted to take some time off."

Taking time off from work was one of Lavender's specialties. Annie wasn't surprised that she assumed everyone would want to melt into a fainting couch for weeks afterward.

"We talked about it, but decided that it would be best for Lavender to continue her training," Martha explained. "I told her that if you'd been bucked off a horse, you'd get right back in the saddle, and she should do the same. Was I right, Annie?"

"Absolutely." Annie immediately put another piece of pork roast in her mouth to avoid elucidating further.

The phone rang, and Martha excused herself to answer it. When she came back, she looked a bit quizzically at Lavender.

"It's for you, dear. It's Sheriff Dan Stetson. He says he wants to talk to you about Ashley."

Lavender burst into tears and fled from the table. Her outburst baffled the dogs, who'd been contently chewing bones in the corner. They watched Lavender run out of the room and then placidly resumed their pastime. Annie and Martha looked at each other.

"She'll be fine, dear. Remember, her first conversation with Sheriff Dan was a bit hard on her."

Right. Annie had forgotten that Dan had pulled over Lavender for speeding in a school zone a few months before, which, in turn, had exposed her half sister's hornet's nest of legal problems back in Florida. Still. Why should Lavender be so upset to talk about a woman whom she barely knew?

CHAPTER 10

SUNDAY, MAY 8

Annie looked at the ground, three feet below. A graceful exit was just not in the cards.

Glancing back at Wolf in the cab's passenger seat, she scooted her body to the edge of her own, grabbed the open door handle, and leapt. She'd forgotten about her high heels. Although they were not much taller than those on her most stylish Western boots, the incline of the sole was much steeper. She made a jarring landing on the asphalt, pitched straight forward, and felt hard gravel grating into her knees and palms.

A string of curses came out of Annie's mouth as she hastily got up and assessed the damage. Miraculously, her nylons were still intact. *They must make them out of titanium nowadays,* Annie thought. If this had happened when she was in high school—and that was where she now happened to be—her nylons would have been in tatters. Her one black dress was covered in dust, but perhaps a wet towel in the ladies' room would remedy that. It was her pride that had suffered the most. She just wasn't used to wearing apparel that limited her stride to eight inches and severely hindered her mobility. And it infuriated her that her first return visit to Port Chester High in twenty-five years had been made in such a spectacularly humiliating way.

"Are you all right? Can I help you?" A male voice came from behind her, and she wheeled around, mortified that anyone else had seen her go splat on the pavement. The man was older than she by a generation, she guessed, and his gut and receding hairline made him appear exceptionally ordinary. He wore tan Dockers and a navy blue jacket, sans tie. His perfectly polished loafers had those silly leather tassels that men must think make a desirable fashion statement.

"Thanks, I'm fine," Annie called back. "I guess I'm just not used to getting down from my truck in a dress."

"Nice-looking rig," the man said admiringly. "I'd love to have your truck. But my wife insists that it's totally unnecessary, the way we live."

Annie laughed. "I couldn't get along without mine on my ranch. What kind of vehicle do you drive?"

"I've got that Prius"—he pointed to the gray car beside hers—"and my wife drives a Subaru. Great for everything except hauling lumber and horses. Which we don't need or have, but it's the only argument I've thought of so far in trying to change my wife's mind."

He was more entertaining than he looked, Annie concluded, and so she stuck out her hand. "Annie Carson. Nice to meet you."

"Ron Carr Junior. Likewise." They shook hands, and then Ron's eyes widened. "Hey, I *know* you—Sheriff Dan mentioned your name when he called to tell me about Ashley's memorial service here today. Aren't you the lady who found her body?"

Annie's heart skipped a beat. As Ron spoke, she'd simultaneously realized who *he* was—Eloise Carr's son. The one who thought Ashley was so nice, just as she had.

"Unfortunately, yes. And I recognize your name, as well. The sheriff told me that Ashley had been caring for your mother. I'm so sorry for your loss." This was the absolute truth. Annie had lost her mother twenty years earlier to breast cancer, and she missed her every day.

Ron shook his head back and forth as if he were trying to clear cobwebs from his brain.

"I still can't believe Ashley poisoned my mother. I met her several times, you know, when I stopped by to deliver Mother's groceries or her medications. They always were laughing and having such a good time. Mother told me she adored having her around. Why would Ashley do something like this? I mean, my mother wasn't in the best of health, but it's not as if she was unduly suffering or had some terminal disease, except for old age."

He looked completely baffled, and Annie felt a sympathetic pang for the man. She was not surprised that Ron had skipped entirely over the possibility that his mother had been responsible for her own death; no one likes to think of one's parents as preferring the easy way out, and she knew of nothing that suggested suicide. But the guy obviously knew Ashley a lot better than she ever would, and she wondered how she could possibly get him to tell her more about the young waif who had flitted into her own life and then left it in such a gruesome way.

"I understand that Ashley had a rotten boyfriend," she ventured. "Maybe he was involved. Or, at the very least, was a bad influence."

"Never met him, although now, after the fact, I remember Ashley coming to work a few times with unexplained bruises. I never asked about them, and she never told me. Now I wished I had. You're right—from what Sheriff Dan told me, it seems a lot more likely that Ashley's boyfriend was somehow involved in Mother's overdose than she was."

The conversation was now on her side of the court, but suddenly Annie didn't know what to say. Talking to a total stranger about the deaths of people you didn't know had that effect on her. She shifted her gaze from Ron to the school buildings in back of them.

"Did you graduate from here?" Ron asked.

"Class of '90," Annie confessed. "I still keep in touch with a few old friends. But I've never quite worked up the courage to attend a class reunion. How about yourself?"

"I'm going to date myself with the answer," he replied with a chuckle. "Class of '68. Half of us went into the army the day after graduation. I got lucky. Had a high lottery number."

"I'll say." Annie had barely known about the Vietnam War when she was growing up. She'd been so young. "I guess the science building was still new when you went here."

"That's right. Although the lab equipment's been replaced since then, I'm sure. We were so excited about looking at stuff under shiny new microscopes. My kids were doing that at eight years old."

They smiled at each other, and then Ron glanced at his watch. "Whoa, ten-thirty already. Maybe we should go inside. The principal said the auditorium probably will be packed. My wife's supposed to save me a seat, but who knows if she's even here yet. The woman takes her own sweet time just getting dressed to get the mail." He said it in a half-grumbling tone that still conveyed deep affection.

As Annie struggled to keep up with her mandated eight-inch stride, she vowed never again to wear a form-fitting dress as long as she lived.

She felt an eerie sense of déjà vu as soon as she walked inside the school doors. The same photographs of past homecoming queens and kings filled the walls; the same smell of sweat, overcooked vegetables, and raging hormones infused the air; and the noise level was as high as Annie remembered. A small crowd of people roamed the halls—some adults, some students, none of whom Annie recognized. Who would have thought Ashley had so many friends, Annie mused, although Dan had told her that the memorial service, or technically, "celebration of life," had been publicized in the local newspaper as open to the public. Perhaps this was an outpouring of people who'd known Ashley and genuinely cared. Or perhaps it was simply an alternative way to spend an otherwise boring Sunday afternoon. After all, the sun had gone behind the clouds today.

She looked vainly for someone she knew, but aside from a few teachers, whom she had no desire to encounter again, she saw no one. Ron had disappeared from her sight almost as soon as they entered the auditorium, no doubt in search of his wife. Finally, with more relief than she wanted to admit, she saw the head of Dan Stetson towering over the rest of the crowd. He was talking to a woman whom Annie assumed was the principal. She threaded her way over to where he stood and waited expectantly for his hello. He ignored her.

After two minutes, Annie couldn't take it anymore.

"Dan!" Her tone reflected her high degree of irritation.

The sheriff peered at her, and then stepped back. "Annie? Is that you? I didn't recognize you with your clothes on. I mean, with those clothes on." His face suffused with red, he turned toward the principal, whose cheeks also had turned bright pink.

"For the record, Dan always sees me fully clothed." Annie felt she had to clarify his blunder. After all, she was talking to the principal, who looked as if she was perfectly comfortable wearing constricting dresses and four-inch high heels every day. "It's just that normally I'm wearing jeans and cowboy boots, not a dress."

The principal laughed. "I totally understand. If a student sees me walking through the grocery store in my sweats, I become invisible." She held out her hand. "Carla Johnson. Very nice to meet you."

"Annie Carson. You look like a nice principal. I wish Dan and I had had you around when we were going to high school."

Carla gave her a wide, appreciative smile. "Thanks. I've been here since 2009, and it's been quite a learning curve for me. This is my first job in a rural community. It's a huge difference from the urban environments I came from. The kids are great, of course. They just have different sets of challenges."

Challenges—the ubiquitous, euphemistic word for whatever ailed teenagers these days. Annie decided not to let the principal off the hook. After all, she'd been a rural kid a few years ago, too.

"Such as . . . ?"

"Well, poverty, really. So many of the kids here come from homes that have edged below the poverty level all of their lives. Not surprisingly, expectations for future growth, including higher education, are pretty low. It's rare if more than twenty percent of our graduates go on to college. It's a miracle if they actually get a degree. It's not because they can't do the work. It's just that they're not particularly motivated at home to go beyond their parents' educational level."

"Well, you're looking at two success stories now," Dan said proudly. It was true, Annie realized. It had taken a lot of menial jobs, careful budgeting, not to mention large government loans, but she'd managed to get her B.A. from Central Washington University in Ellensburg in less than the usual four years. Dan had attended the UW in Seattle on a football scholarship before going on to the police academy. He told anyone who'd listen that he still could fit into his old Huskies uniform.

"You're both such great role models. In fact, I'd love it if you could come here before school lets out to speak to graduating seniors. They'd get so much from what you could share."

Annie trained a discrete glare in Dan's direction. This is what comes from unnecessary bragging, it said.

"Why sure, Carla. We'd be happy to speak to the kids, wouldn't we, Annie?"

"Sure." Annie managed to choke out the word.

"Terrific. Well, I must run." Carla glanced at the big round clock overhead, put there just to make sure students knew when class started and had no good excuse for being late. "I'm making a few announcements before the kids take over." She walked off briskly, the epitome of good sense and deportment. Annie wondered how she managed to walk so quickly in a pencil-thin skirt.

"Nice of Carla to arrange this for Ashley's friends," Dan commented. "Her mother didn't intend to do a thing. As it is, the county's picking up the cost of burial."

Annie was shocked but said nothing.

"Let me show you the cast of suspects." Dan took Annie's arm and led her into the back of the auditorium, where staff was doing last-minute checks on a soundboard. He seemed to know he'd peeved Annie by volunteering her time without asking.

"That's Ronald Junior and Jane Carr, over on the left, in front," he said in a sotto voce tone while pointing with one beefy arm.

"I know," Annie whispered back. "I met Ron coming in. Seems nice enough. Why'd he and his wife decide to come?"

"Told me he wanted to remember the good things about the girl who took care of his mother," Dan said. "Pretty darn nice of him, under the circumstances."

"Dan! Mrs. Carr might have done herself in, you know."

"Doubt it. Ronald says he called his mom the night before she died, and she was full of good cheer, looking forward to a visit from one of her grandkids the next day."

Then again, maybe not.

Dan pointed to the opposite side of the auditorium. "That's Candice Lawton, Ashley's mother, over there on the aisle."

"You mean, the woman who wants to sue me? This I've got to see."

Annie tiptoed halfway down the far aisle to get a better look. Ashley's mother probably was close to her in age, but that's where the similarities stopped. Her polyester pantsuit couldn't hide a girth that stretched bigger than Dan's, and even sitting, bags of fat rolled around her knees. Her long hair, all gray, hung limply despite being pulled back, and exposed a solid face that portrayed no emotion. She had small eyes, a small mouth, and, Annie decided, looked just plain mean. She could understand why Ashley might think living with a jacked-up, sometimes violent boyfriend was better than what was back at home; she was certain living with Candice had been no picnic. Annie noticed that none of the students were approaching her to give their condolences.

She made her way back to Dan, who then identified several of Ashley's friends who intended to speak. Although Ashley had graduated two years before, many in the crowd appeared to be still high school age. She was sure Ashley's sudden death was a huge source of gossip right now—the information the Sheriff's Office had disseminated was pitifully small, barely worth a paragraph in the newspaper's online Sheriff's Log. It merely stated that the body of Ashley Lawton, a twenty-year-old female who had graduated from Port Chester High in 2014, had been found on a local ranch, possibly the result of suicide, although the case was still under investigation. No other details were listed.

To Annie's surprise, the ceremony itself was surprisingly entertaining. A variety of friends spoke from the stage and related several funny and heartrending stories about the young woman. She learned that Ashley's favorite person was her paternal grandmother, who had died when Ashley was fifteen, and that Ashley had a special fondness for older people in general. Her favorite poem was by Robert Frost, "A Road Not Taken." She was a skilled horsewoman, and had adored her 4-H horse, Jumper. Two of Ashley's favorite songs were played, and Annie was relieved that neither was rap music. Absent from the stories was any mention of Ashley's home life, past or present. The ceremony ended by all her friends coming up to the podium, placing a small stuffed lamb next to a photo of Ashley, and delivering a final message to their beloved friend. Ashley loved lambs, the audience was told, and had become a vegetarian as a result. As far as Annie could tell, it was her only flaw.

She glanced at Dan. He nodded back. "Looks like we know the original owner," he muttered.

"Yes," Annie whispered back. "But do you know if Ashley stayed at the campsite or whether someone was just carrying around her stuffed animal?"

"Dunno yet. But we will."

When the lights went on, the auditorium erupted in a hundred conversations, everyone clambering to get to each other or out of the building. Dan excused himself and quickly made his way to the front, near the Carrs. Annie watched him go, but her attention was soon drawn to a heavily tattooed young man jogging down the steps. *It must be Pete Corbett, Ashley's boyfriend,* she thought. His flight ended abruptly when he reached Candice Lawton, who was still wedged into a seat. Annie fleetingly wondered if the woman would be able to get out without a crowbar. She watched Pete—if that's who he truly was—lean over and say something to Ashley's mother. Annie couldn't see Candice's face, but she could see the young man's, and he looked intensely serious. She then saw both Pete and Candice turn and look directly at Ron Carr and his wife, who now were standing and talking to Dan. They were long, hard looks, and not at all friendly.

Curious, Annie started the long walk toward the stage, but before she took a dozen steps, she was waylaid by a group of Ashley's friends, several of whom had just spoken onstage. They were so glad to see her here, they said. Ashley had told them she had visited her ranch and that Annie had offered her a job and a place to stay. Oh, my god, that was so cool of her, they gushed, because Ashley really didn't have a home and her boyfriend could be so mean, you know? Seriously. But what they really wanted to know was, why did Ashley die, because, like, she wasn't depressed at all after you gave her the job, and it was just so strange, and, like not like Ashley *at all*, and is it true she died on your ranch? The cops wouldn't tell them nothing, but someone thought it was true. Was it?

Annie was so stunned by this outpouring that she simply shouldered her way past the girls and ran for the nearest exit. It was only when she was driving by Martha Sanderson's tidy little house that she wondered why Lavender hadn't been in the audience. Then she saw Kim Williams's patrol vehicle parked in the driveway, and knew the answer.

CHAPTER II

MONDAY, MAY 9

It had been a long week for a cowgirl. Annie had awakened at six o'clock on Monday without her alarm clock, and plunged into her routine. Last week had set her off-kilter, she'd decided, what with finding dead bodies and abandoned campsites and spending far too much time talking with Dan Stetson over evidentiary details that didn't make a bit of difference in her business.

Then there was Ashley's memorial service. When Dan had told her about it on Saturday, she'd felt compelled to go, although being among so many strangers filled her with trepidation. She'd compensated by spending the rest of the day on her couch in her sweats, eating junk food and watching old movies. Her horses, of course, received their usual excellent level of service. But she'd felt so discombobulated by the recent series of events that she hadn't had the energy to do much else. Even when her trail-riding buddies had called and tried to wheedle her to bring Trooper out and play, she'd declined. She needed to hibernate, and hibernate she did, only emerging to take care of the horses and engage in her nightly call with Marcus, who was the epitome of sympathy and concern.

But now the dreaded memorial service was over and she'd tossed the memory of wearing a constraining dress to the recesses of her mind—just as she'd tossed the dress to the recesses of her closet. It was time to get back on track.

She started with a long session on Layla, who still needed a lot of TLC from her trainer. The Walker was no longer skittish when Annie brought out her saddle, and she didn't toss her head when shown her bridle, but she still tended to involuntarily tremble whenever Annie gave a cue to change what she'd just been doing. And then there was the apparent ghost to contend with, who lived in the round pen, somewhere on the northwest side. Every time Layla came to it, she tried to veer inside the circle, sure the unseen bogeyman was about to grab her. She wasn't the first horse who'd flinched at that particular area, even though there was no underbrush or trees or unlit area within twenty yards of the pen. Annie just accepted that some horses saw things that she didn't, and walked them through their fears. Most of the time, that is. Many years before on a trail ride, she'd once urged a horse whose hooves apparently were glued to the ground to go forward. When the horse wouldn't budge, she finally dismounted and tried to lead him on foot. What she found ten feet ahead of her was a precipice with a hundred-foot drop. She'd learned then to trust her horse's instincts, but drew the line at ghosts.

"Come on, Layla," she whispered into the horse's left ear, her heel resting on the horse's left side. "You can make it. Walk right through Casper. He's a friendly ghost, remember?"

Layla danced a bit on her front legs and then dropped her head and sighed. This is what Annie was waiting for. She gently encouraged the horse again. The Walker delicately stepped through the forbidden area, with only a slight hop at the end. The walk wasn't worthy of a show cup, but it was a whole lot better than it had been.

Hannah showed up at two, ready for a lesson, and to continue Layla's, Annie saddled Trooper and ponied Layla on a short trail ride on the ranch. As usual, Hannah was stuck with Bess, but for once the little girl had more pressing things to talk about than when she could ride a big horse that knew how to gallop.

"Let's go find the fawn, Annie!"

"I've got a better idea. Let's all ride down the road until we get to the ice-cream stand."

It was an easy sell. Although the campsite Annie had discovered a week ago was now completely cleaned up by the Sheriff's Office, Annie didn't want to answer any more questions about its demise than she had to. And Hannah would be sure to have several. Instead, Hannah learned, to her delight, that Bess liked strawberry ice cream as much as she did.

After dropping off the little girl at home two hours later, she drove into town to buy supplies at the local Cenex. Then, remembering that she needed stamps, she pulled into the post office. That errand tended to, she turned toward home, but hesitated when she saw a lineup of Suwana County Sheriff's Office vehicles outside Laurie's Café just across the road. She couldn't resist. She pulled into the parking lot, promised Wolf she'd bring him back a treat, and exited the truck without falling on her face. She was back to wearing Levi's.

Dan, Tony, Kim, and two other deputies Annie didn't

know were seated at the largest circular table in the place. They were the only guests; it was late in the day, and the dinner crowd hadn't started to arrive, even those who relied on the senior specials, available only between the hours of five and six PM.

"What's up, guys?" Annie said, strolling to the table. "Someone walk out on their bill and the owners had to call you in?"

"Very funny, Annie," Tony answered. "We're in a highly confidential strategic meeting and figured this was the place to hold it."

"Where you can get coffee and a slice of pie to help you think." Dan leaned back in his chair and slapped his considerable belly. Annie saw remnants of two orders in front of him.

"Good thinking. Public places are always the best spots to talk in private."

"Is she getting more sarcastic as she ages?" Kim asked her colleagues. Tony and Dan vigorously nodded yes.

"I am so maligned." Annie pulled up a chair and inserted it between the two deputies she hadn't recognized.

"Hi, I'm Annie Carson," she told the deputy seated to the right of her. "I find most of the dead bodies in Suwana County."

"Better than a trained K9," Dan threw in.

Looking slightly aghast, the deputy swallowed and held out his hand. "Bill Stetson," he said, a bit uncertainly.

"Stetson? Did I hear you right? Are you related to that thug over there?"

"He's my cousin, twice removed," said Dan. "My aunt's daughter's boy. Or something like that. Joined the force six months ago and is doing real well." He was practically preening.

"Nice to meet you, Bill. Hope the sheriff isn't being too hard on you."

" 'Course I am, Annie. He has to show everyone else that he's not getting special favors. Right, Bill?"

"Right, Uncle Dan. I mean, Sheriff."

The man to the right of Annie now spoke. "I'm Jack Clauson. I'm not a relative of the sheriff's, but our mothers go way back. Both were our den mothers in the 1970s. I've been with the force since '92, but usually I'm holed up in the basement. I'm the department's one computer geek."

Annie looked at the slight man, who had wispy, receding hair, and a very nice smile. "You make sure they unlock the chains occasionally so you see the sunlight," she said seriously.

"Not a problem. There's not a lock or a password I can't break. I'm a regular Houdini."

"We were just talking about you, Annie." Kim leaned forward. "We actually were going to ask for a little help."

Annie sat up nearly as erect as Kim. "Really?" She sounded as if she were ten years old and being told she could go on the big roller coaster. The vow she'd taken only that morning to stick to her horse business and let everyone else take care of their own had vanished with Kim's remark.

The top-secret meeting continued back at the Sheriff's Office, where the atmosphere turned far more serious. Kim and Dan had taken her into their full confidence, and Annie knew how critical it was that she adhere to her promise to keep what she was about to learn to herself.

"I won't even tell Wolf," she said solemnly.

As usual, Dan told her, the forensic lab in Olympic

was backed up, and so the DNA samples taken from Eloise Carr's bedroom and bathroom, Annie's hay barn, and the campsite still were unidentified.

"Although I'll be surprised if Pete Corbett's DNA isn't all over the place," Dan had said, knowingly.

Annie looked at him with a trace of concern. Dan had a tendency to glom on to the first suspect he encountered as the guilty party—and, as she knew from recent experience, he wasn't always right. The man Dan had suspected of committing three homicides a few months ago was completely innocent, and now courting Annie on the phone nearly every night. *The humiliation of not identifying the real killer until it almost was too late must still rankle him,* Annie thought. She hoped he wasn't making the same mistake again. But she kept quiet. She didn't have enough information about the case to make an informed judgment on Pete Corbett's culpability.

"Meanwhile," Dan continued, "we can't let the grass grow under our feet just because the state lab is twiddling their thumbs. We do have Pete's fingerprints on the empty Sudafed packets so we know he was shacking up on your property, Annie. *And* making meth, at least enough for his own personal use. 'Course, Pete denied knowing anything about a meth lab or even using the drug, if you can believe it. Although he sure looks the part, if you know what I mean."

Annie did. She had occasionally seen the before-and-after photos of meth addicts tacked up in public buildings. The changes to a person's face and skin after meth use were horrific, and incredibly quick to take hold. Unfortunately, meth was relatively easy and inexpensive to make, which made it wildly popular in poor rural areas such as her own.

"We haven't found his fingerprints in the barn—yet." This was from Kim. "But we did in Eloise Carr's bathroom, and specifically on the cabinet that held most of her meds."

"Do you have enough to arrest him?" Annie dreaded asking the question. She was afraid Dan would say yes. But the sheriff seemed to have learned from the blunders he'd made in Marcus's case.

"With what? Yeah, it's illegal to trespass and squat on another person's property, but that's not much of a crime compared to murder. As far as being in Eloise Carr's home, he says she invited him, which would be against Elder Home Care's rules, but there's no one around now to contradict him. We know he does drugs, but unless we find him manufacturing, selling, or holding, there's not much we can do."

Dan sounded exceedingly exasperated, and Annie understood why.

"And, to top it all off, we put him on the box and he *passed*." Now Dan was indignant. "He must have prior experience and knows how to beat it. No other reason for it."

"What did you ask him?" Annie was curious.

"After the preliminaries?" Kim reached for her file. "Did you have anything to do with the death of Eloise Carr. Did you have anything to do with the death of Ashley Lawton. Do you have any knowledge of how Eloise Carr died. Do you have any knowledge of how Ashley Lawton died. I deemed each of his answers credible. No equivocation in my mind."

Kim and Annie looked at each other with commiserating smiles. Kim was one of the few deputies on the force trained to administer polygraph tests. Annie was sure that Kim's interpretations of Pete's answers were right on. And the truth was, as long as the killer didn't return to her ranch, Annie felt she had no dog in this fight. She was sorry about Ashley's death but knew that, over time, she'd become reconciled to its tragic occurrence.

Then she remembered she was involved. Or at least someone she knew was.

"Um, I saw your police vehicle at Martha's yesterday," Annie told Kim. "How'd that interview go?"

"Another unremarkable event," Kim said airily. "Lavender obviously thinks that all cops are scary, but she was totally forthcoming and, on the whole, believable. Unfortunately, she had little to add to the party. She'd met Ashley only that morning, and aside describing the shock of finding a deceased elderly woman in bed in a little bit too much glowing detail, she didn't tell us anything that helped."

"Well, thank god for that."

Kim looked at her, her expression puzzled.

"No, I mean of course I'm sorry Lavender didn't help the investigation, but I'm glad that she hasn't managed to involve herself in a potentially ugly situation. She has a tendency to make bad choices."

"Ah, yes." Kim laughed. "I have a kid brother like that. He'll be thirty-six next month and still lives at home."

"So how can I help?"

With a nod from Dan, Kim continued.

"Dan mentioned that several of Ashley's friends approached you at the celebration yesterday."

"Nearly ran me over is more like it."

"We'd like to know what they know of Ashley's relationship with Pete Corbett, as well as with Eloise Carr. We're hoping that you'll agree to talk to them on our behalf."

Annie was flabbergasted. "Why don't *you* interview

them? You're the go-to deputy to interview small children, nasty teenagers, and other disagreeable characters."

"I did, Annie," Kim said. "But I represent law and order, and in my experience, kids whose backgrounds aren't exactly squeaky clean tend to clam up around cops. They're afraid to say anything bad about the person who died, and they're sure as hell afraid to tell us something that might incriminate them. That's the distinct impression I got from talking to Ashley's friends."

"We don't want you to act in any professional capacity, Annie," Dan hastened to add. "But Ashley's entire circle is into horses, which is common ground among all of you."

Annie scoffed. The idea of her having anything in common with the ditzy young women who'd approached her yesterday was risible.

Ignoring her response, Dan went on. "We thought you might take them up on their offer to get together to talk about Ashley. You might get an inkling of something that we can follow up on ourselves."

"Right," Kim agreed. "Just get them talking, figure out what they might know about the case—or Pete's involvement—and let us know. We'll take it from there."

"Aren't I making myself a witness in any future trial?"

"Well, good point, Annie. Yes, you are. But you'd just be laying the groundwork for the police work that followed. We don't want you to investigate. We just want you to probe a little."

Annie privately thought there wasn't much difference between "investigating" and "probing," but she also liked the idea of doing something to help the case along. If Pete Corbett truly was responsible for two murders, then he needed to be caught, charged, and tried for the crimes. And the aching guilt she felt over Ashley's death was not subsiding as the days passed, no matter how flippantly she referred to the event.

"OK, I'll bite. Any idea on how to proceed?"

Kim and Dan looked relieved.

"We thought you might start with Lisa Bromwell," Kim said, writing down contact information for her witnesses as she spoke. "Lisa's got an Appy that's just recovering from colic. I figured you could ask about her horse as a good opener."

"How am I supposed to know her horse just colicked?"

"You'll think of something, Annie." That was Dan, ever helpful. Annie stood up, dusted her jeans with her hands, and got ready to leave. She'd had enough banter with cops for one day. It was time to do something important, such as feed her horses.

"Now that I'm an unofficial undercover agent for the Suwana County Sheriff's Office, what kind of salary am I looking at?"

Kim and Dan looked at each other.

"Well, we'll pick up the tab at Laurie's Café anytime our paths cross."

"As long as you don't order more than coffee."

Annie's long peal of laughter followed her out the door and all the way to the parking lot.

CHAPTER 12

Sometimes Northwest weather could fool a person. The forecast might be for bright and sunny skies, and then a gully washer would come over the mountains at high noon and let up only after midnight. Other times, when the forecast was for gray clouds and constant drizzle, the sun came out with the dawn and shone bright and hot all day. This was one of those days, and it made Annie feel more hopeful than she had in a long time. Summer was coming.

Then she remembered the task she'd promised to perform on behalf of the Suwana County Sheriff's Office. Funny, it didn't sound half as appealing as it had the previous day, when she'd been swept up with law enforcement machismo. What had she gotten herself into? Just when she was trying to get her life in order, she found herself under the unofficial thumb of Sheriff Stetson, precisely where she did not want to be.

Marcus had certainly made his feelings known the previous evening, when she'd admitted Dan had enlisted her help.

"It's not as if I'm being asked to join the SWAT team and help kill the terrorists," she'd explained, trying to inject a bit of humor into a conversation that had suddenly turned somber.

"Yes, but it seems to me that you're being a bit used," Marcus had countered. "Why can't the Sheriff's Office figure out a strategy for getting these women to talk without involving you?"

"Like waterboarding? Or taking away their Nordstrom cards?"

Marcus had refused to buy into Annie's levity.

"You got way too involved in my case, Annie," he went on. "Of course I'm immensely grateful that you did—I might not be sitting in my own home, talking to you, if you hadn't. But I was hoping that life would get back to normal for you. For *both* of us."

Now that hurt. She wanted the same thing.

"Look, Marcus, I'm just going to talk to a couple of girls, that's all. If I find out anything, I'll pass it on. If I fail, I can say I've tried. And I haven't told you everything. Ashley's death was . . . suspicious. I feel somehow responsible for her dying on my property. I know it's crazy, but if I can do this one thing to help find the truth in her case, I think I'll be able to put her death out of my mind. Right now, every time I open the hay barn door . . .

She couldn't finish. She already was reliving the scene. On his end of the line, Marcus let out a long sigh.

"All right, Annie, do what you need to do. Just promise me that you'll be careful."

The conversation had ended shortly thereafter, and

Annie couldn't shake her discomfort over their parting words. She and Marcus had never disagreed before. It was unsettling.

She glanced at her calendar on the wall, a freebie from the local hardware store and the only one she owned. In a few days, she'd be talking to Marcus again, only this time, via Skype. Her meeting with Travis Latham, a neighbor whom she'd met while investigating Hilda's death, and the board members of his new nonprofit—which included Marcus and her—was coming up soon. Marcus was unable to fly up from San Jose, but at least she'd be able to see him. The plan was to discuss Travis's imminent acquisition of Hilda's ranch and how the board planned to use it. If asked, Annie wanted to be able to report on the health and well-being of Hilda Colbert's pedigreed horses that had once lived there.

Since the fire at Hilda's ranch, which had preempted the horses' hasty removal, they'd been boarded at a therapeutic equine center near Cape Disconsolate, about fifty miles north of her own stables. She hadn't seen the herd since the day she and Tony had loaded them into the commercial trailer that had transported them to their new, temporary home. Normally, Annie would have tagged along, but there had been no time— her lambing season had just begun, and she was tied to the farm. Regular phone calls and e-mail from the facility had reassured her of the horses' rapid recuperation, but it was high time that she visited the facilities for herself, and today would have been the perfect day.

Well, almost perfect. As she mucked her horses' stalls, it occurred to Annie that it would be a fine idea for Jessica Flynn to accompany her on her trip north. She trusted her vet implicitly and knew that Jessica would do a more expert job in determining the state of the horses' health than she would. The fact was that

Hilda's horses had lingering health issues—they'd barely escaped a raging fire in the dead of night, and all of them had suffered from smoke inhalation and flying cinders and just plain fear. Considering the trauma they'd lived through, they were doing remarkably well, at least according to clinical reports, but it wouldn't hurt for Jessica to take a look at them and judge for herself. Annie reminded herself that Sarah had thought Layla's care was exemplary, too, until she'd paid a personal call to the boarding facility.

To her surprise, Jessica picked up on the third ring.

"Hi, Jessica, it's Annie. How's the mule doing?" Delivering Molly the mule to Jessica one week before now seemed a distant memory. Annie felt guilty for not checking on the animal sooner.

"Molly's great, thanks for asking. As we predicted, her hooves are going to need frequent visits from our best farrier over the next six months or so, but fortunately there seems to be no lasting damage. Her feet are tender, and she's a bit lame in the hindquarters, but I think that'll go away over time."

"Great. How'd she check out in general? Is she ready for a foster home yet?"

Dan had brought Annie up to speed on the Bruscheau case before they'd left Laurie's Café the previous afternoon. Larry would be cooling his heels in the Harrison County jail until his trial, which was probably six months out, and his wife had fled rehab and taken off for California, parts unknown. Jim and Susan Bruscheau now had legal custody of all three children and the bulk of the family menagerie, but still hadn't made a decision on the mule. Foster care, Annie assured Dan, was the way to go until a final decision was made about the animal's permanent residence.

"She has strangles, not surprisingly, and a couple of

other nasty hosts that could have caused big problems down the line. But our deworming program is doing its job. She's now up-to-date on all her vaccinations. The sores on her neck are healing nicely, and her hair's already starting to come in over the wounds. Overall, she looks pretty darn good. If asked, I'd say she still has a long life ahead of her."

"Fantastic!" Annie felt immensely relieved. "As usual, you are the miracle vet. Should I put the word out among our foster caretakers?"

"Not yet, Annie. I want to make sure her foot problems are fully resolved before I let her go to another home. And I may dig in my own heels, myself. Molly and I have bonded, and I'd just as soon she stays here than go someplace new. If you want, the kids who had her could visit Molly at the clinic. But I think she's best served right now by staying put. She's a good influence on the horses that have to spend the night at the clinic. It's that calm and steady mule demeanor, you know."

"I do. Trotter has the same effect on my horses and the ones I train." It was true. Every new horse at her stables was first paired with Trotter. The little donkey had a tranquil composure about him that soothed even the most agitated equine. Trooper had arrived at Annie's ranch after a near-death experience from a roadside accident, but with Trotter at his side, he had acclimated to his new environment in just a few days.

"Listen, Jessica, I've got another favor to ask—one that pays, for once."

"Heart be still. Tell me more."

"Remember the horses we saved from the fire at Hilda Colbert's ranch several months ago?"

"How could I forget? It was the most horrific example of human depravity I've ever seen."

"Well, at least the horses are doing fine. Or that's the

report that's e-mailed to me every week from the administrative staff. But I really should run up to Cape Disconsolate for a hands-on wellness check. I'd be very happy if you'd come with me to give your professional opinion."

"Where are they stabled?"

"A place called Running Track Farms. It primarily boards racehorses. It was the only facility I found that could house all eighteen. It's quite the palace."

"Eighteen horses? We're talking a full day here."

"Yup. But the horses' new owner is more than happy to foot the bill."

"Marcus? Then I'm not worried about being paid. But I'm concerned about finding time. The only day in the near future that might work is this Friday, my one day off, and that's if I cancel a dental appointment, a meeting with my CPA, and—this is the potential deal breaker—an appointment with my massage therapist."

Annie knew that Jessica always scheduled a massage after meeting with her accountant. She told Annie it was an excellent antidote to one of the most hideous aspects of running one's own business.

"Just say yes, Jessica. It'll be fun, almost like a day off. It's a chance to meet eighteen gorgeous horses that are getting a second chance at decent lives. Plus, I'll drive."

She could sense Jessica's indecision.

"I'll throw in lunch at the greasy spoon of your choice." Annie's tone was wheedling, and she didn't care.

"Deal. I've been dying to try out that fifties-style burger place that got written up in the paper. Be forewarned, though—I've been known to eat two double burgers in one sitting."

"Hah! Your personal best is no way near close to mine."

Now came the tricky problem of getting Lisa Bromwell
to talk to her. She wondered which one of the heavily
made-up girls who'd accosted her in the school auditorium she'd turn out to be. Annie hunted for a phone
book and finally found one underneath Sasha, who was
sleeping under her desk. Gently removing the puppy,
she opened the book, glad to see that it had not been
used as a urinal. Sasha associated newsprint as the place
to relieve herself, and generally was rewarded for remembering this crucial fact. Annie hadn't had the
heart to discipline her last weekend when Sasha had
happily peed all over the Arts section of the Sunday
New York Times.

There were several Bromwells in the book, none with
the first name of Lisa. Annie sighed, thought of what
she would say, and punched in the first listed number
on her cell.

"Hi. My name's Annie Carson. I'm trying to reach
Lisa Bromwell." As she spoke the words, she envisioned
repeating this line until late in the afternoon. Instead,
she got lucky. All the Bromwells in the county, it
seemed, belonged to the same tribe, and they were only
too happy to divulge personal information about other
family members.

"You want to talk to Lisa?" asked the woman who answered the phone. "That's my husband's niece. She's
probably over at her dad's, tending to that horse of
hers."

"I heard that her horse had colicked. How's it doing?"

"Well, I guess it survived, but Lisa's in a state. The
horse has colicked or nearly colicked almost every
month this year. She's beside herself, trying to figure
out what she's doing wrong."

"Well, I'm a horse trainer, not a vet, but I've lived
through enough colic scares to last a lifetime. Lisa said

she wanted to talk to me when we met at Ashley Lawton's memorial yesterday. Maybe I could stop by and look at the horse."

"Well, I'm sure Lisa would appreciate it. Horse means the world to her. Means more to her than the rest of us, anyway. Did you say you went to the funeral of the girl who killed herself? She was a good friend of Lisa's. It's such a shame when something like this happens. A permanent solution to a temporary problem, I've always thought. I wonder if she cared how much she'd upset everyone by what she did."

"Well, that's hard to say." Annie tried to tiptoe around the subject. "I think if you're to the point where you want to kill yourself, you don't really care about what anyone thinks. I think the pain is just too bad."

"Lisa said she never saw it coming. Said everything was looking up in her life, just got a new job helping some horse lady . . . say, that wouldn't be you, would it?"

Annie's heart sank. Was she going to have to contend with the little fib Ashley had spread around with everyone she encountered? She'd have to figure out a diplomatic answer now.

"It's true, I talked to Ashley the day before she died," Annie admitted. "She seemed fine to me, as well." She rushed on. "But I would like to talk to Lisa, if it's possible. Maybe we could help each other better understand what happened."

She couldn't believe she'd just uttered such a pathetic platitude. It was enough to make her gag.

"You sound like such a nice person. The kind of person Lisa needs in her life right now. Would it help if I gave you directions to her dad's place? And what was your name again?"

*   *   *

Lisa's family lived near Chester Bay, south of town, and near a well-used public horse trail that afforded spectacular views of the water. Many horse owners lived in this area; the proximity to riding trails was just too good, and the neighborhoods had none of the standardized suburban look found elsewhere. It was one of the few places where people could still build a substantial home on substantial acreage and keep their horses in their own backyard. Property values were twice what they were in the valley, where Annie had built her ranch. That was the price of being so close to the water.

A winding driveway led Annie into the Bromwell compound, which consisted of a large, new farmhouse-style building with a wraparound porch and several horse-related buildings in back. Annie parked her car and decided to eschew the front doorbell and try to find Lisa first.

She discovered her in the round pen, walking a tall chestnut gelding. She looked as if she'd been crying, and try as she might, Annie could not place her with any of the exuberant women who'd been so keen to talk to her. She approached slowly and cleared her throat before reaching the pen. Lisa turned around. It was clear by the look on her face that she was expecting someone else.

"Hi, Lisa, I'm Annie Carson." Annie walked up with a smile. "We met yesterday, remember? You and your friends wanted to ask me some questions. Your aunt told me you were out here, so I thought I'd try to find you. I'm sorry about your horse; she told me that he's been colicking."

"Oh. Hi." Lisa didn't seem half as excited to talk to Annie as she had the previous day. "I thought you were the vet. Hunter's doing a lot better now, but I thought I was going to lose him last night." She wiped her eyes with the back of her flannel shirt, which was not very clean.

"May I come in and look at him?"

Lisa nodded. Annie unhitched the pen gate and walked inside. She was glad that she'd kept Wolf and Sasha at home; Hunter looked as if he'd been through a siege and didn't need to meet two active dogs right now. His magnificent head hung low, and his eyes drooped. Lisa was now at his rear, combing out his tail, but Hunter seemed not to care very much if his owner made him beautiful or not.

Annie knelt down by his left fetlock and took his pulse. It was close to normal, thank goodness, and not racing. She next stood up and gently opened his lips. His gumline was pale pink—not the robust hue one would hope to see with a well-hydrated horse, but at least it wasn't white, or worse, purple—a danger signal that something was seriously wrong. She turned to Lisa.

"Any piles yet?"

"He pooped a bit about three o'clock in the morning, and a bit more this morning. The vet's supposed to be out to tube him again."

Annie knew Hunter wasn't out of the woods yet. His eighty-foot-long large and small intestines still weren't operating normally, and if they didn't get back on track soon, his condition could easily turn into a crisis, solved only by emergency surgery or—if Lisa couldn't afford this expensive alternative—euthanasia. Annie felt intense sympathy for the young woman. Tending a colicky horse was every horse owner's nightmare while the danger lasted, and the situation could persist, unresolved, for days. She observed Hunter's owner, who looked as if she hadn't slept well for several nights. She wondered

why, considering Hunter's condition, she had even bothered to attend Ashley's celebration of life. But then, saying good-bye to a good friend was important, as well.

"Have you and the vet talked about hydrating him
with an IV drip?" she asked. Every horse owner, she
knew, no matter how long or short that title may have
applied, knew best how to take care of their animal, so
suggestions on health care had to be delicately phrased.

"I've *told* Dr. Wiggins we should do it," Lisa said angrily. "Hunter's not drinking. But he said it wasn't necessary. He just keeps tubing him."

Tubing a horse was not fun for the horse or for anyone to watch. The vet inserted a long rubber hose up
the horse's nose and, using a hand pump, transferred a
large bucket full of saline and milk of magnesia into the
horse's system. Annie hated when this procedure was
required, even though she knew it was pro forma for
colic cases.

Annie arched one eyebrow, a skill she'd honed sitting
through many boring high school classes, and replied, "I
think you're right. I once had a horse that colicked during one of our winter floods, and the only way he survived until he could be transported to the mainland
hospital was to keep him on a continuous drip. I kept
him on it for six days and nights until the water receded
and we could move him. Of course, the vet was out
every day. But that drip saved him."

"Would you tell Dr. Wiggins that?" begged Lisa, starting to cry. "I can't lose Hunter now. I've just lost Ashley.
I can't lose anyone else."

Annie dug out a relatively clean bandanna from her
Levi jacket and handed it to her.

"Come on," she said. "Let's put Hunter in your foaling stall right now so the vet can set up the drip as soon
as he arrives."

* * *

Two hours later, Annie and Lisa sat on milking stools in the foaling stall while they watched Hunter shift his weight from one back leg to another. The horse's eyes were closed, but the two horsewomen knew that Hunter was resting, and not in pain. A bag of fluid on an aluminum rack stood near him, where a slow but steady flow of electrolytes seeped into his body. A small pile of manure—the first that looked even remotely normal, according to Lisa—was in the corner. To the women, it was gold. It meant Hunter's gut was beginning to move again, and his chance of survival had just skyrocketed.

"So you really think it's the sand?" Lisa asked, handing Annie a can of Coke.

"Makes sense," Annie replied, taking a long swig of the sugary stuff. "I've got it on my ranch, and I'm twelve miles inland. Your stables are practically waterfront property. I'm sure your pastures are full of it. I'm guessing he's out on pasture pretty much all day?"

Lisa nodded morosely.

"There's your cause for Hunter's recurring symptoms. Over time, he builds up enough sand in his large colon to cause an impaction-type colic. You don't *see* him ingesting sand; you see only the colic. So you treat the colic, Hunter gets better, but then he goes right out to where the sand is. Even Dr. Wiggins conceded it could be a problem. The stethoscope pretty much forced him to."

At Annie's gentle insistence, the vet had listened to Hunter's gut, which was still dangerously devoid of the usual healthy gurgle of gut sounds. But what he did hear was the soft, rolling sound of the ocean—exactly the sound that sand in the gut mimics. He was none too happy to have a civilian nicely suggest that too much sand ingestion was what was causing the horse's chronic colic attacks, but he also was too much of a professional to protest—much. He grudgingly wrote out a prescription for a sand cleanser, and Annie promised to bring some of her own over to Lisa in the next few days.

"I was so happy to put him out on fresh pasture again," moaned Lisa, her head resting on her horse's thigh. "All that new grass. I thought I was doing what was best for him."

"Oh, stop." Annie said the words humorously, but she meant them. "Isn't that all we ever do—what we think is best for our horses? Anyway, now you know how to fix the problem. Stay on the sand clearance program and I'll bet you Hunter doesn't colic again, knock on wood."

Lisa face softened and a tear slid down her face. But she looked immeasurably relieved.

"Thank you so much for coming over. You saved my horse's life."

Annie hated compliments to her face. She never knew how to react to them. She stood up, stretched, and walked over to Hunter.

"Oh, pshaw. Happy to help. But I'm curious. Did you and Ashley get your horses together?"

"How'd you know? Oh, of course—because of their names. Yes, we both got our horses when we were ten and big into 4-H. We thought it would be cute to name them Hunter and Jumper. That's what we planned to do, of course. Dressage and eventing and all of that fancy stuff. Instead, Ashley ended up using Jumper for barrel racing, and Hunter was always the lead horse in drill team events and parades."

"A perfect job for such a handsome guy. Ashley said Jumper had been sold. Do you know where he went?"

"Dunno. Ashley's father sold him when we were both on a church mission one weekend. Ashley was so upset I thought she was going to . . ." She paused, then looked away. "For a while, I actually thought she might kill herself. Or her father. But then her dad took off with a new girlfriend a few months later and Ashley never saw him again. At least, she never mentioned him again."

"That must have been tough."

"It really was. Have you met Ashley's mother? I mean, after seeing Candy, you can kind of understand why her dad left. But as much of a jackass as he could be sometimes, he still acted as a kind of buffer between Ashley and her mother. That woman is *mean*. Ashley couldn't wait to leave. And Pete offered her a way out. For a while."

"You know, Ashley didn't say anything about her boyfriend when we talked."

"That would be like her. She was embarrassed that she'd made such a big mistake, living with such a loser."

"Do you think she was scared of him? I heard that she filed a restraining order against him not too long ago."

"Nah. Pete's really a wuss when you get to know him. He just sat around and smoked dope all day. And lived on handouts from his parents and from what Ashley earned from her job."

"He wasn't violent toward her?"

Lisa looked at the ground. "Well, he might have hit her once or twice, but only when he was high."

"Seems to me that Ashley wouldn't put up with that kind of behavior very long."

There was no way for Annie to know if Ashley would have or not, but it seemed the appropriate thing to say to keep the conversation going. She was right.

"She didn't. Ashley hated drugs. After the last time Pete freaked out on her, she left. She stayed with me and my family for a while. Then Pete got all misty eyed and convinced her to come back. But the truth is, by then, Ashley had found someone new."

Now this was interesting.

"Really? She had a new boyfriend when she died? Even though she was still living with Pete?"

Lisa stirred the dust in the pen with the toe of her cowboy boot.

"Well, don't tell anyone, okay? I didn't want to tell that deputy, you know, Kim, anything bad about Ashley. Although I guess the police are going to find out soon enough."

"Lisa, listen to me. You really should tell Kim the name of Ashley's new boyfriend. It could be important."

"That's the problem. She never told any of us."

CHAPTER 13

"**A**nnie, if you want to talk to Dan, you're going to have to go where he is, right now. It's the only chance you'll have of catching him all day."

Esther's voice was kind but firm. She'd had forty years' practice at the art of speaking to the public and was an undisputed pro. Annie knew there was little point in trying to convince the Sheriff's Office's only dispatch officer and sometimes receptionist that her news merited Dan's special attention. She wasn't the one who decided these things. Esther was.

"Fine. Where is the sheriff at the moment?"

"Port Chester Episcopalian Church."

"What? Has Dan gone all religious on us?"

"Don't be silly, Annie. It's Eloise Carr's memorial service today. Dan'll be there, but then he has an all-afternoon meeting with the county commissioners. So if you want to tell him anything, now's your time. Service starts at noon." The click that followed told Annie that Esther had turned off her headset.

Annie was not amused by these marching orders. She'd deliberately waited until now to tell Dan about Lisa's new information because, frankly, she wanted time to think about it herself. Obviously, Ashley's list of potential killers had now doubled. But it would help if Annie could deliver a name. She was going to have to talk to all of Ashley's friends, she knew, if she expected to get any new clues as to his identity. But she couldn't justify putting off passing along the information that she had any longer.

But the little black dress, undoubtedly more appropriate attire in an Episcopalian church than a high school auditorium, would not be worn. It already had been put in a bag to take to the local Goodwill.

She arrived at the church a few minutes past noon, glad the slacks and blazer she'd worn allowed her to make full strides, because she needed them now. Entering the church through the nave, she stood for a few minutes to adjust her eyes to the low light; stained glass windows surrounding the interior were the only source of light, and today, not much sun was filtering in.

"What are *you* doing here?" She jumped before realizing it was Dan who had whispered the words. He was standing to the back of her, nearly invisible in a cloistered nook.

"I'm trying to find you," she hissed back. "Do you think I like going to funerals?"

"No more than I do. Well, settle back in one of the rear pews with me. We've got a good hour before we come up for air."

Annie fumed inwardly that if she'd only been on time, perhaps she could have caught Dan before the service began and then made a hasty exit. She would have been if she hadn't had a last-minute visitor to the ranch, albeit a welcome one. Every month, Ian the Chip Man, as she privately called him, arrived on her farm, driving a Kubota with a small trailer hitched to it. She never knew when he was coming but was always glad that he did; he came bearing sweet-smelling cedar chips, which he wordlessly deposited into her shavings shed. The chips were perfect for layering the beds in her horse stalls, and the price was exquisitely right— zero. Cal and Mary Trueblood owned the local paper mill, which had been in the family since 1856. A few months back, they had graciously told Annie she was welcome to all the chips she wanted from their sawmill. Annie had eagerly accepted their kindness. She'd just learned that Trooper was allergic to pine shavings, and the cost of buying bags of the cedar replacement was wreaking havoc with her austere budget.

So, even though Ian's arrival meant that she would be late for Eloise Carr's service, she welcomed Ian in and hurriedly had told him to just put the shavings in the usual place, adding her effusive thanks. But today, Ian had a message to deliver.

"Mrs. Trueblood wants to talk to you," was Ian's blunt declaration. "She says she'll call you, and it's important. Said she'd be happy to come to you, or you can meet at her home."

"Sure," Annie said cautiously. "Did she say what she wanted to talk about?"

"Nope. Just said she wanted to talk to you."

Annie spent the entire drive into town trying to fathom the reason for Mary's interest in getting together. Aside from knowing that the Truebloods owned the local paper mill, she knew precious little about the family. She hadn't the slightest idea of what Mary wanted to discuss. She was so focused on Mary's mysterious desire to talk that she forgot she was about to attend her second memorial service of the week.

An organ started to play "Jesu, Joy of Man's Desiring," music that always brought tears to Annie's eyes—it had been played at her mother's service as well. She tried to pay attention to the priest intoning a prayer in front of her but instead found herself surreptitiously looking across the adjoining pews for any familiar faces. Ron and Jane Carr were in the front row, flanked by two families with small children—they must be Ron's children and grandchildren, Annie realized. To her surprise, she caught a glimpse of Lavender's long, brown hair in the row behind the Carrs. A shimmering, silvery halo was barely visible next to her. Ah, yes. It was entirely possible that Martha had known Eloise Carr. After all, they were in the same age category: old.

An hour later, Annie dutifully sang one last hymn while Dan hummed off key, and the service ended. They remained seated with the rest of the congregation as the priest and his entourage gravely made their way up the center aisle, followed by the Carr families. Ron, Annie noticed, looked as if he was going to burst into racking sobs any moment; his wife, Jane, patted him ineffectively on the arm and whispered something to him. His children—assuming they were the adults who followed—looked utterly solemn. Their kids just looked bored. Annie wondered if they even realized that they'd never see Grandma again; the oldest appeared to be about six, a bit young to assimilate the meaning of death, she thought. The baby in one woman's arms would never know her grandmother's touch or smile, or hear any of her stories.

Knowing that Eloise Carr had not died naturally now

disturbed Annie more than before. Either Eloise had taken her own life or it had been taken from her. Neither was the way a life well lived was supposed to end. Annie had spent an hour learning just how well lived Eloise Carr's life had been, and how much she would be missed.

Annie's cell phone vibrated in her saddlebag purse. She pulled it out and saw a text from Lisa: "Hunter is better!!! Three piles this a.m.!!! U R wonderful." A long series of happy emoticons trailed the message. Annie breathed a small sigh of relief and turned to Dan, who was looking over her shoulder. She snapped the cell phone shut.

"I visited Lisa Bromwell yesterday."

"So I gather. Learn anything?"

"Ashley had a new boyfriend when she died. Someone other than Pete."

"Holy crap!"

"Dan, quiet! We're in a church." A man in a dark suit walked silently past them and gave Dan a distinct look of disapproval. Dan got up and motioned Annie to do the same. They walked outside into the vestibule, now empty. The reception was being held in the chancery, and Annie assumed most people already were there. It was one o'clock, and her stomach growled. She hoped that Eloise's family had put food on the tables besides tea and coffee—substantial food, not just cheese and crackers.

"Sorry, Annie. But we found Pete's and Ashley's fingerprints all over the camp. I assumed they were still a couple at the time of her death."

"Only for outward appearances. According to Lisa, Ashley was back living with Pete but had started seeing someone new during their brief separation."

"Who is he? Don't keep me in suspense."

"Afraid I'm going to have to. Ashley never told her friends who her new beau was."

Dan groaned and leaned on the stone pillars behind him. "She must have told someone."

"We can only hope. How long until DNA tests are done?"

"We put in the usual rush order, but we're still looking several weeks out. Suwana County doesn't rank very high on the triage list in Olympia. Not when King County gives them most of their business."

"Well, I'm going to see Lisa this afternoon. I've been helping her with a sick horse. I'll try to get more information, and talk to some of the other girls."

"Whoa now, Annie. You've gone far enough. You've done exactly what we wanted you to do—ferret out information that Kim wasn't able to get. We'll take it from here. You want to help a kid with her sick horse, be my guest. But no more sleuthing."

His blunt fiat brought Annie's blood pouring into her face. She glared at Dan. "You can't just ask me to do something and then, after I perform *beautifully*, pull me off the case on a whim."

"I do that every day with twenty-five deputies. And it's not a whim; it's a reasoned law enforcement decision."

"Well, I'm not one of your deputies."

"No, you're not. Which is why you should stop acting like one now and go on home. Anyway, I have to run. I'm already late for my meeting. Good work, Annie. We'll talk later."

For a large man, Dan could move surprisingly fast when he knew he was about to get verbally reamed.

* * *

Five minutes later, with most of her equilibrium restored, she decided to pay her respects to the Carr family. After all, Martha and Lavender were there, so she wouldn't be among total strangers, something Annie abhorred. Wandering down much more modern halls than the august sanctuary would have suggested, she found the chancery by the sound. Laughter was coming from the room, which suggested that the people who'd come to pay their respects to the deceased had evolved to the stage of telling good stories and recalling fond memories.

Martha was talking to Jane Carr, while Lavender was in earnest conversation with Ron. Annie hesitated, then decided to take care of her own comforts first. After six ham canapés, two chicken wraps, and two cups of hot tea, Annie felt revived enough to join the party. As she picked up an éclair from the dessert table, a man about her age looked at her with amusement.

"Nice to see a woman who isn't afraid to show her appetite."

Annie could have taken umbrage at this remark, but chose not to. After all, she was technically still in a church, and besides, she really was sated with good food. Also, she suspected the speaker was a member of the Carr family.

"Glad you're enjoying the show. When you own a ranch, you tend to work up an appetite. Several times a day."

The man smiled. "Good for you. My wife eats like a bird. Drives me nuts. I'm Ron Carr the Third, by the way."

"Annie Carson. I met your father a few days ago at the high school. I thought it was nice of him to attend Ashley's service."

"Well, up until now he thought the world of her. She did such a good job of taking care of Nana Ellie. Now, he's not so sure. I guess the evidence is beginning to point to homicide, which is pretty unbelievable to take in."

"Really? The sheriff hasn't shared that with me yet." *As if he would,* her Good Angel reminded her.

"He showed us a couple of keys this morning, before the service. Ones that Ashley had on her when she died, I guess. One of them was Nana Ellie's house key. Since Elder Home Care still has the one we gave them way back when, Ashley must have stolen it from Nana's home."

Annie remembered Dan showing her the keys as well. One looked like an ordinary house key. It must be the one to which her grandson was now referring.

"You said there were two keys. Did you recognize the second one?"

"Nope. Odd-looking one, too."

For some reason, Annie felt compelled to stick up a bit for the dead girl.

"I can see how troubling it must be to realize that Ashley essentially had free rein of your grandmother's house. Do you think there's any chance that she gave Ashley an extra key, just in case?"

"Completely against company rules. If Nana didn't answer the door, Ashley's instructions were to call in to her supervisor. But that's not all. Sheriff Dan said Ashley recently had been arrested for possession of drugs without a prescription. I think it's pretty clear that Ashley was helping herself to Nana's pills and selling them on the street."

"I see you've met Annie, son." Ron Junior had approached them without her noticing. She did notice, however, that he now had recovered his composure. All earlier signs of grief had disappeared.

"I was admiring her exemplary appetite, as compared to my wife's." The two men exchanged a look. *There's more to that story than I'll ever know,* Annie thought. Maybe the wife was anorexic or bulimic. She looked around for an emaciated woman and saw the woman who'd earlier been holding the baby. She'd taken off her jacket, and Annie could see her pencil-thin arms and nearly transparent frame. *You wouldn't be able to pull a single hundred-ten-pound bale of hay off a truck,* Annie thought, *let alone stack it.*

Ron Junior turned to Annie and smiled.

"Thank you for coming today. I know you didn't know my mother, but I appreciate the gesture. And I keep hearing good things about you wherever I go. Sheriff Dan tells me you're involved in reclaiming that ranch up north, the one that was burned to the ground. He says you're turning it into a nonprofit for troubled youth."

We're in the infancy stages, for heaven's sake. Sheriff Dan should keep his mouth shut more often. Annie smiled back.

"That's right. Travis Latham—do you know him?— wants to turn it into a working ranch for young men at risk. The current owner thinks it's a great idea. He has no interest in rebuilding the equestrian buildings on the same scale as before and wants a more rough-and-tumble environment. We're just now starting the process of transferring the property over to Travis, who in turn will deed it to the not-for-profit organization that will manage the operation."

"Sounds just like something Travis would do," Ron replied. "He's quite the legend in these parts—built his investment company from scratch, made a fortune, and then got emotionally flattened by the death of his grandson. I remember going to that memorial service. Not a dry eye in the house."

"Yes, Alex's tragic death is the impetus for this project. Travis wanted to find a way to honor his grandson's life *and* try to help the kind of boys who were responsible for his death."

"I've been wondering how that property would reinvent itself." Ron took out a leather business card holder from his back pocket and handed Annie a card. "If you need any help with the closing, let me know."

Annie looked at the card and then at Ron with undisguised surprise. It read: "Carr & Sons. Three generations of real estate experience. Call for a free appraisal today." Wasn't soliciting business at your mother's memorial service just a bit tacky?

"You're a real estate agent?" The words were out before she could stop them.

"Yes, indeed. I'm the second generation, Trey here is the third. And it won't be long before little Marky over there with his mom becomes the next Carr to take over the business. Isn't that right, Trey?"

Trey looked a bit uncomfortable at his father's boasting; she didn't blame him. Either that or he hated the nickname "Trey."

"Well, thanks for the offer, but since the owner and Travis are on the same page, I'm not sure we need a real estate agent's help. There's not much to negotiate. But I'll pass along your card at our next meeting."

"I understand." His face displayed a trace of disappointment that his words did not. "It's a real good thing that Travis is doing. You tell him I said so."

"Will do."

She said a hurried hello-and-good-bye to Martha and Lavender before leaving. Martha, as predicted, had known Eloise through her bridge club and through church activities.

"She made the best chicken liver spread in the valley," Martha said, "and was kind enough to share the recipe with us, too, without 'forgetting' about one of the ingredients. It was the eggs. Lots of hard-boiled eggs, that's what made it so special."

"Well, I think Ron Carr is just the nicest man," Lavender broke in. "I told him that I was with Ashley that day, and he just took my hands and told me how brave I was. And said how much his mother would have liked knowing me."

"You told me you fainted in a heap. I don't suppose you mentioned that to Mr. Carr?"

And with that rejoinder, Annie made an exit almost as speedy as Dan's.

CHAPTER 14

FRIDAY, MAY 13

A squeal came from Annie's passenger seat. She chuckled, intent on her driving.

"A Paso Fino farm! Look, Annie! On my right! I had no idea anyone was breeding Paso Finos on the Peninsula!"

"I know, I saw them the first time I came up here. They are drop-dead gorgeous, aren't they? And their gait is supposed to be just made for trail riding."

"Let's go buy two!"

"Sure, on the way back. As soon as we buy the trailer I forgot to hitch to my rig."

It was eight in the morning, and the sky overhead promised another warm, sunny day. Annie and Jessica were sailing along the highway en route to Cape Disconsolate and in very fine moods. Annie was still glowing from the praise Lisa Bromwell had heaped on her yesterday for her astute diagnosis of Hunter's tendency to colic, not to mention bringing him back to life. Jessica, Annie suspected, was just happy to be away from her clinic for a day—with the knowledge that her postponed meeting with her CPA was now another month out.

As they traveled along the coastal highway, each lost in her own thoughts, Annie recalled the image of the horse she'd seen upon arriving at the Bromwells Thursday afternoon. Hunter simply was a different animal. His head was erect, his eyes were clear, and he was alert and energetic. Best of all, the pile of his manure had quadrupled since the previous day. Lisa was ecstatic and accepted the sand cleanser Annie had brought as if it were a gift from the gods. Her parents came out to join in the accolades. Annie left Chester Bay an hour later feeling absolutely buoyant—and for reasons other than Hunter's miraculous recovery.

"I wish you could meet all of Ashley's friends," Lisa said as Annie stood by her door. "We'd like to thank you for all you did to try to help her."

Annie had one hand on her truck door handle. Inside, Wolf and Sasha had awakened from their naps and were sitting up, their tails frantically trying to wag in the cramped space.

"Lisa, I'd be happy to meet with anyone who knew Ashley," she replied honestly. "But please don't think you or anyone has to thank me." *Because you never made the offer in the first place, and don't deserve any thanks,* her Good Angel reminded her.

She looked at Lisa and smiled. "Besides, if I hear any more nice things about myself it'll start going to my head. But sure, let's get together."

They'd agreed to meet on Saturday night at a local bistro. Annie was amused that she, a bona fide adult, was being sought after by a group of women who were half her age and who had twice her energy. The thought that both Dan and Marcus would thoroughly disapprove of her getting together with Ashley's friends flitted across her brain and was quickly discarded. Ashley's friends had asked *her*, after all. Her Good Angel loudly tsk-tsked. Annie silently told her to shove it.

She was now driving through Shelby, near where Hilda's equestrian center had once stood. Her gaze automatically was drawn to the road leading up to the property. All that remained were the remnants of the electronic gates leading into the decimated ranch, the two jumpers etched in metal in the ironwork now grotesquely twisted and bent, stark reminders of the havoc that had occurred here a few months earlier. Annie knew that once Travis acquired the property, the gate would be the first thing to go; he wanted no reminder of its previous owner. Still, the stables and arena really had been spectacular, she thought. They'd just belonged to the wrong person.

As if reading her mind, Jessica broke the silence in the cab. "Too bad I didn't get to see the place when it was still intact. It must have been something."

Jessica had arrived moments after the fire, after it had consumed every building except the main house and finally been extinguished. She'd spent twelve nonstop hours tending to the horses that had been removed to the lower paddocks before the flames, fueled by three tons of hay bales, had sent the arena and stable roof crashing down. After doing what she could, Jessica had approved of the horses' transport to the county fairgrounds, but this was just a stopgap measure; no other facility could board them all, and Annie had insisted that the herd stay together. The next day, Annie had discovered Running Track Farms, sixty miles north, which miraculously had sufficient open stalls. She could not have found a more appropriate rehabilitation center. Running Track had two on-site vets and medical facilities that included state-of-the-art therapeutic equipment. Annie was hard-pressed to think of any equine injury or disease that the center couldn't handle.

The memory of that day had a sobering effect on the women's moods, and their conversation turned to another morbid topic—the recent spurt in predator sightings and deaths of small farm animals in the county.

"Johan Thompson swears he saw a cougar on his property," Jessica reported. This was not good news—Annie wintered her sheep on his land and fleetingly wondered if Trotter's services as ewe protector would now be required year-round.

"What's the count so far?" Annie asked, not really wanting to know.

"Five lambs, one llama, and two goats," was the prompt reply.

"Jeez! It's a little late in the season, isn't it?"

"Yes, which is why Sergeant McCready is asking anyone who loses an animal to report it immediately. He's privately told me he suspects at least one predator on the prowl may be human, not animal. He's asked if I'll perform a necropsy on the next carcass."

"Fish and Wildlife wants to hire you to confirm the cause of death?"

"Yup. Four of the lambs were killed in the same week. McCready said the travel patterns are too widespread to account for a single predator. So either unbeknownst to us, a traveling zoo unleashed a lot of tigers all at once, or the killer is someone who has a driver's license."

"Well, that is downright scary."

"Indeed. I hate to see any animal killed, but I'd rather believe it was done by an animal acting on instinct and need rather than a deranged maniac."

"No kidding. Let's grab some breakfast. If we're up against a psycho animal killer, we need to be well fortified."

They arrived at Running Track Farms at ten-thirty, and Annie had to admit that the equestrian center pretty much put Hilda's to shame. It was a well-known layover for racehorses that rested and recuperated here during the off-season months, as well as the permanent home for dozens of dressage horses, licensed stallions, and their offspring. Clinics on dressage, driving, jumping, and other equine disciplines were commonplace, although the instructors usually were internationally known in their respective fields.

Annie didn't know how much Marcus was paying for the horses' care and feeding. She wasn't sure she wanted to know. But she was impressed by his dedication to taking the best possible care of animals that he'd barely met, and never ridden.

"Make sure everything is up to your exacting standards, Annie," he'd told her on the phone the night before. "Nothing's too good for my herd. Although it still feels very odd to know I own eighteen horses with pedigrees that far outstrip mine."

When Annie had reminded him that he also owned five mares currently in foal, boarded in Montana, Marcus had groaned.

"Tell them their benefactor sends his love. Along with his checkbook."

A sign by the electronic gate politely asked visitors to please use the voice box to introduce themselves to the staff on duty. Annie dutifully complied.

"Annie Carson and Jessica Flynn. We're here to see Marcus Colbert's horses. All eighteen, if there's time."

"Oh, hello!" a bright, cheery voice responded. The voice had an accent—British, Annie thought. "We've been anticipating your arrival. You made good time, didn't you? One moment and I'll buzz you in." Annie looked at Jessica with a touch of skepticism.

"Chipper little thing, isn't she?"

"Bet you the accent is fake."

Their assumptions were dashed when they met the owner of the voice.

As they walked toward the front office, a tall, willowy blonde in her midforties strode toward them, her smile wide and welcoming.

"Hi, I'm Patricia Winters, the operations manager. I'm so happy to meet you both. I've only been here a month, but I've heard so much about you, and your daring exploits in saving the horses." All this was uttered with a pronounced English accent and attire that matched. Patricia was wearing tan English riding breeches and a navy blue hunting jacket with a crest that looked, Annie thought, terribly important. Her long, blond hair was pulled back into a loose ponytail, and Annie could see small, rose-colored pearl earrings adorning each petite earlobe.

"She looks like she walked off the set of *Downton Abbey*," Jessica whispered to Annie.

"What's that?"

There was no time to talk, as Patricia had now reached them. After introductions and handshakes were over, Patricia led them into a large conference room inside the front office building. A large walnut table stood in the middle with plush chairs all around. The walls held photos of horses and riders jumping in competition and performing other equestrian feats. Annie was sure she recognized Patricia in one of the photos. Her body was elongated at the same angle as that of her horse as they prepared to make a jump that looked at least six feet high. *They looked magnificent together,* Annie thought. She was sure the two had cleared the fence with several feet to spare.

"We've so enjoyed having Mr. Colbert's equines with us," Patricia began. "I know you'll want to meet with our veterinarians, and of course see the horses themselves. To save time, I've created a brief dossier on each horse, so you can review its progress and see where we are now."

She passed out a large pile of folders, each labeled with the name of the horse on the front, as well as the name of the attending veterinarian.

"This is incredible," murmured Jessica, as she opened the first file. "I'd love to implement something like this at our clinic."

Fat chance, Annie thought. Jessica's staff consisted of one other veterinarian, fresh out of vet school at Pullman; two vet techs; one receptionist; and three part-time helpers who cleaned clinic stalls, fetched and carried, and did anything else that needed to be done. Annie knew that Jessica alone worked an average of twenty-eight days a month. She suspected she barely had enough time to pay her bills, let alone create executive reports on each farm visit. But it was a nice thought.

From the head of the table, Patricia smiled. "We didn't have much time to pull these together, so they're not quite as complete as I would like. But I was able to download much of the information from our computer. Every task performed on behalf of an individual horse, no matter how small, is entered into the system, so it's not difficult to create a chronological history of its treatment."

She opened the first file, which documented the recent life of Knight in Armor, a 17.2-hand Danish Warm-blood. As Annie recalled, Kim Williams had transported this massive horse down to safety in Hilda's lower pastures. Later, she learned that it was the first time Kim had ever been around a horse. Annie still could not fathom the courage she'd shown that night as she navigated a terrified horse out of its stall, down a hill, and into a paddock, with nothing more than a lead rope slung around its neck.

"Knight in Armor is one of our biggest success stories," Patricia said with pride. "He suffered the least smoke inhalation, so his lungs had fewer smoke particulates than some of the other horses. We've detected no thermal damage to the upper airway or burn damage to the nasal passages or throat."

"Excellent!" exclaimed Jessica. "Was there a specific kind of treatment that worked best?"

"Hyperbaric oxygen therapy, after intravenous fluids had stabilized the horse's blood pressure," Patricia responded. "The treatment's still a bit controversial, but we are firm believers in its efficacy. In fact, most of Mr. Colbert's horses received hyperbaric oxygen therapy at some point, and we think it's the reason most escaped without any scar tissue or other lasting symptoms that might pose problems down the road. It simply speeds up the healing process."

Annie could see that Jessica's brain was practically on fire; she was so enthralled with the innovative treatments used here that she looked as if she would implode if she weren't able to soon see them for herself.

Patricia must have sensed this, too, because she said, "Why don't I introduce you to the veterinarian staff now? You can take the dossiers with you and read them at your leisure. When you're done chatting, let the medical staff know, and I'll meet you at the dressage court. We've reserved it this afternoon so you can see each horse perform. Of course, all of the horses have been pretty much on bed rest since they arrived. But they've had access to the paddocks attached to their stalls, and they've been walked twice daily as soon as their health permitted. By now, I think everyone's up to showing you a brisk walk, controlled trot, and light canter."

"Wonderful. Thanks so much for setting this up. We can't wait to see how the horses are doing. Can we, Jessica?"

But Jessica already was halfway out the door.

Six hours later, Annie and Jessica were back on the road again, heading south this time. Their conversation consisted of unusually short sentences, punctuated with short silences in between.

Annie started first.

"Wow."

"Unbelievable."

"Did you see the water treadmill?"

"Yup. In use."

"Incredible."

"And the cold saltwater spa?"

"Wish Bess could soak her tired bones in it."

"I wish *I* could soak my tired bones in it."

"Did you check out the solarium?"

"No! Where was it?"

"By the hyperbaric chamber."

"Damn. I think I was watching the staff muck stalls when you were in there. Did you know that it takes a shovel, rake, broom, and two kinds of muck forks to clean a single stall there?"

"Why?"

"Dunno. But the stalls look like feather beds when they've finished."

"Wow."

"Patricia was pretty cool."

"Very cool."

"I wonder if the vet staff is hiring."

"Forget it, Jessica! We need you here at home. Besides, I don't think they let molly mules board there."

"OK. Can't go unless Molly comes, too."

"Glad we got that settled."

"Did you see how relaxed everyone was?"

"Hey, I'd be relaxed too, if I lived in a spa."

"Horses look great."

"Yup."

"Wow."

On their way out of town, Annie noticed a billboard with two familiar faces emblazoned on it—Ron Carr Junior and Ron Carr the Third, or Trey—shaking hands, Ron Junior's hand on Trey's shoulder, and standing in front of a McMansion with a "SOLD!" sign in front. The rest of the billboard repeated the same message as on the business card Ron had thrust into her hand a few days ago: "Three generations of real estate experience. Call for a free appraisal today!" The toll-free number took up the remaining space.

She said nothing to Jessica but made a mental note that the Carr family seemed to take their business very seriously. Maybe they could be helpful in Travis's plan to rebuild Hilda's facility, especially if there were zoning or construction issues that only locals knew about. She hoped she'd remembered where she'd put the card, and it wasn't someplace where Sasha could chew it up.

"Oh! There's the diner that you promised we'd stop in. Next exit. Annie, are you listening to me?"

"I'm on it. I'm just trying to figure out how I'm going to find homes for all those beautiful, rehabilitated horses."

Once inside the diner, with massive hamburgers and vanilla shakes in front of them, the two women continued the conversation.

"Except for the Appy, it looks like the herd is all ready to go to their new homes," Annie said, wiping her chin with her oversized napkin. "Wherever and whatever those are. Talk about having my work cut out for me."

Jessica nodded thoughtfully. "It seems such a shame to separate them. But it's inevitable, I suppose. Why not ask Patricia for help? She looks as if she knows her way around the elite horse world."

"Good idea." Annie felt a smidgeon better. She'd e-mail Patricia tomorrow.

"In fact, I think it's worth a return visit just to get her take on each horse's specific strengths in the eventing world. Face it, Annie, we can recognize a good roper or barrel racer, but when it comes to jumping and dressage, we're out of our league."

"You don't fool me, Ms. Flynn. You just want to go back to have another chance to drool over the medical equipment. But you're right. If my pride hadn't gotten in my way, I'd have already told Marcus that I'm simply not up to the job. But now I feel it's a little too late."

"Gotcha. Rely on Patricia; I'm sure she'll help. And think of this as a tremendous learning experience. All the stuff you'll learn about how other people use horses. Why, you might turn Trooper into an eventing equine yet."

"Sure. I'll build the dressage court right next to the sheep pasture. You can help me cut the cavaletti with my chain saw."

"I'm serious, Annie! Wouldn't it be great to have dressage lessons in our little hamlet?"

But Annie only smiled and picked up the check, swiping a day-old newspaper on her way out the door.

"I wonder how Luann's getting on with my herd. It's just about feeding time," Annie mused a half hour later, as they made the exit toward Annie's farm. Luann was Annie's nearest neighbor and a good riding buddy, and the two women frequently subbed for the other on days when it was impossible to get home by twilight, the standard feeding time.

"I'm sure everyone's fine. Just don't tell them tomorrow morning about where you've been today."

"Not on your life! If I ever install a whirlpool on my property, the first creature that's going in it is me!"

CHAPTER 15

SATURDAY, MAY 14

Annie's horses may have been in the dark as to where their mistress had been the previous day, but thanks to Jessica's penchant for social media, word of her journey up north spread fast among the two-legged population. By ten o'clock the next morning, three of Annie's riding pals had called and demanded full details of her adventures at Running Track Farms. One had even inquired if Marcus might be up for adopting adult women.

"My Morgan would benefit so much from that water treadmill Jessica described," Sandy had told her. "And I'd be the perfect child—no expectations of college, and I'm done with marriage, so no weddings to cover. Just my horse."

Sandy was older than Marcus by a good ten years.

Annie knew her friend was kidding, but she still issued a stern reply.

"Marcus has no desire to adopt another horse, let

alone you. Don't forget he expects me to find homes for his existing herd. You'll simply have to find another millionaire."

Annie realized that what she really was telling Sandy was that Marcus was off-limits. If she had to admit it, she did feel more than a tad possessive of him. Whatever their relationship entailed, at this point. It was hard to gauge when your new kind-of-boyfriend lived 850 miles away and you talked only by phone.

Tomorrow, that arrangement would marginally improve; on Sunday afternoon, the first formal meeting of the board overseeing Travis's new nonprofit organization would take place, and everyone would be able to see each other. Marcus had hired a tech geek to install Skype on Travis's computer. Of course, his own system was already set up for face-to-face conference calls.

Annie had balked when he suggested that she install the software as well.

"When we talk, I'm usually in my jammies with seven layers of moisturizer on," she'd said, half-jokingly. "Only my animals get to see me in that state."

Marcus's response had brought a blush to her cheeks— which, fortunately, he was unable to see—but Annie refused to back down. She'd already set aside a full hour on Sunday morning to attend to her dress, hair, and makeup.

Today, however, her only scheduled appointment was in the evening, when she would meet with Lisa and friends at the Crossroads Bar, an upscale drinking establishment in Port Chester. That was hours away, so she settled down with a pot of tea and spent an enjoyable three hours perusing the files Patricia Winters had prepared for her and Jessica. She marveled at Patricia's attention to detail and the careful labeling of each section. She was amazed at how much nutritional feed, not to mention hay, each horse had consumed over the past two months—but she now recalled Jessica talking earnestly with one of the staff vets on this very subject. Apparently, the more the horse consumed, the faster the healing process progressed. Too bad the same theory didn't work with humans.

When she turned the last page of the last file, she got up and put her teapot and mug in the sink and her tea leaves in the inside compost bucket. It was time to ask for help—something Annie never liked to do. But she really had no choice. Annie had amassed her five horses by rescuing them. She had no idea how to go about telling the dressage and jumping world that eighteen selectively bred and enormously expensive equines were now for sale. She didn't even know how to price them; Hilda had acquired most of them many years ago, and Annie had no idea how their value back then compared to their value now. She sighed and turned on her anti-quated computer.

To her relief, Patricia responded almost immediately and with much enthusiasm.

"I'm happy to help, Annie," she wrote. "Let me consult my calendar and I'll provide you with some possible dates to consider. Frankly, it may take several weeks to properly evaluate all the horses, but I agree, we can get started with many of them. I'll make sure their pedigree papers are all in order. In the meantime, you might want to take a look at the following magazines, which many people consult whilst searching for that perfect hunter jumper or dressage horse. This isn't how Mr. Colbert's horses will be sold, of course—word of mouth is more appropriate for this caliber of horse—but it will give you an idea of how second- and third-tier horses are often promoted."

A long list of magazines, many of them published

outside the United States, followed. Patricia had included the link to each of their websites. It looked daunting. But it was a start. Annie mentally patted herself on
the back. She had reached out for help and received exactly what she needed. One thing she knew for certain.
If word of mouth was the established way to sell outra-
geously expensive equines, Patricia was going to be
front and center, not she. Annie knew that talking to
her pals at the local grange and feed store wasn't exactly what Patricia had in mind.

At eight o'clock, Annie pulled up in front of Crossroads Bar. It wasn't quite time for the local band to start
playing, but the noise level already was at a near earsplitting level. *I really am getting too old for this,* she
thought, as she pulled open the main entrance door
and got the full onslaught of what she'd heard inside
her truck with the windows rolled up. She glanced
around and eventually espied Lisa, sitting on a bar stool,
surrounded by a group of women. Lisa saw her at the
same time and raised her drink, inadvertently sloshing
some of the liquid over the edge of the glass and down
her arm.

"Whoops!" she yelled to Annie, then leaned back
and laughed at her clumsiness. Lisa obviously had been
parked there for a while.

Annie threaded her way through a series of packed
tables and waitresses who looked as if they'd rather be
anywhere else. Still, the staff was an attentive bunch.
Annie had hardly sat down on the stool Lisa and one of
her friends had snared for her when a young woman
appeared at her side.

"What can I get for you?" Her tone hardly could have
expressed less interest in hearing Annie's reply.

"Um . . ." Annie stalled while she glanced at what Lisa and the others were drinking. "A gin and tonic, I guess." She'd once heard a friend of a friend refer to it as "my summer drink; the only thing I'll imbibe from May through September."

"Bombay Tanqueray Beefeater Gordon's Seagram's or Hendrick's." The words reeled off the waitress's tongue, and Annie stared at her until she realized she was naming different brands of gin.

"Um, Hendrick's." It was the only one she remembered.

"Good choice." This was intoned with about as much enthusiasm as the last sentence. Annie had a feeling she could have said, "I'll have what's left in the bathtub," and it would have elicited the same response.

Conversation proved nearly impossible at the bar—not because Ashley's friends didn't want to talk—in fact, their words spilled over one another's in their eagerness to communicate. It was the noise level and proximity of everyone else in the crowd that made it impossible for Annie to catch more than a single sentence. She wasn't even sure she'd caught all the women's names. She decided to take charge; after all, she was the oldest in the group.

Grabbing her drink, she shouted into Lisa's ear, "Let's get out of here before the band starts. I think there's a patio out back."

"Good idea," Lisa shouted back, and gestured with her drink to her friends. This time, the drink hit the glass of another patron and the contents of both went flying. Lisa and the man whose drink had just been emptied erupted into raucous laughter. In fact, their antics were received with great hilarity throughout the bar. But Annie felt unease rise within her. If Ashley's friends were as intoxicated as they appeared, what pos-

sible help could they be to her now? And was their behavior indicative of how Ashley acted on a Saturday night
out with the gang? She hadn't seemed like a party girl,
but then, what did Annie know? She'd never been one
even when she hit the right age group. Getting drunk
for the sake of getting drunk always had seemed stupid
to her, not to mention a waste of good money.

Mercifully, the patio was relatively empty and certainly much quieter. It seemed most people were waiting for the band and didn't want to give up their seats.
But music was not on Annie's agenda, and when the
gaggle of women finally had arranged themselves
around a table, and the ever-present waitress had received everyone's next drink order, she began with the
speech she'd practiced on the way over.

"I'm sorry we didn't have a chance to talk more
when we met at Ashley's celebration," she said, smiling
at each woman and making deliberate eye contact. "As
you know, I've got a ranch to tend to and I'm a one-
woman show right now. I know Ashley would have been
a tremendous help to me if she were alive today. I met
her only the one time, you know, so don't know much
about her. What can you tell me that will help understand why she might have felt so depressed?"

Her opening gambit put an instant pall over her lis-
teners and seemed to help sober them up. Everyone
looked uneasily at each other. Finally, Lisa spoke.

"We don't know, Annie. She said when she moved in
with you, she'd be leaving Pete for the last time. We
can't understand it ourselves. We thought *you* could
help us." The women all nodded in agreement.

"Well, let's start with what you know. Did Kim
Williams tell you anything about Ashley's death?" This
was underhanded, she knew, but she had to know the
extent of their knowledge.

"You mean the cop who talked to all of us?" This came from a wisp of a woman with long, black hair. She hardly looked old enough to drive, let alone drink.

"Yes, that's Kim. I've known her for a long time. She helped me save the horses in that big barn fire a few months ago." That got their attention and probably raised Kim a notch or two in their minds, Annie thought.

"She was awesome," said another in the group, whose name was Danielle, Annie recalled. "Really, really nice. Not what I thought a cop would be like at all."

Annie smiled. "There are a few nice cops in the department. Most of them are women." This elicited a laugh, and the tension around the table eased perceptibly.

"Well, Kim actually didn't tell us a lot," Danielle went on. "Mostly she wanted to know what we thought of Ashley's . . . death. The last time we'd seen Ashley. How she was acting. You know, that kind of thing."

"When *did* you all last see Ashley?" Annie asked. She was curious.

Another series of sidelong glances passed around the table.

"Oh, come on," Annie said, a trifle impatiently. "I don't care what you were doing. I just want to know the truth. She was found on my ranch, you know. How do you suppose that makes me feel?"

Annie recalled that where Ashley died was one of the questions posed to her at the memorial service. If she gave this tidbit up and inspired a tinge of pity, maybe she'd get new information in return.

"Well, we didn't exactly tell Kim this, but the truth is, we were celebrating Ashley's future with her," Lisa said. Danielle, who was seated next to Lisa, quietly began to cry.

"Yeah, we were so happy for her. You know, new job,

new home, new boyfriend, all that. Everything was going so good for her." A woman with curly red hair offered this statement. For the life of her, Annie could not remember her name.

"So, a party. What would have been wrong with telling Kim about that?"

"We were drinking, smoking a bit of weed . . . that's all," the redhead went on, a bit defensively. She threw up her hands. "I don't know. We just felt we should keep it private."

Keep it private. Dan and Kim had been right. These young women had no clue as to what might be helpful to a police investigation, and so they had erred on the side of protecting their friend. Of course, none of them knew that Ashley's death was internally classified a homicide. As far as they knew, Ashley had decided for unknown reasons to hang herself later that night. Their fierce loyalty to their friend was commendable. Their judgment sucked.

Annie took a sip of her G&T and tried again.

"Where did Ashley go after the party? You must have known."

"She said she was going to stay with her new boyfriend," Lisa said. "We joked around a little, and begged her to tell us who it was, but she just laughed and said we'd find out soon enough."

"Yeah, Ashley wanted to get married so bad," added the woman Annie thought was Courtney. "You know, her childhood wasn't all that great. I think she was in love with the idea that she could create a family of her own. A happy one, with her own children someday."

That made sense to Annie, although the chance of that ever happening, she knew, probably had been remote.

"Where did her new boyfriend live?"

"He lived someplace north of Port Chester, maybe around Shelby," the redhead chimed in. "I don't know. It's only a guess. But I know he was going to pick her up at the bus stop and take her to his place. Ashley said it was really fancy, nothing like Pete's dump."

"And she seemed happy?"

Vigorous nods all around the table. Annie decided to move on to another topic.

"How about Pete? How was he taking all of this?"

Loud noises of disgust filled the air.

"Oh, Pete," Lisa said with disdain. "He was all broken up about it. Cried for days. Called all of us the week after she moved out, wanting to know where she was. 'Course, we never told him."

"He also wanted to know the new boyfriend's name," Danielle added. "We *all* did. But Ashley kept telling us she had to wait until the time was right."

Annie wondered why Ashley had refused to share this small piece of information. Maybe he was a member of the mafia. Or maybe he was just a married man.

"Lisa, you told me that Ashley lived with you for a few days. You two must have had a lot of late-night talks. What was it about Pete that finally convinced Ashley to leave him and move in with me?" It pained Annie to perpetuate Ashley's story, but there wasn't much use in correcting it now.

Lisa fidgeted a bit, then sucked down the rest of her drink. Annie knew it had to be at least her third, if not her fourth.

"Pete sold drugs for a living," she finally said. "He had a pretty big meth problem himself, and about a year ago he started selling on the side to support his habit. Ashley couldn't stand that about him. She was the straightest chick among us." Uneasy laughter floated around the table. Well, at least Annie's intuitive belief that Ashley was relatively levelheaded had been right on.

"You all must have known about the death of the woman Ashley had been caring for," she said, carefully watching for their reactions.

"Mrs. Carr!" Danielle sat up straight. She looked happy again. "Ashley loved Mrs. Carr. She said she was as close to her as she'd been to her own grandma. Her grandma died about five years ago, when Ashley was fifteen. She took it really hard."

"It must have been tough finding her body."

"It definitely shocked her," Lisa said. "But, like, Ashley knew she was going to die sometime."

"Why didn't she continue to work for Elder Home Care?"

Lisa shrugged. "Said she needed a break. Said after a while taking care of old people was just too heavy on the soul."

That phrase again—the same one Ashley had used when they'd met. Annie could tell that the women were getting a bit antsy with all her questions. After all, they'd invited her to join them so they could meet her and learn about her exciting life as a horse trainer. Instead, here she was grilling them just about as resolutely as Kim had, Annie suspected. It was time to wrap things up and get back to being strictly social. And make sure everyone around the table had a safe ride home that night.

"You guys really loved her, I can tell. And I can't tell you how bad I feel that Ashley's life didn't work out the way she'd planned. I was ready to welcome her to my ranch, and looked forward to getting to know her better. But there's one thing I don't get. How did Ashley know to look me up? I mean, she said I'd given a talk to your horse group years ago, but honestly I didn't think anyone remembered me, or thought that I needed help."

The women looked at each other, as if doing so would help them recall how Ashley had found Annie's name.

"It was a friend of hers, someone we'd never met," said the woman Annie was now nearly positive was named Courtney. "Someone who knew you and thought Ashley would be the perfect person to help you on your ranch. Ashley said you seriously needed an extra hand."

"Really?" No one had approached Annie with this observation before. They wouldn't dare.

"What *was* her name?" asked the red-haired girl, tapping her brightly colored nails on the table.

"It was a flower."

"No, not a flower. More like an herb."

"Something you put in a sachet."

"It's on the tip of my tongue. La–La—Lavender! That's it, Lavender!"

Annie grabbed the arm of a passing waitress. "Another gin and tonic, please."

CHAPTER 16

The only thing that stopped Annie from confronting Lavender on her way out of town the next morning was just a wee bit of a hangover and the surprising amount of time it had taken to make sure she was perfectly coiffed and dressed for her first ever Skype meeting. But it didn't stop her from cursing her half sister as she drove past Martha Sanderson's quaint home.

"Damn you, Lavender! You meet a woman for the first time and the first thing out of your mouth is how much *I* need help. How *dare* you? If anyone needs help, it's you. But you'll never acknowledge that. Oh, no. It's just everyone else's life you have to fix."

The inquisitive whines of Wolf and Sasha from the back cab, where they were resting in their crates, made her realize that they thought their mistress was referring to something they'd done. She spent the rest of the trip singing doggie songs to them and telling them they were the most wonderful dogs in the world. Both Wolf and Sasha frequently joined in on the chorus.

Wolf had been to Travis Latham's house many times on previous visits, but this was Sasha's first meeting with Travis, and Annie had high hopes for the encounter. Travis had suffered a stroke several years ago, which left him fully intact mentally but with a distinct limp and reduced gait. He refused to put in a handicapped rail or alter his home in any way that his children and doctor strongly suggested, and instead made the laborious trip up and down the eight steps to his front door every day to retrieve his mail.

"Everyone says my walking will improve with physical therapy," he'd once grumbled to Annie. "Well, this is my physical therapy. Take it or leave it."

It made sense to her. When she'd first met Travis, he needed two crutches to ambulate throughout his home and garden. Now he needed only a cane.

But he had drawn the line at having a dog, and Travis had owned big, active retrievers all his life up until his stroke. Annie had started training Sasha as a companion animal; she hoped that Travis would bond with the Belgian and it would be a match made in heaven. Annie was well aware of the high exercise needs of the breed, but Travis had several grandchildren and a large fenced-in yard, so there would be ways to accommodate Sasha's need to romp and explore. The pup already had displayed such a warm, loving nature that Annie felt certain that she would happily adapt to the role of being Travis's right-hand dog.

She turned right onto Chesapeake Road as if she were a homing pigeon and cheerfully ignored the NO TRESPASSING signs that had caused her some unease on her first visit here. Travis had left his gate open—it was steel, six feet high, and an excellent barrier to unwanted persons. Today, however, it was wide open, and Annie could see rows and rows of colorful annuals lining the wraparound porch. She wondered if Travis had been able to plant any of the flowers himself this spring or if his daughter-in-law, who was good-hearted but a bit too protective, in Annie's view, had insisted on doing the job.

Annie was the first board member to arrive. Bounding up the steps, dogs in tow, she reached the door just as Travis was opening it. He looked the epitome of a country gentleman, Annie thought as she gave him a quick hug. His attire certainly fit the part—baggy corduroy pants, a crisp tartan shirt, and an elegant vest with the gold fob to a handheld watch draping from one pocket. But it was Travis's face that truly showed his character. His craggy features displayed a sureness that could not be toppled by the fiercest adversary. Yet when he smiled, as he did now, he showed himself as someone who still intended to enjoy life to the fullest, even as he struggled with his infirmaries. She wondered how she ever could have considered him a suspect in Hilda Colbert's death. Then again, she recalled, once she'd met him, all suspicion had vanished.

Holding her at arm's length, Travis turned his steely gray eyes upon her and nodded approvingly.

"You look good, Annie. Life must be treating you well."

Aside from a murder on my property and a meddling half sister, it's been swell.

"It is, Travis. You look great, too. May the dogs come in?"

"Of course, of course." Travis gestured with his cane, and Wolf and Sasha trotted in, tongues out, inquisitive as always.

"Sasha, come." The Belgian really didn't want to—there was a new, huge house to explore—but Annie's weeks of training had paid off. Sasha walked obediently to Annie's side, sat, and looked expectantly up at her.

"I'm impressed." Travis's words were sincere.

"Wait until you see what comes next. Sasha, shake hands."

Sasha raised her right paw and extended it forward a few inches.

"Travis, meet Sasha. Sasha, meet Travis."

Travis pulled a nearby chair toward him and gingerly sat down. He slowly leaned over and gently took Sasha's paw into his fingers.

"Delighted to make your acquaintance."

Travis spoke seriously, as if he were addressing an important personage. Sasha gazed back at him, her brown eyes glued to his. Annie was pretty sure it was love at first sight. Then Sasha gave a loud bark.

"*Sasha*! What do we say about indoor voices?" Drat the dog. She knew better than to bark inside a home.

"Why, she's simply answering me," said Travis. "Let the girl speak her mind. I'm pretty sure she was saying she was pleased to meet me, too."

Now Annie was sure it was true love.

The rest of the board—Dan and Tony—arrived within the next fifteen minutes. This gave Annie time to brew a pot of tea, set out tea cookies, and sneak a few dog biscuits that Travis now kept on hand for canine guests. Over the past two months, Annie had gotten into the habit of stopping by the Latham residence whenever she made a Costco run in Shelby. By now, she and Travis were comfortable friends, and Annie navigated his kitchen as competently as she did her own.

She brought out the tray of cookies and set them on Travis's mahogany dining table, a massive piece of furniture that could comfortably seat ten people. Pads, pens, and a printed agenda were placed as four individual settings on the north side. Travis's large-screen display sat a few feet away, attached to a MacBook Air that was discretely in one corner.

"It looks very official," she said approvingly.

"Thank you, Annie," replied Travis. "I haven't held a formal dinner in here since the Thanksgiving before my wife died. It's good to feel that it's being used again."

Marcus was due to call in at two o'clock sharp, so by 1:55 everyone was seated and poised to begin. Annie ran a discrete hand through her hair, and Tony kicked her under the table. She kicked him back.

The phone rang and everyone started. Then the screen was filled with Marcus's face. He was seated behind a desk in a big leather chair, but instead of his usual Armani suit, he was wearing a polo shirt that once again, Annie noted, showed off his extremely hairy and sexy chest. He looked exactly as when she'd last seen him, now two and a half months ago, she thought. Then she noticed a long scar that traversed the left side of his neck and ended in front. The original gash had long since healed, but the remnants were shocking. The scar looked long and wide enough to have sliced Marcus's neck off, or at least slashed his carotid artery and jugular vein. She almost gasped, but realized that her reaction, this time, could be seen and just not heard. She tried very hard not to look as upset as she felt.

Tony, bless his heart, came to her rescue.

"Marcus, good to see you," he said in a hearty voice. "That's quite the battle scar you're wearing."

Marcus gave a broad smile back. "I show it off when I'm feeling my oats. Today happens to be one of those days."

"Glad to hear you're back to being your old self," Travis added. "Because we need all the brain power we can muster today. We've got a lot to get through."

"I'm ready whenever you are, Mr. Chairman. I've got the agenda you e-mailed right in front of me."

Travis turned on a tape recorder next to him and immediately took the floor.

"We're calling our first board meeting to order on Sunday, May fifteenth, at exactly 2:01 PM. I can't tell you how delighted I am to see all of you, proof that our plans are truly under way.

"First, let's review where we are right now. As you know, Gil Houseman, my attorney, has established a Washington nonprofit corporation on our behalf, which is registered as Alex's Place. You're all now officially members of the board."

Everyone around the table smiled broadly. Travis next explained that he was currently talking to Seattle architects to get bids for the new construction.

"But there's really not much they can do until we all decide exactly what the footprint will look like," he continued. "I'd like that to be our main topic of discussion today."

Annie felt a surge of excitement rising within her. She was thrilled at being part of designing the ranch of her dreams. Everything that she had constructed on her property had been done right, of course, but staying within budget had always been foremost on her mind. With Travis's operation, no such hindrances existed. She tuned back into the meeting. Travis was again speaking.

"But first, we do have to address one important piece of business, and that involves the subject of money. Marcus, you own the property outright, I understand; the title is free and clear. You've agreed in theory to sell it to me at fair market value. As you know, I've asked you to present your offer at this board meeting so we can settle this point once and for all and move forward. I'm prepared to meet any reasonable offer without quibbling."

Annie fingered Ronald Carr's business card in the pocket of her blazer. She wondered if she should suggest his help.

All eyes were on Marcus, who leaned back in his chair and rocked a bit.

"I have given it a great deal of thought, Travis, and what seems reasonable to me is that I donate the land to the nonprofit organization as one of its first gifts. It seems only right to me that I do so. After all, you had the property by rights when my wife purchased it out from under you—something she never shared with me, you understand—and considering all that's happened since she owned it, I think it only fair that it be returned to you without anyone having to incur any further costs."

Marcus must have seen a line of stunned faces on his side of the screen, because he sat up and said, "I'm serious. You'll have plenty of costs building the place. I intend to contribute to that, as well. But I'm afraid you'll have to go along with me on this one, Travis. It's a nonnegotiable decision."

Annie looked at Travis, who looked as if he was having difficulty comprehending Marcus's words. Then his face aligned into its usual noble features, and he said gravely, "Marcus, your generosity is unheard of. I accept your gift with humbleness and thanks. You are a true philanthropist. We are most fortunate to have you on our board."

A sustained round of applause arose around the table. Annie could see that Marcus was on the verge of complete embarrassment and was not surprised when he broke in to speak.

"Thanks, everyone. Now let's move on to the interesting part—the construction phase."

For the next three hours, the group intensely discussed the future needs of the new ranch, both for the boys who would reside there and for the various farm animals under their charge. At the end of the discussion, the list included horses, cows, pigs, goats, chickens, and possibly llamas.

"They spit," Annie said flatly. "And they always have a supercilious gaze."

"Yes, but they produce beautiful wool," Travis insisted. "And we do want this to be as self-sustaining a ranch as possible."

"Why not sheep?"

"Annie, we know you're partial to the ovine sector, but they do take up a lot of pasture," Dan said. "And if we try to rig the ranch so there's an agricultural component as well, we'll need that acreage. Plus, they're darn good guardian animals."

"I'll concede the point, but don't blame me when you get pasted by one."

At five o'clock, Travis suggested calling the meeting to a close.

"I think we've made significant progress today," he said. "I'll give our digital recording to my personal assistant to write up the minutes and then e-mail them to all of you before our next board meeting on Sunday, June fifteenth. But before I end the meeting, is there any new business that we haven't discussed?"

"I have one suggestion," Annie said, and all eyes turned toward her. "I'd like to suggest adding another board member—Jessica Flynn. Many of you know her as my vet; she oversees the health needs of half the horses in the county, but you may not know that she also works on mules, cows, and other farm animals. I think she'd be a valuable asset to our board, particularly in the planning stages. She also might have ideas how to help any boys who have an interest in the veterinary field, either as a tech or doctor. She's spread pretty thin—she volunteers her time and services to the Suwana County Rescue Brigade among other rescue groups—so I don't know how she'll respond, but I think it's worth an ask."

"Absolutely," said Dan, and everyone around the table murmured their assent.

"I concur, Annie," Marcus said from the LCD screen. "And, Travis, if I may, I have just one idea I'd like to run by the board before we close."

"Be my guest."

"Annie filled me in yesterday on how my horses are doing at their rehabilitation center."

The board members fell quiet. Annie was grateful that Marcus referred to the horses as his, rather than Hilda's, even though his dead wife had purchased every one. Despite Marcus's incredible generosity today, Annie knew that it was difficult for Travis to shred that last vestige of bitterness he felt over Hilda's cheating him out of the property five years ago. Marcus was doing his best to avoid using his dead wife's name.

"For the most part, they seem to have fully recovered from the fire, am I right, Annie?"

She nodded, interested to know where this was heading.

"Well, the wisdom of the vets and Annie and anyone else who's seen the horses is that they're ready to find new owners. But my question is, is that really necessary? Would these horses be happier as hunter jumpers or dressage horses or whatever else they've been trained to do, or as horses that are simply cared for and ridden on a ranch? I don't want to disparage their illustrious heritages, but I ask because we want horses, and I'm simply wondering if we can procure some from the ones we already own."

There were no immediate responses; it appeared that every board member was weighing Marcus's idea very carefully.

"They're worth a lot of money, Marcus," Tony offered. "The organization obviously can't afford to buy them at their market value."

"It would be another donation."

"You must need a lot of tax deductions this year," said Travis, half-jokingly.

"Always. But that's not the point. We've been left with a big chunk of land and a lot of horses, and I just want to make sure that we make the best use of what we already have."

Annie decided to take the lead. "Marcus, I've asked Patricia Winters, the operations manager at Running Track, to help me assess each horse's value and strengths. I expect we'll be meeting several times in the coming months to do that. From what I've already learned—and there's a steep learning curve still ahead of me—it seems more likely that your horses will be better suited to experienced riders who can bring out their best. But I'll ask Patricia to make sure I'm correct in that assessment. As far as populating the ranch with horses, I truly think we have to look no further than the several animal rescue centers in the county. A lot of good horses are housed there, not just the neglected and abused ones but horses that have been given up simply because their owners can't afford to take care of them anymore. I think we'll have plenty of choices locally."

"Thanks, Annie. I appreciate your honesty and your

willingness to follow through with finding the right answer."

Annie blushed, and blushed even more when she realized Marcus could still see her.

Wolf and Sasha had been as good as gold throughout the meeting, so afterward Travis insisted on giving them a turn on the old run he'd installed on his property for his retrievers. Tony went with him. Annie could tell he was still wound up from what had been discussed today. Tony had never been a scofflaw growing up, but he had been born into extreme poverty and was one of those young men whom Carla Johnson had described as unlikely to surpass his father's level of employment. In his case, this meant grooming horses at the local racetrack. The chance to help other disadvantaged kids transcend their limitations at home excited him in a way Annie had never seen before.

Annie took the opportunity to lure Dan into the kitchen as she washed up. She knew she'd never get his help with putting things away, but she could count on his interest as long as there were tea cookies still on the plate.

"I ran into a couple of Ashley's friends last night," she began casually.

Dan reached behind her and turned off the faucet. "Is that a fact?"

Annie turned and gave him a bland smile. "Isn't a girl allowed to go out sometimes to have fun off the farm?"

Dan snorted. "And I'm guessing you just happened to choose the same watering hole as they did."

"Yes, amazing, isn't it? Anyway, they mentioned that

Ashley was going to meet her new boyfriend the night she died. Just thought you should know."

"What I'd really like to know is his name."

"Sorry, can't help you. Someone said something about him living in Shelby, but it was only a guess."

"Anything else?"

"He lives in a much nicer place than Pete, who, by the way, isn't just a drug user, he's a bona fide drug dealer. So what are you going to do with this information I picked up in such a serendipitous way?"

"Come in tomorrow and make a statement. And talk to Kim. She needs to reinterview all of Ashley's friends." Dan sounded reluctant to ask this of her. It was thoroughly annoying.

"I'll try to make the time."

"Make the time. And Annie?"

"Yes, Dan?"

"Don't think I don't appreciate your help. But I've been rethinking my decision, and involving you is just a bad idea."

"You can't be referring to my results."

"What in the Sam Hill do you think, Annie? Of course we're glad for the information. But not if you get hurt while you're digging up dirt."

"I'll be fine."

"That's what you thought the last time."

"Well, I'm still here, aren't I? Alive and kicking?"

"Forget it, Annie. You narrowly escaped a scar worse than Marcus's. You've got the heartfelt thanks of a grateful sheriff. But from now on, you're off the case."

CHAPTER 17

"So that's the story."

"About half of it, I'd say."

"Gee, Kim, I did the best I could. I guess I just don't have your ten years of police experience talking to sullen adolescents."

Despite her flippant remarks to Dan on Saturday, Annie had delivered her statement to Kim on Monday as soon as she'd had a chance to shed her mucking clothes, shower, and grab a muffin to eat in her truck.

The deputy draped a well-toned hand over Annie's clenched ones. "You did great. Hey, you got way more out of them than I did. It's just that I don't believe that Ashley's four closest friends in the entire world don't have a clue as to whom she was seeing on the side. Those women know more than what they told you. Count on it."

Annie was seated in a chair next to the deputy's desk, close enough to know that Kim was still seething over what she'd just related to her about her conversation at the bar. Kim's eyes, normally a warm chocolate brown, now appeared black and looked as if they could bore a hole in the head of any unfortunate witness and easily extract any information that had carelessly been omitted the first time around.

Save me from ever being in Kim's crosshairs, Annie told herself. *And God help those young women when she talks to them again.*

"So is Pete off the suspect list?" Annie asked cautiously.

"No, Pete is not off the suspect list," Kim replied, her irritation showing once more. Then she smiled. "Sorry, Annie. It's just that I find it difficult to comprehend the reasoning process of anyone under the age of thirty anymore. I know, they think Ashley's death was a suicide and don't want her reputation besmirched any more than it already is. But don't they understand they have a responsibility to tell the Sheriff's Office everything they know and let us decide what's important?"

"No," Annie replied bluntly. "They don't. They think they're perfectly capable of deciding what's relevant and what's not. I'm sorry, Kim, but that's the normal mind-set of people who are barely out of their teens."

Kim sighed. "You're right. But it gets tiresome trying to pry information, most of which *is* irrelevant, out of their underdeveloped brains."

A short silence ensued, during which both women privately bemoaned the lack of common sense in the generation that had followed them. Each was certain they had never gone through this stage themselves.

"Oh!" Annie leaned forward. "Speaking of underdeveloped brains, there's something else I wanted to bring up. Did you know that Lavender was the one who told Ashley to ask me for a job?"

Kim stared at her. "I don't believe so. I would have put it in my report if she had. Are you sure?"

"All four women were positive. They haven't met her, but they remembered her name. In fact, Ashley described Lavender as a friend. Since they only met the morning they discovered Mrs. Carr's body, that seemed a bit odd."

"Indeed," Kim said flatly. "It appears that I'll be spending my week reinterviewing every single female I've spoken to so far on the case."

"What a drag. Isn't there any other way to try to find the guy's identity?"

"Well, as a matter of fact, there just might be. Ashley's personal effects, such as they were, turned up squat, but Jack Clauson's promised to deliver his report on her smartphone this week. A lot of the texts were deleted, so it's taken him this long to reconstruct them. I'm hoping we'll find a name in there. I probably should have waited for Jack to finish his work before approaching the girls. But you know Dan—he's hot to interview witnesses before the forensics are all in. He's always afraid people will think too much if we wait too long."

"Try to be nice to Ashley's friends, Kim. If they know I talked to you and you beat them up too badly, they'll be all over me, and I don't think I could withstand the attack of four irate twenty-one-year-olds."

Kim laughed. "I promise. We didn't have Ashley's autopsy report when I first talked to them. So I'll be merely touching base because I have new information I'd like to discuss with them."

Annie felt considerably better. She didn't particularly want to destroy the trust she'd built with Lisa Bromwell, or anyone else, for that matter. Perhaps it was better that she stay outside the investigation from here on out. Going undercover was turning out to be more of a headache than an adventure. She even decided not to ask Kim what "new information" Ashley's autopsy had provided. At least, not yet.

Annie's Good Angel patted her on the back but still looked worried.

Annie's mind was on high overload as she exited the Sheriff's Office. Ever since she'd made the split-second decision to give Ashley a try at her stables, she'd been thinking about the time she spent tending to the daily needs of her horses. Until now, she'd never really thought about the hours it took to feed, groom, exercise, and see to the general health of her herd—not to mention the time it took to procure supplies, muck stalls, and make sure her horse structures and fences were all in good working order. But now she did.

For eighteen years, she'd been the sole employee on her ranch, and for all that time she had deliberately kept it that way. In the early years, she simply didn't make enough money as a horse trainer to spread the work around. When she decided to raise sheep and market their wool, her income more than doubled. So did her workload. Still, for reasons that escaped her now, she'd never contemplated bringing in someone to share the work. She hired people, of course, when she needed specific tasks done. Leif, for example, had been shearing her sheep twice a year since day one. But now, at age forty-three, wasn't she entitled to a little more help?

She considered her next stop a good case in point. Once a month, Annie lugged all her recyclables to the county transit center, along with any items that merited a permanent home in the county dump. Why couldn't she hire someone to do it for her? If she did, perhaps she wouldn't always be scrambling for time to do her primary job—train horses. Perhaps, with help, she'd be able to take on more clients. Her stables were certainly large enough to accommodate more horses.

The e-mail she'd received from Patricia Winters that morning had added fuel to her new discontent over how she spent her days:

> *Annie,*
> *I've looked at my calendar and have set aside the following possible days to get together to evaluate Mr. Colbert's horses.* [A list of six dates followed, from the rest of May through June.] *Since Running Track is a bit of a drive from your own stables, perhaps you would consider spending several days up here so we could accomplish our work most efficiently. The centre has built a number of cabins throughout its campus for owners who wish to spend a block of time with their equines. We would be happy to give you one of these accommodations at no charge. Mr. Colbert is one of our most important clients, and we would be quite pleased if you could spend three or four days with us. Please review these dates and get back to me at your leisure.*
> *Sincerely yours,*
> *Patricia*

The thought of spending several days at Running Track was tantalizing, and Annie would have loved to hit Reply and tell Patricia that she would be there at her first opportunity. But that was the problem. What opportunity? She could hardly ask Luann to take care of her horse and sheep herds, morning and evening, for three or four days. Well, she could, but it seemed like a huge inconvenience to her friend, who had even more horses to care for than Annie did. Up until this point, Annie's life had been so circumscribed that the need for more than minimal help had never arisen. Now it had, and she wasn't sure how to solve her problem.

She was so intent in her thoughts that she nearly missed the turnoff to the transit center. Making a sharp left at the last possible minute, she narrowly missed being sideswiped by an oncoming truck, whose driver honked his horn at her sudden ill move. Annie snapped to attention. It was time to table her thoughts until she had adequate space to ponder them alone—preferably with a glass of Glenlivet in her hand.

She pulled into the recycling center parking lot and got out. Wolf and Sasha were in the rear cab in a state of near ecstasy; they recognized the smell of one of their favorite places. Annie's goal was to keep both inside during her time at the dump. Sasha had already shown just how sneaky she could be in getting out of the truck. The previous month, she'd managed to roll in the garbage *and* consume something of questionable taste. It took more than a week to get the smell of doggie upchuck and rotting trash out of the rig.

It was a busy day at the center; the good weather seemed to have stirred many Suwana County citizens into a frenzy of spring cleaning. Annie looked around to see if she recognized anyone. She did. To her utter surprise, she saw Tony, dressed in jeans and a T-shirt, sitting in an old Ford Fairlane, two rows away from her own parked truck.

"Hey, Tony!" she yelled. Instead of answering, Tony glared at her and put a finger to his lips. Puzzled, she jogged over to his car. The passenger window was rolled down by the time she arrived and Tony was bent over, hovering low in the seat.

"Go away," he whispered. "I'm on surveillance."

Oh. Annie stepped back, then leaned forward. "Who are you surveilling?" she whispered back.

Again, Tony looked daggers at her. "Who do you think? Our only viable suspect."

"Pete? You poor thing. Can I bring you some doughnuts?"

Tony sighed and pushed the passenger door handle. "If you insist on blowing my cover, you might as well come inside," he whispered. "But for just a minute."

Annie promptly stepped into the car and rolled up the window. She looked at Tony, curious.

"Does Pete work here? I thought he sold dope for a living."

Tony offered Annie his jumbo-size bag of potato chips, and Annie gratefully grabbed a handful.

"Nope. But we got wind that he makes a pilgrimage to the dump every Monday. He allegedly doesn't go through the line, just hands off a trash bag or two to an attendant. Without paying."

"Aha." Citizens who brought their rubbish to the dump went through a specific process. They drove their cars onto a weighing station, attendants removed their garbage from the vehicles, and their cars were weighed again. Customers then paid for the privilege of transferring their trash to the dump heap. The cost was calculated by the displaced weight.

Tony plunged his hand into the bag and began tossing potato chips, one by one, into his mouth. "If we catch him actually passing along drugs or materials used in the manufacture of drugs, we'll have enough to arrest him. So here I am."

"Sounds exciting."

"Believe me, it's not. At least, not until something happens."

"So what kind of car are you looking for?"

"A Dodge Ram, turbocharged, silver with red trim. Should be easy to spot, since our boy has it jacked about ten feet off the ground."

"And what's the plan?"

"Catch him on camera making the drop, retrieve the bags with this handy subpoena I've got in my pocket, and bring it back to the shop to analyze."

"Isn't that illegal?"

"What?"

"Filming him."

"Hell, no. This is a public space, and I'm not using audio."

"Oh."

They munched in quiet.

"I probably should get back to my truck," Annie said a few minutes later. She was getting sleepy from inactivity, and she wasn't sure her windows were rolled down sufficiently for the dogs to get much fresh air.

"Good idea. Go home and ride a horse. It's a lot more fun than what I'm doing."

"So true," she said carelessly, stepping out of the car. At that moment, the sound of loud and raucous rap music filled the air, and a Dodge Ram roared into the parking lot.

"Go! Now!" hissed Tony, and Annie obediently trotted back to her car, where, to her relief, her dogs had plenty of fresh air. But now she had no intention of doing anything except watching the show.

The tattoo that scaled up the driver's arm easily identified Pete as the driver, but the tinted windows in the cab made it difficult to see if he had any passengers with him. Annie watched Pete put the truck in park, open his door, and jump down, leaving the engine running, the door wide open, and the rap music at its mega volume. Now she could see more clearly who was inside. A petite female was hunched in the middle, next to a large male in the passenger seat. She glanced over at the Fairlane; Tony seemed to have disappeared from view, although she was sure he was recording the scene unfolding before them. She looked back at the truck. Pete was hauling two large, black garbage bags out of the truck bed. They appeared to be heavy; Pete was having difficulty wrestling them to the ground, and his male passenger either wasn't up to offering his help or had been advised not to do so. Once both bags were out of the truck, Pete whistled, and the passenger door opened.

The man who emerged was twice the size of Pete and looked older. He had a scraggly black beard and a potbelly that Annie was sure would cause him back problems in the future. Each man took a bag and dragged it over to the pocket-size office next to the receiving center. Annie watched the bags disappear inside the office, and then a young man with a long ponytail came out. Everyone certainly seemed friendly; the three men casually chatted with one another for a minute or two and then high-fived each other before Pete and his friend headed back to the Dodge Ram. Annie was surprised that what had been described as an illegal transaction was conducted so openly and seemingly without fear of being caught.

Pete's exit was as spectacular as his entrance; he revved the engine, backed up twenty feet at twenty miles an hour, and peeled out of the parking lot toward the highway that led to Port Chester.

Tony, Annie knew, would be delivering the subpoena and yanking the bags in the next nanosecond. She wondered if the man on the receiving end would be arrested at the same time. Probably not, she thought, until Tony was sure of the bags' contents. Would Mr. Ponytail alert Pete and his friends about Tony's interception after the fact? Annie's guess was that he would. Which meant someone should be tailing Pete to see whether he was tipped off.

Annie looked at her dogs. "Up for a little adventure?" she asked. Without waiting for the answer, she turned the key in her ignition and rocketed toward the exit.

CHAPTER 18

When she emerged on the highway, the Dodge Ram was nowhere in sight, and for one heart-stopping moment Annie thought her high-speed exit from the county dump had all been for naught. The two-lane road had a double yellow line down the middle, so passing any vehicle was strictly illegal. Traffic was seldom heavy on the five-mile stretch between here and the outer limits of Port Chester, but it was constant, and no one was in a hurry. Then, finishing the turn on a wide corner, she saw Pete's truck. There were perhaps eight cars separating her truck from his, but with the Ram's elevated undercarriage and the now relatively straight road ahead of them, it wasn't difficult to keep the truck in her sights.

Except that Pete obviously was on the move with places to go. He tore around an old orange farm truck that was hindering his journey and roared ahead, once more passing out of her vision.

"Hell's bells!" she muttered. Behind her, both Wolf and Sasha were barking with excitement. They'd never seen their mistress drive so fast before and thought it terribly exciting.

Annie, who had never tailed anyone in her life, simply prayed she knew what she was doing.

She came to the first stoplight in town and glanced around her. No Dodge Ram. Her heart sank. She was now on the main drag, which had offshoot streets everywhere that led into myriad small neighborhoods. If Pete had turned onto any of them, she'd never be able to find him. The light turned green and she inched forward, unsure of what to do. Then she felt the pulsating beat of rap music and the muffled sound of angry lyrics being spit out between each thump, and looked to her left. There was Pete, in the takeout line of the local Mc-Donald's. Apparently even drug dealers on the go had to eat. Annie discretely made a U-turn after she'd passed the golden arches. She entered the parking lot on the opposite side of the takeout line and pulled into an empty parking space, leaving her engine running. Her heart was beating like a jackhammer. The dogs had stopped barking, but their breath was coming fast. Their hot, quick pants tickled the nape of her neck. She looked around her environs and in her rearview mirror. From where she sat, she should be able to easily pull in behind Pete as he exited the drive-thru lane. What worried her was whether she would be noticed as she did so. The exit from McDonald's gave drivers four options of where to turn. If he chose the main drag in either direction, her truck would be relatively anonymous. If he chose either of the other two routes, her truck would stick out like a sore thumb. She waited, and tried not to think about her own growling stomach. A

double cheeseburger would taste great right now, but
there was no time. Now she knew why Tony kept junk
food in his surveillance car.

Pete chose the main drag, and Annie sighed with relief as she carefully pulled out behind him. He was now
at a stop sign and had to turn either right or left, but
predictably his turn signal failed to provide a clue.

Cursing inconsiderate drivers, Annie waited impatiently to see where he would go. He turned right, but
Annie was unable to pull in behind him after making
her own full, complete stop. Perhaps traffic laws should
be suspended while on surveillance, she thought, as she
watched three cars zoom by before she was able to fall
into the line of traffic. Fortunately, the height of the
Ram truck gave her a distinct advantage. After going
through two roundabouts—which forced Pete to slow
down to an almost legal speed—he turned right again,
onto a long country road that Annie knew led to several
housing developments. Now no cars separated them,
but this was a well-used thoroughfare, and Annie didn't
think her presence would be considered terribly unusual. She was fairly certain that Pete had no clue he
was being followed, but what did she know? This was
her maiden voyage, and she'd forgotten to read the
manual on how to tail vehicles without being spotted.

She was several car lengths behind him, but slowed
down even more when Pete came to another stop sign.
Chugging along at a snail's pace, she waited until she
saw the direction in which he was now headed. Pete was
definitely not stopping in any of Port Chester's suburban
neighborhoods, where one could expect to see manicured lawns, tidy flower beds, and community parks where
children played. No, Pete was headed to the outback,
where dilapidated homes jumbled together. In this area,

Annie knew, the lots were tiny, the sidewalks nonexistent, and weeds more prevalent than grass in the postage-stamp lawns. Annie could imagine a meth lab in any one of the homes. Judging by the number of chimneys spewing smoke in mid-May, she assumed that many homeowners used wood as their primary source of heat.

Even Pete was slowing down now, and Annie fleetingly contemplated parking her car and going on foot; there was no question that a late-model F-250 with an extended rear cab would be a distinct anomaly in this neighborhood. Pete had rolled down his window, and she could see him looking out, peering at the house numbers going by him. He stopped his truck for a moment, and Annie, now one block behind him, slammed on her brakes and then quickly pulled over, as if she was parking. Pete didn't seem to take any notice of her antics behind him. A moment later, he gunned his engine, turned right, and disappeared.

"Damn!" Annie hissed from the confines of her truck. But then the pulsating rap music started again, and she knew that Pete could not be far away. She turned to her dogs and dug out treats from her jacket pocket. Opening their crates, she told them to be good for just a little while longer, and then slunk down on her seat to wait for Pete to emerge.

A half hour later, Pete had yet to make an appearance, although the rap music continued as loud as ever. Maybe he wasn't in one of the homes, Annie thought with a trace of panic. Maybe the sound came from just another rap music lover who'd decided to crank up a boom box while Pete was passing by. If she'd lost him now, she'd be in a fine fury. But what could she do?

Behind her, Sasha gave a small whimper. Annie recognized the sound; it meant Sasha had to pee, and she couldn't blame the pup, as she'd been cooped up in the truck for nearly three hours. She would have to indulge her Belgian's needs. Then it occurred to Annie that taking Sasha for a walk might be an excellent way to scout out the neighborhood and figure out if Pete and friends truly were in the vicinity.

She grabbed Sasha's leash and rooted in her glove compartment for a small pair of binoculars, which she knew would be there. Attaching the leash snap to Sasha's collar, she told Wolf sadly, "Sorry, boy. You have to stay here and guard the truck. We'll be back soon—promise." Taking both dogs out, she decided, would be just a bit too conspicuous. Besides, Wolf's control over his bladder was far better.

After Sasha's call of nature was met, Annie strolled up the shabby street with the Tervuren, taking in the drawn drapes, closed doors, and general closed-off look of her surroundings. No children played in the streets; there was not a single dog being walked except the one on her leash. She turned left at the corner before the one where Pete had turned, and walked up a small slope. Aha—there was an alley running behind the homes facing the street, and yes, there was Pete's truck, parked at an angle behind the home squarely in the middle of the block. The music was still blaring from inside the truck, but she was certain that there were no occupants in it. Annie couldn't see any activity from where she stood, and wondered if she dared walk by the truck to try to glimpse inside. Walking past the front of the house was useless; like every other home on the street, everything was buttoned down so no one could get a glimpse into what must have been the living room. Unless someone walked out the front door, she was out of luck.

The back door bounced open, and Annie jumped. She quietly told Sasha to "heel" and continued her walk up the street, this time with a sense of purpose, averting her eyes from where she'd just been staring. She could hear voices, however, and whoever was out there was not in a good mood.

"All right, all right!" The man who was talking obviously felt put out. The rap music abruptly stopped and a truck door slammed. "Happy now?"

"I can't stand your music. I don't see why you play it." This was from a woman with a high, whiny voice.

"Well, I don't like yours, either. All that country twang. Makes me sick."

The screen door slammed and the voices faded back into the house. Annie felt herself relax. That had been close—although how out of place it would have been for the couple to see a woman walking her dog, she didn't know.

But she did know that she had to find a better viewing place, because any conversations she might overhear or people she might see probably would be in the alley. She reached the top of the rise and looked around. The house and Pete's truck stood thirty yards downhill from her, easily visible from this height. But where could she and Sasha perch? She could hardly stand in the backyard of one of the houses on the next block. Or could she? None of the neighbors in this area seemed to take pruning or weeding too seriously, and Annie espied a thicket of blackberry bushes in the corner of the nearest home. Could she crouch in front of them and remain unseen? There was only one way to find out.

Annie was glad she'd worn her parka, because it helped protect her, to some extent, from the incipient thorns that were in full force, even if the berries were just beginning to emerge from the bushes. She'd picked up Sasha and put as much of the squirming puppy as she could inside her jacket to keep the puppy's exposure to thorns as minimal as possible. When she was sure that they could not be seen by anyone but the most eagle-eyed homeowner, she set Sasha down, gave her a treat, and pulled out her binoculars.

She could barely see inside the house but was aware of activity within. If she'd had to guess, she would have said that people had congregated in the kitchen. At this point, there was really nothing to do but wait. She noticed that every home had one or two aluminum trash cans out in back; the alley must be the route that the city garbage trucks used, she thought. She wondered if Tony would be interested in the contents of these cans, as well.

Ten minutes later, a blue Toyota pickup turned in from the street Annie had taken earlier. The truck looked dwarfish compared to the Ram. It stopped when it was practically head to head with the Ram, and a man got out. Annie trained her binoculars on him, but he was inside the house before she could identify any of his features. The slope of the hill was just high enough so she couldn't make out the license plate. To do that, she'd have to stand at the same level, and she wasn't sure she was up to the task—not when Sasha was with her, at any rate. The last thing she needed was for Sasha to make a run for it while she was jotting down a license plate. After a few seconds of indecision, she decided to risk standing up. Standing on her toes and peering through her binoculars, she concentrated on the plate and thought she could make out an "A" and a "J."

Annie heard laughter now coming from the back of

the house. She quickly hunkered down again and set her binoculars resolutely on the back door while pulling the coil of leash closer to her. "Good dog," she murmured absently to Sasha, who, in fact, was being a very good dog and had lain still even as she had moved about.

The back door burst open once more, and this time several people spilled out at once. Annie cursed herself for refusing to buy a smartphone; taking a photo would have been handy right now. She concentrated on memorizing what lay before her—two women and three men gathered in a circle, lighting up what Annie first assumed were cigarettes, and belatedly realized was some kind of drug. It looked as if a pipe was being passed among them. Annie could see each recipient take a drag and then throw back his or her head, presumably sucking as much of it in as possible.

"Where's my beer?" The voice belonged to the woman whom Annie recognized as having sat between Pete and the other man in the Dodge Ram. Her words were slurred, and her neck and shoulders twitched and jerked for no particular reason at all. Annie thought the woman was behaving most oddly.

"Hey, Melissa!" Pete bellowed. "Bring us a six-pack."

"Get it yourself!" A woman's voice came from inside the house. The quality of her voice suggested years of smoking and double shots at neighborhood bars.

Pete cursed back but stomped into the house, returning a minute later with a six-pack in his hand. He set the beer on the stairs and opened one. By now, the woman who'd made the request seemed to have forgotten all about it. To Annie, she seemed to be in a world of her own.

Pete was talking to the group. Annie couldn't understand his words; she only saw the rest of the crowd move toward him as if they wanted to listen very closely to what he was telling them.

Then the other woman, who had not yet said anything, stepped back angrily.

"No way! I'm not your mule. Find someone else. I'm done." She spat out the last words angrily.

Annie saw Pete grab her arm. "Clarissa, don't be an ass. You owe me. You know you do. It's just this one time."

Clarissa jerked her arm away and took another step back. "No! Maybe you could get Ashley to do your dirty work, but I'm not interested."

"I don't care if you're not interested." Pete's voice had taken on a menacing tone. "And I'm not asking you. I'm telling you."

Clarissa turned and ran down the street. Pete and the rest of the group watched her go; no one made a move to stop her. When she'd turned the corner, she continued to run. Annie wanted to see where she was headed but was afraid to take the binoculars off the main event below.

Then Pete laughed. "She'll be back. I've got it covered."

One of the men spoke up. "Yeah, Pete. You've got such a way with women. That's the reason Ashley took off with—"

Pete's arm shot out and he slugged the speaker, who staggered back a few feet. Regaining his balance, he lunged at Pete's neck. The remaining woman screamed and ran into the house.

Annie glued her eyes on the fight below. Everything happened so quickly that later Annie wasn't sure that her memory had everything in the correct order. She mostly remembered seeing the guy who'd been slugged kicking Pete on the ground and the man with the blue

Toyota running out the back door, getting into his car, and racing away.

It was then that Annie decided that for once, maybe she'd take Dan Stetson's advice. Turning to her puppy, she said, "Well, Sasha, I think this is about the time when concerned citizens dial 911."

CHAPTER 19

By mid-morning, Annie had rethought her idea of hiring help for her stables. She was so tired of people intruding into her life that all she wanted to do was go back to bed and pull up the covers. Whatever needed doing on the ranch, she'd do it by herself and be perfectly happy, thankyouverymuch.

The onslaught had started at six o'clock that morning with a phone call from Dan, who, as usual, was irate about Annie's latest escapade.

"You just *happened* to be walking your dog in the prime meth zone of Suwana County?" he asked sarcastically.

"You know I'm training Sasha as a companion animal," Annie explained in an exaggeratedly patient voice. "She needs exposure to different kinds of people and environments. It's good to try new neighborhoods."

"Huh! Guess you found a new neighborhood, all

right. I can't believe you fooled those officers in Port Chester. Had you been in my jurisdiction, anyone on the force would have known you were up to no good."

"What, there's an APB out on me now? Isn't that a little unfair, Dan, considering that every time I extend myself on your behalf, I turn up good intel?"

"Intel. You've been watching too much television. Wait, you don't watch television. Oh, forget it, Annie. I've got the police report in front of me, so don't think you can squirm your way out of telling me what happened. Unless you were fudging a bit to the Port Chester boys last night."

That was a low blow. Annie considered hanging up the phone, something Dan did regularly whenever he was on the losing side of a verbal battle with her, but she thought better of it. She really wanted to know what Pete had been up to, and she suspected that between Tony's and her own legwork yesterday, Suwana County deputies had been kept busy most of the night.

"It's just like I told the nice officer," she said sweetly. "I was walking my dog when I heard sounds of a domestic altercation. I saw two guys slugging it out in an alleyway. I called the cops. Period."

"And the fact that Pete Corbett happened to be one of the combatants is just one giant coincidence?"

There was silence on the other end.

"Cough it up, Annie. I already know the truth."

Of course, thought Annie. *He's talked with Tony.*

"Well, it *was* a coincidence that I ran into Tony at the county transit center. And if you don't believe me, check my truck—my recyclables and trash are still in the bed. Tony told me what was up, and I watched from the safety of my truck. It looked to me like everyone was pretty cozy during the drop-off. Since Tony was concentrating on getting the bags, I thought I'd see what Pete was up to. I wanted to see if his friend at the dump would tip him off about the bags being confiscated."

"Well, of course he didn't. Tony took him into custody the same time he took the bags into inventory."

"Oh. I didn't know he'd be arrested, too."

"That's because you're not a cop. Even though you're doing your best to pretend you are."

"That's not so, Dan! A woman died on my property! You and I know it's murder, not a suicide, and I think I'm entitled to find out what happened just as much as you are!"

Annie was shouting by now, and she realized, with some amazement, that she had yet to consume a single cup of coffee. She plugged in the machine. Whenever she talked with Dan about the case, she couldn't have too much ammo.

The conversation ended on a more civilized note. Annie agreed not to investigate any further without clearing it with Dan first, although the odds of the sheriff okaying anything she wanted to do were about a jillion to one. In return, Dan agreed to keep her informed of any new information on the case that might impact Annie's safety. When she shamelessly whined for more information *now*, Dan grudgingly told her that the bags Pete had dropped off at the transit center had, indeed, contained meth—a rather large quantity, in fact. The man who had received the bags hadn't talked yet, but it would be in his best interests to do so. Dan told her the case needed a fall guy who might cop a decent plea in return for naming all the players in Pete's local drug ring.

"There's just one problem," Dan said at the end of their hour-long conversation. "Pete's AWOL. According to your statement, everyone hussled inside while you were calling 911. By the time the officers showed up, Pete was gone. His truck was still parked in the back, but he and the two people you described being with him at the dump had taken off. Nearly all our man-power is looking for them now."

Annie hadn't known that. After she'd seen the black-and-whites from Port Chester pull into the alleyway, effectively blocking the truck's exit, she'd clambered off the rise to meet them. For a good two hours, she and Sasha had been parked with a nice female officer who chatted with her about the weather, admired Sasha, and let her go after she'd provided a statement. Unlike Dan, this officer hadn't divulged a thing about what was happening inside the house. Annie had assumed Pete was in handcuffs, along with the rest of his gang.

On the top of the kitchen hutch, Annie's Seth Thomas clock gonged the hour. It was seven o'clock—far past the horses' normal morning feed time.

"Gotta go, Dan," she said wearily. Her early morning adrenaline rush had left her feeling enervated, and she still had six horses to feed. "But if I see him or anyone else on my property, I'll be sure to let you know."

"Be careful, Annie. I don't think Pete knows you're involved, but act as if he does, you hear me?"

As usual, Dan hung up without waiting for her reply.

The next call was the one Annie had been wondering about for several days. She was in the middle of mucking her stalls when the landline in the stables gave its signature shrill ring. Annie picked it up with her left hand while she continued to desultorily toss used shavings into her wheelbarrow.

"Annie Carson speaking."

"Annie, it's Mary Trueblood."

"Hi, Mary. How are you?" Annie's greeting was less than inspired, but Mary didn't seem to notice.

"Ian said he dropped off a load of chips for you the other day and told you to expect my call."

Annie perked up. "He did. I can't tell you how much I appreciate your generosity. The chips are great, and they really save on my horse budget." All of this was perfectly true. Annie wondered if the point of Mary's call simply was to discuss the merits of cedar versus pine chips.

"You're doing us a favor by taking them off our hands. But that's not what I wanted to talk to you about, Annie. It's something I'd prefer to do in person. Will you be at home today? Could I stop by late afternoon for a chat?"

Annie had hours of ranch chores ahead of her and wished she could say she had a root canal scheduled this afternoon. But she didn't.

"Sure, Mary, I'll be here, and probably will be down at the stables or working in the round pen. What time do you think you might stop by?"

"Shall we say four o'clock?"

"Fine. I'll see you then."

"See you then, Annie."

She hung up the phone feeling thoroughly puzzled. Obviously, Mary had something on her mind, but for the life of her Annie couldn't figure out what it might be.

The third disruption occurred just as Annie stepped out of the shower. Her cell phone buzzed insistently on her dresser, and she picked it up, her hair dripping over her wood floor and, to her cat Max's disgust, him.

"Annie? It's Patricia Winters. From Running Track Farms."

Normally, Annie would have been delighted to talk to Patricia, a fellow horsewoman, but she still hadn't figured out how she could arrange care for her horses so that she could spend several glorious days learning all about the merits of pedigreed horses. By the time she'd finished talking to the Port Chester police and finally returned home yesterday, it had been high time to feed her own horses and check on the ewes. The contemplative evening she had envisioned gave way to a long nap on the couch after a makeshift dinner. At ten o'clock, she woke up, dumped the rest of her largely untouched glass of Glenlivet in the sink, and fell into bed.

"Patricia," Annie now said. "How nice to hear from you—at least, I hope so. Is everything okay with the horses?"

Patricia laughed. "Spoken like a true horse owner. First confirm that every horse is safe and healthy, and then ask me how I'm doing."

Annie laughed back. "Sorry, it's just an ingrained habit. Horses first, you know."

"Well, the horses are absolutely fine. Even Cinder is doing better. We may have her scar tissue issue licked."

Cinder, Annie knew, was the Appaloosa who had suffered the most smoke inhalation. She was relieved that like Cinderella, for whom the horse was named, Cinder was going to have a happily-ever-after life.

Patricia went on. "Have you given any thought to when you might come up? And does my idea of spending several days at once make sense to you?"

"It does make sense," Annie admitted. "And I'd love to do it. The difficulty is finding someone who can take care of my horses while I'm gone."

"Oh, I do understand." Patricia's voice reflected her

empathy. "No one's quite good enough to take care of our little darlings, are they? Well, keep me posted. I'll hold the dates I e-mailed you as long as I can. Just let me know how you fare with getting help."

The rest of the morning Annie scoured her address book and her brain in her attempt to find someone who had the flexibility to take care of both sheep and horse herds during her prolonged absence. For the life of her, Annie couldn't think of a single person.

She worked with Layla while she waited for the expected visit from Mary Trueblood. It was amazing how much progress she'd made with the Walker after remembering one crucial fact. Annie had always known that horses' two-sided brains absorbed information differently. It wasn't all black and white, of course, but generally speaking horse people considered the right side the flight-or-fight side and the left side the one that absorbed and remembered new information. Many well-known horse gurus insisted that only when a horse was taught to perform a task on both sides of its body did the lesson fully sink in. Annie was a proponent of this way of teaching, but she had forgotten just how important it was with the horse at hand.

Under "the bully's" rein, Layla's right brain was continually fired up on all cylinders; she was afraid most of the time, so instinct took over whenever someone was on her back. It made learning new things extremely difficult, because right-brain behaviors simply took over. When Annie worked with her, Layla was far calmer and wanted to please, but remnants of her former training still crowded into her memory bank. Annie had discovered that if she took the time to teach both sides of Layla's body, she seemed to integrate Annie's "asks" much faster and with greater accuracy. In fact, Annie was marveling at the lightness with which Layla now sidestepped across the round pen in both directions when Mary Trueblood's Lexus pulled into her driveway.

"Over here!" she shouted as Mary got out of her car. The lesson was over, anyway, and Annie was glad she had something to do with her hands while Mary made whatever pronouncement was coming.

"What a day!" Mary exclaimed as she walked up to the round pen. "If this sun keeps up, we're going to have one of our best summers in recent memory."

"It's been great," Annie agreed as she loosened the cinch on Layla's saddle. "You never know what May will be like on the Peninsula, but this weather is enough to make me think about planting a garden."

"Oh, you really should, Annie. You've got the room, the right southern exposure, and I suspect your compost pile would make anything grow."

Mary's own gardens attested to her green thumb. The Trueblood property was exquisitely landscaped with shrubs and flowers that began at the end of the driveway and enveloped the manicured yard in front of their home. And Annie had once glimpsed Mary's extensive organic garden in back of the house, which, thanks to a large greenhouse, produced vegetables almost year-round.

"Sure, in my spare time," Annie joked, as she pulled off Layla's saddle and slung it over the round pen fence.

"Gardens really don't take that much effort, or skill, despite what most people think," Mary said. "It's just planting the seeds and watching them grow. I'd be happy to give you some starts, if you'd like."

"Really? That's awfully nice of you. Maybe I should give gardening a try." The thought of picking ripe tomatoes and strawberries had a certain appeal. Plus, she could choose precisely what she wanted to plant.

Kale, for example, would not be seen in her garden. Nor would many root vegetables.

Annie picked up a brush and started grooming Layla, who was quietly standing in the middle of the pen. "I hope you don't mind my doing this. I'll turn her out in a few minutes and then we can talk."

"Not at all. What a lovely horse. Is she one of yours?"

"No, Layla is being rehabilitated after having what I call a 'jerk-and-spur' on her back. A friend of mine had to stable her while she underwent chemo. When she was ready to bring Layla home, she found out the extent of the damage he'd done."

"How infuriating," Mary said. "There's nothing I hate more than a bully." Annie silently agreed as she brushed out Layla's tail.

After a moment, Mary spoke again, more tentatively. "You know, Eddie also was a bully."

Annie stopped brushing for a moment, then resumed the task. She was silent only because she didn't know what to say. She knew that Eddie Trueblood was meant to have taken over the family business but instead was a source of heartache and disappointment to his parents, his reckless behavior eventually involving drugs and crime.

"It was just a matter of time before Eddie did something that would land him in real trouble," Mary continued. "We never knew where he was staying or what he was doing—or who his friends were. The truth is, we really didn't want to know. The only time we could count on seeing Eddie was when he wanted money for one of his hare-brained business schemes."

Mary spoke resolutely now, with none of the quiet despair she'd voiced before. "We couldn't save our son, but we would be very happy if we knew we could help other boys who are on the cusp of going in the same direction as Eddie. Cal and I have discussed it, and we would like to contribute to that new center you're planning with Travis Latham. We can contribute money and construction materials, and would be happy to help with fund-raising, as well. I'm on the board of several local organizations and have experience prying checks out of residents who can well afford to make charitable donations. And I know just who they are."

Annie had no doubt that she did—the Truebloods were one of the "first families" of Suwana County; their local roots extended further than nearly anyone else who now lived here. Nonetheless, she was stunned by Mary's magnanimous offer.

"Mary," she began, intending to tell her just how much her generosity would mean to Travis and the rest of the board. But as she began to speak, the sound of pounding hooves filled the air, and she turned toward the pasture to see her five horses galloping straight to the gate, the white in their eyes exemplifying their fear.

Not another predator. Her mind immediately flashed to her ewes.

"Stand back, Mary!" she called out. "I'm going to let them into the paddock." She strode to the pasture gate, flung it open, and stood aside. The horses merged as a blur into the pen without bickering over who went first. Relieved, Annie stepped into the paddock with them and began calming them with her voice and hands. They clustered around her, which meant they considered her their leader right now. Once she was sure no one was unduly traumatized or physically hurt, she opened the paddock gate to the stables to give the horses access to their stalls. She then turned to her guest, who was standing silent by the barn, her own eyes wide.

"Mary, something out there scared the bejeezus out

of them, and I have to investigate. I don't know how long I'll be gone—do you want to finish our talk later?"

"I'd like to come with you, if I might. If there's a predator out there, I'd like to know about it, too."

"Hop into my truck."

She hoped Mary would not be upset by the sight of her Winchester .30-.30 in the gun rack. She'd returned it to its usual place last Sunday after Dan had officially called her off the case. Now, she was glad she had.

Annie bumped along the rough road that flanked the ten-acre horse pasture and had been carved out not by road machines but by use and time. Although both of Annie's hands were firmly on the wheel, her eyes were glued to the great expanse beyond. Something had frightened the horses, and it had to be more than the average coyote that made his way, sometimes with a band of brothers, across the grass. The horses would notice these intruders onto their territory but seldom made a fuss, at least during the day. Coyotes were not going to bother a herd of healthy horses that could and would kick them into oblivion if given the chance.

A cougar, on the other hand, could move with lightning speed and rip out a horse's underbelly before the rest of the herd knew what was happening. This was what worried Annie now.

"What about the sheep?" Mary shouted above the sound of the truck's tires pounding over the uneven dirt.

"We'd have heard them if they were in trouble," Annie yelled back. "And Trotter would be braying his head off. But we'll check them, just to make sure."

Mary gave a half scream. Annie slammed on the

brakes, and both women rocked forward from the sudden halt. Mary held a trembling arm out in front of her.

"Back there! In the woods. I saw something move. I'm sure I did."

"Good eyes," Annie told her as she yanked open the truck door with her left hand while fumbling for her Winchester in her right. "Stay here for now. I might need you to move the truck."

Crouching down, she trotted forward several yards and took cover behind a small grove of alders. She brought the Winchester to her shoulder and sighted it. All was quiet for a moment. Annie heard only the sound of her own ragged breath. Then she saw a flicker among the trees, beyond the neat white fence line that marked the end of the pasture, from somewhere within the forest beyond. She pushed the cross-bolt safety off with her thumb, levered one round into the long chamber, and waited. A half minute later, another flicker appeared from the far-off wood. It was metallic and glinted in the sunlight.

Annie slowly lowered her rifle. She heard the sound of running behind her and turned. Mary was nearly upon her. Clasping Annie's arm, she repeated nearly word for word what Hannah had told her more than two weeks earlier.

"Annie! It's a man! I saw him running behind the trees. And I think he has a gun!"

CHAPTER 20

"I can't understand how Wolf materialized by the sheep pasture," Annie told Marcus the next morning. "I swear he was locked in the farmhouse when I left to work with Layla. How could he have gotten out?"

"The ability to evaporate and reappear at will is a well-known trait among Blue Heelers," Marcus solemnly told her. "Especially when they're concerned for their mistress's safety. I'm just glad the sheep were untouched by this human predator."

As soon as Annie had seen the glint of metal within the forest, she knew her only course of action was to call 911. She hardly wanted to provoke a shoot-out with a stranger, even though he was trespassing. What if the figure turned out to be a kid with a toy gun? But here, she'd been completely stymied. Yesterday had been one of Esther's rare days off, and once Annie had uttered the word "trespass" to the substitute operator, she'd been told to enter her 911 report using the appropriate link on the Sheriff's Office website. Annie had fumed but done as she'd been told. So far, no deputy had responded.

"Do you know I had to send an e-mail to report the trespasser? 911 is now reserved only for 'crimes in progress.' "

"How infuriating. I assume you'll share your feelings about this new response system with Dan?"

Annie appreciated Marcus's solidarity more than she could say.

"You know I will. Not that it will do any good."

Marcus cleared his throat.

"Annie, I have a rather awkward request to ask of you."

"That sounds intriguing." She was more than ready to change the subject.

"Not really. And I hate to ask, but I don't know who else to turn to. I've had all of Hilda's belongings that survived the fire boxed and ready for storage. The moving company will take them to your local storage unit, but they can't open up an account on my behalf, and apparently I can't set up an account over the phone. Would you mind terribly renting a couple of large units and making sure the boxes get in there safely? I'd like to have everything out of the house by the time Travis takes possession."

"Of course, Marcus. I'd be happy to help."

In truth, Annie was not particularly happy about Marcus's politely worded request. She would do anything to help Marcus, of course—but the attendant pleasurable feeling from knowing that one has done a good thing was conspicuously absent.

Annie had never met Hilda; she'd known her only by reputation, and what she'd heard was not particularly complimentary. Hilda was known as the rich, stuck-up horse owner who browbeat people and horses with equal opportunity. Anyone or anything that displeased her had received her quick condemnation and often, ferocious wrath. When Hilda was brutally murdered last winter, Annie suspected that everyone around her silently heaved one collective sigh of relief. How Marcus, her husband of twenty years, had withstood her fits of temper and irrational rage was beyond Annie's ken. On the plus side, Hilda had set the bar ridiculously low for anyone who came in her wake. Annie had simply been her usual lively and agreeable self around Hilda's widower and he'd promptly placed her on a pedestal. For a woman who secretly suspected few men would tolerate her solitary, horse-driven lifestyle, this was extremely re-assuring.

So of course she would do what Marcus had so nicely asked her to do.

But first she had an ax to grind that was legitimately within her purview—to give Dan a piece of her mind regarding his so-called modernized response system.

To her relief, Esther picked up the back line at the Sheriff's Office. The dispatch operator was as unhappy as Annie about the change in emergency responses, and the two women spent a good five minutes disparaging the faulty wisdom of the county heads who'd agreed to implement, admittedly on a trial basis, a computerized method of tracking nonurgent 911 calls.

"And who decides at the end of this trial period whether, in fact, this was a good idea?" Annie asked, scorn lacing her words.

"Who do you think, Annie? The same people who approved it in the first place."

"Who are not likely to admit that they made a mistake."

"Exactly."

"So complaining to Dan won't make any difference?"

"Believe it or not, Dan's on the side of the righteous this time. He did everything but beg the commissioners at their last meeting not to downsize my job. When they refused to budge, he warned them that horrendous crimes would go unsolved if the system was implemented for even a single day."

Annie felt a small surge of affection for the sheriff. He might irritate the daylights out of her practically every time they spoke about the case, but at least he saw sense once in a while. Esther went on.

"And as far as I'm concerned, Annie, your call should have been routed immediately to a deputy. You reported a man possibly with a weapon trespassing on your property. Those facts alone were enough to warrant sending out a deputy or two. Why didn't you insist on an immediate response?"

"It was the word 'trespass.' It's listed on the website as one of the nonurgent crimes that don't need immediate attention. I felt I had to play by the new rules."

"Anytime a weapon is involved, it demands our *urgent* attention. It's precisely the reason this system is doomed to fail. And that's exactly what I'm going to tell Dan as soon as he comes in."

Annie felt as if she couldn't have chosen a more competent or articulate messenger of her feelings.

Tony arrived a half hour later, just as Annie was preparing to drive in to the local storage company. She gave the deputy her statement in short order, provided him with Mary Trueblood's phone number, and was about to step into her truck when Hannah Clare came skipping up to the farmhouse door.

Hell's bells! Annie had forgotten that the child's riding lesson had been postponed until today—Hannah's mother had reluctantly concluded that a competing orthodontic appointment made the usual Monday session too unwieldy. Hannah had recently graduated from riding in the round pen to trail rides around Annie's property, but today Annie was less than thrilled with continuing their game of discovering new trails off the tried-and-true paths—not when an unknown, possibly armed man was lurking on the ranch again.

She sent the young girl off to the stables to collect her saddle and turned to Tony.

"What am I going to do?" she asked in consternation. "Hannah already came dangerously close to the site where Pete had been staying before, and as far as I know, Pete's back here now because somehow he knew I tailed him on Monday and he's out to get me. But Hannah's got her heart set on riding. What can I possibly do or say that won't upset her?"

"Let's give her a lesson in police work on horseback. Give me a horse to ride and we'll all go together and sniff out clues. We won't go very far, and nowhere near Pete's old camping grounds, but we'll make it fun. She'll be with me, and I doubt anyone will approach us with my Glock in plain view. Besides, I haven't been on a horse in ages. You hardly ever share them with others." Tony managed to look hurt for two seconds before Annie broke into laughter.

"Well, Tony, this is your lucky day. I'm going to let you ride Trooper. Just be aware that Hannah will be insanely jealous."

For the next hour, the three riders traversed the horse pasture with exceptional care. Annie had caved in and let Hannah ride in front of Tony on Trooper, which sent the little girl into near paroxysms of joy. Annie had saddled up on Baby, her Saddlebred who'd just started under saddle and needed the experience of being away from the rest of the herd. Annie did not tolerate herd-bound horses, and it was easier to break a horse of the annoying habit of having a hissy fit whenever she was separated from her pasture-mates by giving the horse a new adventure of her own.

Their careful scrutiny of the pasture did not turn up any weapons, but it did reveal several items that Annie had been missing for years, as well as a few that she hadn't even known were lost. A work glove, an old string halter that was past repair, and a few rusty tools had emerged from the ground following the spring rains, and Hannah whooped with delight every time a new treasure was discovered. Judging by the decibel level of Hannah's cries, Annie was sure that any trespasser was fully alerted to their presence and therefore nowhere in sight.

Later, as they unsaddled their horses, Tony quietly said to Annie, "I'm going to return with a metal detector and a lot more help. If it was Pete you saw yesterday, he's probably hanging out somewhere close. We need to do a thorough search of your property and the ones around it."

"Do you think he'd be stupid enough to return to his old haunting grounds near the logging trail?" Annie asked in a low voice. "The sheep didn't seem affected, which makes me think he has at least enough brain cells to avoid returning there."

"You never know. And remember that we don't know for a fact that it was Pete you saw. It just seems more likely since he's on the run and we know he's been on your property before."

Annie didn't like being reminded. "Do what you need

to do, and take as much time as you need," was her prompt response. The truth was, she hoped it was Pete. She was as anxious as Dan and Tony to round him up and put him in a place where he could be found any hour of the day or night—the county jail.

As Annie drove Hannah home, they saw three Suwana County vehicles glide by them, all headed in the direction of her ranch. From the back, Hannah, who'd been rambling on about why Trooper was the most wonderful horse in the world and how Annie really should let her ride him all by herself next week, did her best to turn around in her booster seat.

"Wow, three police cars! I wonder where they're going." Hannah had an insatiable curiosity about big persons' lives.

"Off to catch the bad guys, Hannah," was Annie's breezy reply. She hoped they succeeded.

Procuring two large storage units proved a more cumbersome process than Annie had envisioned. There was paperwork—lots of it—and the owner insisted that every scrap had to be meticulously filled out and then copied on an antiquated computer that churned out duplicates about as fast as Annie could have written them. The owner's skills in addition and subtraction also proved less than stellar, and it took Annie a half hour to convince the proprietor that the prorated figure she'd figured out in her head was, in fact, the correct amount.

More than an hour after she'd walked into the tiny office, she wearily accepted the signed and dated stacks of paper from the owner. He'd done his best to convince her that buying his locks would cost her less than if she purchased them in the local hardware store. Annie wasn't so sure, and she couldn't waste any more time on this lengthening errand. One thing was certain, she grumbled silently to herself—the owner obviously didn't have horses to care for, or they'd all have starved to death by the time he'd calculated their grain rations.

Turning toward the door, she saw a man in perhaps his midthirties seated quietly on one of the plastic chairs in the tiny office foyer. He smiled at her, and Annie realized she knew his face, although his name did not come readily to mind.

"I'm the next victim," he whispered to her. "I'm not sure I'll be as patient as you were."

Then Annie remembered—it was Trey, Ron Carr's son, whom she'd briefly met at his grandmother's memorial service nearly a week ago. What was he doing here?

As if he anticipated her question, he said, "My wife and I have just cleaned out my grandmother's home. It's tempting to toss most everything or give it away, but we thought it might be better to store it now and go through it later, when we've built up our strength."

Annie looked at Trey and realized why she didn't immediately recognize him. At the Episcopalian church, he'd been dressed in a suit and tie. Now he was dressed in sweats and an old T-shirt, and looked positively grubby.

"I don't envy you," she said. "I had the same job when my mother died. I had no idea that she'd kept every one of her wall calendars for the past twenty years. You'd think I could have thrown them away, but she'd jotted down every single social engagement, school function, and riding lesson I'd ever had. They were a microcosm of our family's life. I still have them somewhere in a box."

"I knew we were doing the right thing," Trey said with some relief.

"Definitely. The trick is to remember to go through all those boxes someday. I have yet to learn that one."

Trey grinned. "If we're smart, we'll leave that to our children. Speaking of which, I should see how Marta and the baby are doing. I didn't realize that the, er, application process took so long."

"It's not so bad. You should be done by the summer equinox."

Trey looked over at the proprietor, who was still laboriously filing Annie's papers.

"I'll be right back," he called over to him. His comment seemed to go unnoticed. Trey shrugged, and both he and Annie stepped out of the stuffy office. The sunlight was farther west than when Annie had arrived but still relatively high in the sky, and she felt refreshed just feeling its warm glow on her face.

Trey's car was parked in front, and Annie recognized the emaciated woman she'd seen at the funeral, now seated in the front passenger seat. As then, she was holding a baby in her arms. At the church, the infant had been the picture of tranquil repose. Now he was displaying his distinct personality in the "baby awake" mode. He squirmed and twisted in his mother's arms, obviously unhappy at being in a dormant car for so long.

"Are we done?" Marta asked anxiously as Trey approached the car.

"Sorry, honey, we're just beginning. The man who runs the place isn't exactly the sharpest knife in the drawer. It could be another half hour yet. How's Marky doing?"

Marta groaned softly. "He's cranky. I've fed him but he still won't settle down."

"Maybe you should take him for a drive," Trey suggested. Annie thought that an odd suggestion, but then recalled reading somewhere that babies who refused to sleep in their cribs miraculously succumbed to slumber when taken for a leisurely spin in the family car.

Marta sighed and started the elaborate process of transferring Marky to the backseat and into his infant car seat.

"While you're out, why don't you pick up some hamburgers? Then we won't have to cook dinner tonight."

Marta shot her husband a dirty look. "You know I don't eat hamburgers."

The disdainful tone of her voice had an immediate effect on Trey's mood.

"Well, whatever. I still like to eat, and so does Becka. At least get us a couple and don't forget the fries. Add a chocolate milkshake to mine. One of us has to have strength to take care of this family."

Annie was shocked at the instant tension between the couple, which had arisen over a few simple words.

"I should go," Annie mumbled to Trey, and started to walk toward her truck, parked a few feet away.

"Sorry, Ms. Carson. It is Ms. Carson, isn't it? It really is nice to see you again. My wife and I don't always rip each other's throats out like this. It's just that Marky has some developmental issues that we're trying to sort through, and we're a bit on edge at the moment."

Annie paused. "I'm so sorry to hear that," she told Trey, looking at him with sympathy.

"Well, luckily Becka doesn't have the same issues. I'm convinced she will grow up and be president someday. Marky's just going to lead a different kind of life, that's all."

"I think you have a lovely family," Annie said, thinking the opposite and wondering if Marta's weight issues had any bearing on her son's development problems now.

"Thanks. Take care, now."

Annie drove off, thanking her stars for the umpteenth time that all her children were four-legged animals.

She had prepared herself to see the ranch peppered with patrol vehicles, roaming deputies, and more crime scene tape plastered across one of her buildings. After all, she'd given Tony carte blanche to search far and wide on her property—not that he needed her permission, but it had still been nice of him to ask. So she was pleasantly surprised when the only official Suwana County vehicle she saw in her driveway was Dan's. He and Kim emerged from the woods as Annie was parking. It appeared that they'd been waiting for her return.

"What's the news?" she called out to them.

Dan waved an arm in her direction and pointed toward her farmhouse. Inwardly, Annie grinned. She strongly suspected it was going to be Glenlivet time.

But first, she had horses that need care and feeding. Not to mention a pasture full of sheep. Duplicating Dan's gesture, she pointed off to the barn. Dan nodded. Cupping her hands, Annie yelled out, "And as long as you're on county time, would you mind throwing a dozen bales of orchard into the sheep pen?"

"Already done," Kim called back. "Tony told us what to do. We'll meet you at the bar."

Now comfortably settled around Annie's kitchen table, Dan took one long, appreciative sip of Annie's coveted single malt and sighed with satisfaction.

"That's the best thing that's happened to me all day," he declared to no one in particular.

"I take it your search was not successful?" Annie took a more delicate sip of the amber liquid. Dan was right—single malt just might be able to solve all the problems of the world. Taken in moderation, of course.

"No sign of Pete or anyone else." Kim sounded discouraged. She had yet to take a sip, but then, she paid attention to her body and probably didn't often indulge in the substance Dan and Annie privately thought should be part of the FDA's food pyramid.

"Now, Kim, we did make some headway." Dan put down his glass. "Tony's metal detector picked up several round metallic balls just outside your fenced-in area. They appear to be the same kind we found in our search of Pete's home a few days ago. They're ammo of some kind. We're just not quite sure what kind—yet. Too big for a BB gun, definitely not something you'd want to put in a gun or rifle, unless it was the musket variety, but it's ammo, all right."

Kim took up the conversational thread. "The good news, Annie, is that there's no evidence that anyone's been squatting on your land since we plowed the primitive meth lab site. Whoever came by yesterday and spooked your horses seems to have been just passing through."

Whew. Annie felt much, much better, and just not from the Glenlivet.

"Did you find anything else when you searched Pete's house?"

"We did, indeed," Dan said with immense satisfaction. "Meth, Spice, Europa, sherm, drug paraphernalia, you name it. Plus a notebook with coded writing that appears to be some kind of spreadsheet. Most likely it tracks drug deliveries, money paid and perhaps still owed. We'll sort it out."

"You said that Pete and that woman Clarissa were still AWOL. Who else is in custody at this point?"

Dan and Kim looked at each other and smiled. They seemed inordinately pleased at the swell in jail population over the past several days.

"Well, there's Roy Sharp, the county dump operator who accepted the drugs." Dan started ticking off the names using his oversized fingers. "In the house . . . well, that was quite a party. Port Chester PD gets the credit for nabbing these guys. Let me see if I can remember all these miscreants' names. There's Marty Goldberg, Melissa Clarkson, Ben Franklin . . ."

"Ben *Franklin*?"

"His parents must have had a sense of humor. And one more gal. Who was it, Kim?"

"Zoe Hampstead," came the immediate reply. "I've arrested her for shoplifting and vagrancy too many times to count."

"So . . . has anyone given you the complete story yet? I mean, I know the drug stuff is serious, but we are trying to find out if Pete killed Ashley Lawton, as I recall."

"Not if—*how*." Good old Dan. Why wait for the facts to prove one's hypothesis when you knew, in your heart of hearts, you were right?

"Well, there is Ashley's new boyfriend. He may have been the last person to see her alive. In fact, my money's on him as the killer. Has anyone identified *him*?"

Again, Dan and Kim looked at each other, but there were no corresponding smiles this time. Kim reached down and finally took a tiny sip of her drink.

"Roy Sharp is holding firm," Dan said reluctantly. He hated it when people didn't immediately confess. "We haven't had the pleasure of interviewing him, thanks to his lawyer, but we're being told that he never met Ashley. Oh, and he apparently had no idea whatsoever that the bag he voluntarily accepted contained illegal drugs."

"You think a jury will buy that?"

"Nope. Not when you have witnesses who will testify that they saw Roy taking possession of black trash bags on the sly from Pete every Monday for the past six months."

"You've already *found* these people?"

Dan looked a trifle embarrassed. "We're working on that angle, Annie. Give us time."

Annie felt a twinge of despair. It looked as if Dan and his crew were doing a fine job of dismantling a significant drug ring, and she was delighted at their success so far, even though her ego reminded her that she had played a small part in it. But it seemed the Sheriff's Office was absolutely no further along in solving Ashley's or Mrs. Carr's murder than they had been two weeks ago, and now their prime suspect was missing.

"How about the people in the house? What do they say about Pete? And what about Ashley's mysterious new boyfriend?"

Now Kim looked pained. "Nothing yet. All of them have been through the system and know enough not to talk outside the presence of their attorney. We don't know who represents them, yet—apparently their lengthy criminal records are making it difficult to find lawyers who don't have a conflict of interest—but the bottom line is that we can't talk to them. At least, not until one of their attorneys convinces his or her client to cop a plea. Judy Evans is figuring out the best deal strategy right now."

Judy Evans was the prosecutor in Suwana County. She was pretty and petite and could destroy a defendant's story on the stand so thoroughly that even the courthouse janitor couldn't find enough shreds to sweep up.

"Well," Annie said with a sigh, "it looks as if it all hinges on finding Pete. Although good luck talking to him when you do. He'll just exercise his Miranda rights the same as everyone else."

Normally, Annie was a stalwart supporter of a person's constitutional rights. At the moment, however, she bemoaned the inherent problems with a case in which every defendant and most of the witnesses knew those rights as well as she did, and wisely figured that exercising them was in their best interests.

She looked up at her companions. "Welcome to the world of criminal justice," Kim said kindly.

By ten o'clock, Annie was looking forward to a good night's sleep, but she was interrupted by the sound of her cell phone, still in her jacket pocket. She pulled it out and looked at the number, curious as to who would call her so late. She knew it would not be Marcus; he had informed her the previous night that today was his mother's birthday and, short of a national disaster, he would be celebrating that austere occasion with her from five o'clock on.

It was a local number, but one she didn't recognize. There was only one way to find out. She punched the answer button. It was Mary Trueblood, who just wanted to make sure Annie was all right.

"Thank goodness the police didn't find anything," she told Annie, after learning about the search by the Sheriff's Office on her property. Annie had omitted any mention of the mysterious ammo Tony had discovered.

"Yes, it is comforting," replied Annie, although deep down she did not believe that this meant the stranger might not appear again. She decided, however, to tell Mary about the earlier sighting on her property and the

makeshift camp that for a brief time had been the site
of a small meth lab. Mary lived only a half mile away.
She might as well know the neighborhood was going to
hell in a handbag.

"Such a terrible drug," Mary told her. "I suspect that
many of my Eddie's problems were the result of an early
use of meth. But he wasn't above stealing from our
medicine cabinets, either. We were blind to it for so
long. And when we did find out, we were astounded by
the street value of the drugs pilfered from our home. If
a drug dealer has targeted your home, Annie, I hope
you're keeping that Winchester clean and oiled."

Annie found it deliciously funny to hear Mary, the
paradigm of good breeding, offer the same advice as
Dan.

But later, as she drifted off to sleep, Annie thought
about what Mary had said. She could understand why
Pete might kill Ashley. She knew about his drug dealing
and presumably could have turned him in any time she
felt so inclined. But why would Pete kill Eloise Carr?
Even if Eloise had discovered that Pete was taking her
prescription meds, why would he waste pills that had an
absurd street value on a nice old lady just to make sure
she was permanently shut up? He could have put a pillow over her mouth and accomplished the same thing.
And it wouldn't have cost him a dime in profits.

CHAPTER 21

THURSDAY MORNING, MAY 19

"That sister of yours has really ticked me off."

Kim Williams sounded a tad ominous and blatantly displeased. She'd driven into Annie's driveway at seven forty-five that morning on her way to work. Initially, she'd told Annie she just wanted to make sure that no noxious fumes still emanated from the abandoned campsite. None had for weeks, but Annie appreciated her kindness in inquiring. However, something else was clearly on Kim's mind, and when Annie had asked what was really bothering her, Lavender's name, predictably, came up.

Annie put down her wheelbarrow filled with used shavings, wiped her forehead, and sighed.

"She's my *half* sister. What's she done now?"

"She's done the one thing that always makes my blood boil. She lied."

Annie groaned. "Come on in. This conversation will

require more caffeine. Too bad it isn't five o'clock, or I'd offer you another shot of Glenlivet."

Kim laughed, and followed Annie into her farm-house. The stained Mr. Coffee on the kitchen counter still showed half a pot that was hot and drinkable, and Annie pulled out two clean mugs from her dishwasher. She found a small container of half-and-half that hadn't spoiled and set it on the kitchen table, where Kim now sat erect, looking every inch the athlete she was.

"Did your mother make you walk around with a book on your head when you were a child?" Annie queried. She'd never known anyone who sat up so straight.

Kim smiled. "No, she just told me to be proud that I grew up to be so tall and to make sure everyone saw every inch of my height."

"Good for her."

"Well, it took a while. I used to slouch something awful until I got to the sixth grade and discovered basketball. Then I was happy I was such a string bean."

"So was the coach, I imagine."

"Knowing how to dunk baskets sure didn't hurt when I was applying for college. I think half the force with justice degrees went to school on athletic scholar-ships."

"True. And it's amazing how so many of you have kept that trim, athletic build."

This got a raucous guffaw out of both women. Kim, Annie knew, was a serious bodybuilder and a devoted gym rat after work and on the weekends. Many, if not most, of her colleagues spent their weekends watching games on a couch and drinking beer. Annie knew for a fact that this was Dan's Sunday routine.

"So what's Lavender gone and done now?"

"Well, you know Lavender was with Ashley the day she discovered Eloise Carr's body." Annie nodded her assent, and Kim continued. "The executive director of Elder Home Care debriefed her that same day. We got a copy of his report, of course, but essentially it told us nothing. A week later, the autopsy report came in, showing that Eloise had died from an overdose, Now it was critical that we talked to Lavender. She's a potentially important witness. She might have seen Ashley or Pete steal Mrs. Carr's pills, or heard her say something that implied that one of them was responsible for her death."

"True." It was of some comfort to Annie to know that if either of them had poisoned Eloise Carr, it had to have occurred before that morning, which was the first time Lavender had met Ashley. Presumably, Mrs. Carr had ingested the pills sometime on Monday evening.

"And true to character, Dan wanted me to get the follow-up done without giving Lavender a lot of advance notice, " Kim continued. "Said he didn't want to give her too much time to think."

"Always a good plan. Thinking is usually her downfall."

Kim threw a questioning glance at Annie.

"Just kidding. But Lavender's been known to dance around the truth, if it suits her purpose."

"Exactly what Dan said. So I was on her doorstep as soon as I could find the time. Ashley's death was keeping us all pretty occupied."

"Right. I saw your patrol car at Martha's coming back from Ashley's memorial service at the high school, remember? I also happened to be present when Dan initially called Lavender at home."

"Really? How'd that happen?"

"I was having dinner with Lavender and Martha that Friday evening."

"I didn't know that. How'd she take the call?"

"Well, I wasn't privy to the actual conversation, but as

soon as she knew it was Dan on the line, the waterworks started."

"Odd."

"My reaction precisely. I mean, she told me she barely knew Ashley. And she certainly never met Eloise Carr when she was still alive."

"It was all one big, fat lie!" Kim slapped her hand down on Annie's kitchen counter so hard that both Annie and her coffee mug jumped.

"Sorry," the deputy said sheepishly. "It's just that she completely took me in and it really fries me. If I'd only waited for the results on Ashley's cell before succumbing to Dan's directive, I would have conducted an effective interview. Instead, Lavender gave me the sweetness-and-light version, exactly what you got. And I walk away thinking Lavender knew nothing."

Something in Annie's stomach began to churn. "Ah, are you implying that Lavender was more than just an innocent bystander in this woman's death?"

"Well, she sure as hell knows more than she'd told me *so far.*" Kim managed to inject a sense of impending doom into the last two words. "Jack Clauson gave me a printout of Ashley's text messages this morning. He's really been burning the midnight oil on this case, bless his soul."

The turmoil in Annie's gut worsened. "And what exactly did you find?"

Kim sighed. "This goes under the usual you-can't-breathe-a-word-of-this-to-anyone warning." She waited to get Annie's solemn nod before continuing.

"Lavender and Ashley had been communicating with each other for more than a month. They were burning up the airways with texts. Most of them had to do with Ashley's boyfriend troubles, but there were more than a few that pertained to you, too."

Heat was now rising from Annie's belly. "Do tell." Her tone was icy.

"It's just what you already know—that Lavender told Ashley all about your stables and suggested she ask you for a job. In fact, she practically promised Ashley a job on your behalf."

"Figures. Lavender's so good at running other people's lives."

"In return, Ashley seems to have been instrumental in getting Lavender a job as an aide at the in-home nursing business. In fact, Lavender's application looks suspicious, as if it was filled out by Ashley."

"Wise move. Lavender's spelling is atrocious. I have the letters to prove it."

"And there's more. We're still waiting for copies of all the erased voice messages. The ones that were still on Ashley's phone go right up to the morning of April twenty-sixth, the day the two women discovered Mrs. Carr's body. There's something cryptic about their messages that I still don't understand. *But I will.*"

Annie had no doubt that Kim would wring every last fact that Lavender knew about Ashley and Mrs. Carr's death, and perhaps even Ashley's own demise, in very short order. But she was curious about the messages Lavender and Ashley had exchanged.

"Can you tell me what they said? It's a long shot, but I might know what they're referring to."

Kim looked at Annie critically. "Well, I shouldn't, but since you were so damn good at deciphering the last cryptic message in those recent homicides in our jurisdiction, you might as well have a shot at it. On Monday at 20:50 hours, Ashley texted Lavender and reminded her that tomorrow is 'the day.' Ashley sent another text twenty minutes later reminding Lavender not to forget 'to bring what I gave you.' For the next hour, they texted back and forth, but the only theme is that it's an important day for Ashley that will change her life. Oh, and how excited Lavender is that Ashley will be moving in with you."

Now Annie's hand hit the counter as she stood up, spilling coffee all over her Levi's.

"Every time I hear that story, I get angrier. I just don't get it! I mean, I was nice, but I made it abundantly clear to Ashley that I didn't have any work for her right now!"

Annie was wildly gesticulating as she said this. The truth was, her heart ached at the insouciance she'd shown the day Ashley wandered onto her property. What would it have taken for her just to say "Yes, I have work for you" and thereby changed Ashley's life for the better, as Lavender had so foolishly promised? Annie was convinced that if she had, Ashley would be alive today.

"Annie, it's not your fault." Kim apparently was good at her job of picking up on emotional cues of distraught witnesses. "This is a tragedy, but you're not responsible for it. Ashley's life was spinning out of control long before she approached you. So give it a rest. "

Annie smiled weakly, sat back down, and put her head in her hands.

Before Kim left, she'd delivered Annie's half sister new marching orders—Lavender was to come in for a second interview at two PM sharp, and she was to bring her cell phone with her.

"We can do this the easy way or the hard way," Kim told Lavender on the phone, sounding exactly like Dan when he confronted Larry Bruscheau and his shotgun a few weeks before. "If you fully cooperate, we won't need to get a court order for the cell or arrest you for making false statements to a cop."

Annie heard a high-pitched wail over the phone and smiled grimly.

"If you don't, well, I'm sorry, Ms. Carson, but I can't guarantee that the prosecutor won't decide to file charges against you for lying to a police officer."

"As she should," Annie had bitterly replied when Kim had hung up the phone. "I'll make sure she comes in on time."

"You might remind her that if she deletes any texts, e-mails, or phone messages, we'll know about it and it will go a lot harder for her."

"Will do."

As she watched Kim slowly drive out of the ranch, she wondered how such a bright, sunny day in May could have turned so dark. She should work with Layla, she knew, although every time she did, she was reminded of the perceptive comment Ashley had made on how to back the Walker. Well, she'd just have to get over it. The person Annie felt most sorry for right now was Martha Sanderson, who'd opened her home to her wacky half sister, trusted her, and now was being repaid by the soon-to-be-divulged knowledge that she was harboring a lying witness in a homicide investigation. Poor Martha. She deserved so much better. It occurred to Annie that if Martha was too shocked about Lavender's perfidy, she might ask her to leave. The potential consequences of that disaster were too horrible for Annie to contemplate right now. She headed for the stables.

CHAPTER 22

Lavender was in a sullen mood when Annie picked her up four hours later. Martha was also less than her usual sociable self; her face looked anxious and worried, and she said very little to either of them as they walked out of her home.

"Do not slam my truck door," Annie hissed at Lavender as she walked to the driver's side of her truck. "Try to act your age for once."

Lavender flounced into the truck and shut her door with exaggerated care.

"And *you* don't tell me how I've messed up." Her tone was decidedly petulant, well honed from years of practice.

Annie glanced at her. Today, her half sister was dressed in overalls and a plaid shirt, her brown hair in two long pigtails. She looked twelve years old, just about on par with her emotional age, Annie thought. Maybe her outfit was a ploy. Maybe she thought Kim would go easier on her if she thought she was dealing with a minor. *Fat chance of that happening.*

Stony silence permeated the cab on the way to the Sheriff's Office. Annie interrupted it only once to inquire crossly, "Did you remember to bring your phone?" Lavender did not reply, but merely reached into her purse and waggled it in front of Annie's face.

"I hope you were smart enough not to erase anything," Annie warned her. Judging by the look on Lavender's face, Annie was not sure she was.

Kim and Dan were in the lobby when they arrived. Their faces looked grave, and Kim quickly motioned to Lavender and led her into an interview room.

"And so the little lamb is thrown to the wolves," Annie muttered to Dan as they walked back to his office, where Dan shut the door.

"Not good, Annie," he said. "I'm getting tired of getting half the truth from these women. I might lose my temper if it keeps up."

"I lost mine this morning and still haven't retrieved it."

"Well, Kim'll get the full story from her now, I'm sure of it. It might mean nothing. Or it might break the case. Kim's told me you now know all about the heart-to-heart chats Ashley and Lavender were having right up to Eloise's death. Ashley had to tell someone who her new boyfriend was."

But did she? Annie wondered. Ashley might have had a very good reason for not divulging the name of her new boyfriend. True, she didn't know what it was, but none of the possible reasons were good. At least Dan appeared to be taking the new boyfriend theory more seriously.

A squawk on Dan's shoulder mike interrupted their

conversation. It was Esther, who as usual conveyed her message to the sheriff in near reverential terms. No wonder he fought so hard to keep Esther on board full-time, Annie thought. Who else would give him this much respect on a daily basis?

"Sheriff, your cousin has been trying to reach you for fifteen minutes. He stopped by the convenience store outside of town on his lunch break and thinks he's spotted Pete Corbett inside. He wants to know if he should approach him or wait for backup."

"Damn his hide! What in the Sam Hill do they teach recruits at the academy these days, anyway? Of course he should approach him! Tell him to ask him for his ID, and whether it matches or not, take him into custody. Why am I telling you this when I could be doing it myself? Tell Bill I'm on my way."

Dan bolted from his desk and was out the door before Annie could fully take in the message. She stared after him. So Pete was still in the area, and with luck about to be put in handcuffs. That is, if Dan got there in time.

She wandered down the hall, lightly knocked on Esther's door, and then opened it a few inches. Esther had her headset on and put her finger to her lips but motioned for Annie to sit down. It appeared Esther was doing the play-by-play on the impending arrest.

"Yes, Sheriff. I've told him. Yes, Sheriff. He said he won't let him out of his sight. But he's a bit worried that Pete will make a run for it as soon as he sees him in uniform."

Annie could hear Dan's loud, angry voice even without a headset. Esther gingerly picked up her earpieces and delicately pulled them away from her head, rolling her eyes as she did so. But Annie could tell that she was still intently listening.

"Roger that, Sheriff." A short silence ensued. "On the scene." Another silence, longer this time. Then she exclaimed, "Oh, well done, Sheriff! Will you or Bill be bringing him in?"

The voice on the other end was less vociferous now, so Annie couldn't make out the words. But she picked up enough to know that Pete Corbett was now in police custody.

At three o'clock, Kim emerged from the interview room. To an outsider, her face did not convey any particular emotion, but Annie knew the deputy well enough to know that she had successfully extracted a great deal of new information from Lavender, although it could not have been easy—Lavender had an annoying habit of clinging to her version of events even when the facts were irrefutable. Annie knew this from experience.

She gestured to Kim and asked, "Is the victim still breathing?"

"Sobbing. Used up an entire box of Kleenex."

"Sorry about that." Whatever charming expression Lavender could muster washed off as soon as tears started rolling.

"She's agreed to a polygraph."

"Whoa! This is serious."

"I want her to fully appreciate the consequences of withholding information from the police."

Annie felt a pang of guilt. The last time she herself had been mixed up with a murder case, she'd done the same thing, for reasons she still couldn't understand, and she'd gotten off a whole lot easier.

"Can you do us a favor, while we're putting her on the box?"

"Sure, Kim. What do you need?" At the moment, she would have done almost anything to atone for her own previous omissions.

"Dan wants you to take a look through our mug shot books on the chance that you recognize the woman named Clarissa or the guy who drove the blue Toyota pickup. I've put the books in the second interview room for you. By the time you're done, Lavender should be ready to go home. It would really help us out if we could ID either one of those witnesses."

"No problem."

Annie stepped into the small room, adorned only with a steel desk and two chairs. Not a terribly welcoming place, she thought, but then, she suspected that was the point. She sat down and started to go through the pages, one by one, carefully looking at each face. To her disappointment, Kim had informed her that identifying the license plate of the blue pickup based on the two letters she had been able to spot was impossible—no such database existed that matched vehicles with partial plates. So unless she recognized someone in these books, she realized, these two witnesses might never be found. Unfortunately, the brief glimpse Annie had had of the man who exited the Toyota and gone into the house didn't provide enough time for her to pick out any distinguishing facial characteristics. But she had gotten a good look at Clarissa, first when she was in the circle smoking dope, and later running away, down the street.

In any event, it was interesting to examine the visages of local criminals. It was obvious that on the occasions when these photographs were taken, none of the subjects were having a very good day.

Annie was so engrossed in her task that she was a bit discombobulated when Kim knocked on the door almost an hour later. The deputy entered quietly and sat down. She looked intensely serious.

"I think I've found Clarissa," Annie began, and then got a look at Kim's eyes. "What's up?"

"Lavender failed the polygraph."

"No!"

"I'm afraid so. Fairly conclusively."

"On what subject, if I might be so bold to ask?"

"Whether she knew anyone involved in causing Eloise Carr's death."

"Oh, hell."

"And she was borderline on whether she had been completely truthful in telling us everything about her relationship with Ashley."

"Oh, double hell. What does this mean?"

Kim sighed. "I'll check with Dan, but at the moment, we'll probably do nothing—just give the usual admonitions about not leaving the area and being available to us if we want to talk to her again. Which we will. Soon."

"Can I do anything? Would beating her up help?"

"It might, but I don't recommend it. She's pretty much a puddle as it is, and I don't think she can take any more probing. She's just so damn believable—if I hadn't taken courses in how to uncover deception I'd swear she was telling the truth. I let my guard down during my first interview and am kicking myself now."

"What did she say about those weird messages she and Ashley sent each other the day before they found Eloise dead? You know, the stuff about 'today's the day,' and all that."

"She says that was the day Ashley was going to ask you for a job. 'What I gave you' supposedly refers to a list of references, which Lavender said she typed up for Ashley on her laptop."

"Liar, liar, pants on fire," Annie said bluntly. "Ashley's list of references was handwritten, and not by Lavender—I know her childish scrawl. So what do you think Lavender knows that she's not telling you?"

"I think she knows more about Ashley's private life than she's letting on, and suspects at least one person of killing Eloise Carr, even though I've said nothing to imply that Mrs. Carr's death was anything but accidental."

"Don't you still think this is possible? Or have you definitely ruled out suicide?"

"Sorry, I thought Dan already told you. The tox report came in on Tuesday. Eloise consumed a whole cocktail of drugs—many of which were found in her home, but at least two of which were not, and more important, no doctor had ever prescribed them for her. And, since Eloise didn't drive, she couldn't have procured them herself."

Annie's heart sank. In the back of her mind, she couldn't help but think what Martha Sanderson would make of all this. After all, she was a senior citizen herself, and not terribly mobile. Would she still trust having Lavender in her home, when the police thought she was at least peripherally knowledgeable about the death of another old woman, someone Martha had known?

At least Dan was a happy guy. By the time he'd finished the booking process, it appeared that even his cousin, Bill Stetson, was back in his good graces.

"Chip off the old block!" he crowed to Annie. "Stopped Pete dead in his tracks as he was trying to flee the store."

"Stopped him how?" Annie fervently hoped the use of firearms was not involved.

"With his foot. Tripped him."

Dan's exuberance extended to a phone call from Ron Carr, which Esther routed through as Annie waited for Lavender to appear. Her half sister was taking a long time in the women's restroom, Annie thought, but she was in no particular rush to see Lavender, knowing that all the way back to Martha's she would insist on telling Annie the many reasons why the polygraph results were just plain wrong.

"No problem, Ron! Happy to talk and bring you up to speed about the case." Dan's enthusiasm had catapulted his voice to a volume that made Annie wince.

"You'll be glad to know we picked up Pete Corbett this afternoon. Yup, two-man collar, although my cousin Bill gets most of the credit. He spotted Pete at a local convenience store. I just mopped up."

Ron must have been extending his congratulations, because Dan's face broke into a wide grin. "That's what we think, Ron. We've rounded up most of the players, and pretty soon someone's going to figure out it's in their best interest to talk."

Dan stopped talking again to hear whatever Ron was saying in response. "Well, there's one more little detail we have to wrap up," he said in a more serious tone. "Can't have a case go too smoothly. Never happens. It appears that the woman Ashley was training isn't being entirely truthful with us—yet. She knows something about your mother's death that she hasn't said. But don't you worry. We'll get to the bottom of her story." Dan turned and winked at Annie.

Annie's cell phone buzzed, and she gratefully exited Dan's office and went out to the foyer, where Lavender was now sitting, waiting to be taken home. Jessica Flynn was calling to tell her that Fish and Wildlife had reported another sheep killed and that she would be performing the necropsy in the morning.

"It was close to your place, Annie," Jessica told her. "I thought you should know in case you want to take any extra precautions tonight."

At the moment, Annie couldn't think of a single thing she could do to stop the onslaught of bad news.

CHAPTER 23

FRIDAY, MAY 20

As it turned out, Annie needn't have worried about Martha's reaction to Lavender's disingenuous performance before Deputy Williams. True to her saintlike persona, Martha was primarily concerned about the emotional impact the experience had had on Lavender.

"I'm worried about her, Annie," Martha told her the next morning on the phone. "She was up half the night, sobbing in her bedroom. She won't tell me what's wrong, and every time I ask her, she just says that I wouldn't understand. I'm not sure what to do."

Annie wanted to suggest hitting her upside the head. But she resisted the impulse. It was critically important that Lavender cough up whatever she was keeping from the Sheriff's Office, but Annie knew that convincing her half sister to untangle herself from the web of lies she'd already spun would be an uphill battle and not won by force. She sighed.

"You know she failed a polygraph," she told Martha,

reluctantly. Annie truly didn't want to tell tales, but she thought Martha deserved to know.

"Yes, Lavender told me that straight away. But that's not what bothers me. Someone with Lavender's temperament might easily give responses that register as deceptive when they were really telling the God's honest truth. No, it's this overriding belief that she has to protect someone that has me concerned. Someone entrusted her with a secret, and she's determined not to give it up. Her loyalty is admirable, but it's getting in the way of her mental health. I thought you might know what to do."

Nothing that you'd like to hear. "I'll try to think of something, Martha," Annie said without much enthusiasm. "She's already in hot water with the police and certainly not doing herself any favors by not telling them what she knows. I'll be by this afternoon and see if I can talk some sense into her."

"Thank you, Annie. I know she'll listen to you. She holds you in such high regard, you know."

Against her better judgment, Annie hauled out the boxes of family photos and memorabilia that she'd warned Ron Carr the Third might still be untouched years after he'd neatly stored them. This certainly had proved true in her case. Over time, all of her mother's coveted china, linens, and knickknacks had been brought out into the open and integrated with Annie's own household furnishings. True, the Lenox china on display in her kitchen hutch had not once been brought out and used in the past fifteen years, but still, it reminded Annie of her mother's love of cooking and entertaining, at least when her father was still around. After he'd fled the household with his secretary—who already was preg-

nant with little Lavender—the elaborate dinners her
mother had once made for friends had abruptly stopped.
There was no longer time and even less money for family
entertaining. The full-time job that Annie's mother had
found with the county took almost all her energy, and
any that was left over was spent making sure Annie's life
was on track.

The boxes of photos, however, had remained in
Annie's back closet, sealed and mostly undisturbed. It
was simply too painful for her to look at the pictures, especially the ones from when the Carsons were still a
tight-knit, presumably happy family. The later ones only
revealed the weariness with which her mother went
through life as a single woman with a daughter to raise.
In the first few years following her parents' divorce, her
parents had made an attempt to meld the two families,
but the disparities in lifestyles and personalities soon
proved that a disastrous idea. Soon Annie's visits to see
her father and his new family in Florida stopped, and
Lavender's rare trips to Washington State petered out
as well.

It was the few photographs taken of Annie and
Lavender when they happened to be in the same place
that she searched for now. How she would convince
Lavender to unloose her tongue and tell what she
knew, Annie wasn't sure. But she hoped that reminding
Lavender of their shared family history—limited as it
was—somehow might be helpful.

Jessica drove up as Annie had finished packing the
photos she'd selected. She stepped out onto her porch
to wave to the vet inside her van. Jessica slowly emerged
from her vehicle, looking drained and spent. She displayed none of the exuberance that Annie normally associated with her. Instead, she looked plain exhausted.
Annie ran down her steps to greet her.

Jessica's report on the necropsy she'd just performed was short and to the point, and did not surprise Annie at all. In fact, she'd pretty much come to the same conclusion earlier, after learning about Tony's results with the metal detector on her ranch.

"It's our worst fear," Jessica told her, close to tears. "A small metal ball penetrated the ewe's lung, killing it almost instantly. There are two more in the left rear leg. I can't tell which shot penetrated first, but I do know that there wasn't a chance of this poor thing running away. Of course, animal predators found the body afterward, so you'd never have known a human was responsible without an examination. Sergeant McCready made the right call. Now we know what we're up against. I hope someone nails the guy and strings him up by his thumbs."

"Amen to that." Annie's anger, never far from the surface, engulfed her now. "By the way, that's what the Sheriff's Office found on my property a few days ago—small metal balls. Dan said it was ammo of some kind. That means someone's after my sheep, as well."

"I feel as if we should do postmortems on every animal that's been killed in the past month."

"I've already got one for you on my property—a just-born lamb that Wolf discovered weeks ago. It wasn't one from my flock, but I couldn't understand how such a wee thing had wandered onto my back pasture. Now I'm wondering if the guy was just setting up target practice."

"Annie, stop. That's too horrible to think about."

"Don't worry. We'll find out who's doing it and make sure they're prosecuted to the full extent of the law. We just have to figure out what weapon was used."

"That's easy. Slingshot. No doubt about it."

"Really? You're sure about that?"

"Positive. My brother had one growing up. Used to shoot small game birds with it. It's lethal. My mother wouldn't allow it inside the house."

Annie thought of calling Dan with Jessica's epiphany but decided to hold off. She knew just how much the sheriff resented hearing her relate something he did not already know. Besides, she hoped she'd be able to tell him a lot more of what he didn't know after her little chat with Lavender.

Martha greeted her at the door with a warm smile. The aroma of fresh-baked bread filled the small house, and Annie's mouth began to water. If she was going to be fed, perhaps her errand of mercy wouldn't be as onerous as she'd thought. Lavender was sitting on the love seat in the parlor, swinging her legs to and fro. She appeared to be reading an old *National Geographic,* but Annie wouldn't have bet on it. If a celebrity didn't adorn the cover, Lavender generally wasn't much interested.

Taking a deep breath, Annie approached her half sister.

"Lavender? I've brought some old photos of us. I thought you might like looking at them with me."

Lavender threw down her magazine, crossed her arms, and pouted.

God, this was tiresome.

"You were pretty small, but you used to visit my mother and me, do you remember? It was only for a few years. You used to come out during the summer."

Being a lot older than Lavender, Annie had hated having to babysit her back then, and she wasn't even paid for it; she was expected to take care of her baby half sister for free. She was surprised now that her mother even had agreed to let Lavender come visit. But then, her mother always was nicer than she was. Most people were.

Lavender continued to stare off into the distance. At times like this, it was hard to remember that her half sister had actually passed her thirtieth birthday. Annie sat down and took out the manila envelope that held the photos. She stuck her hand in and pulled out one at random. It was of Annie and Lavender, visiting the horse that Annie's mother had leased for her daughter that summer. It was the best summer of Annie's life, as far as she was concerned. Lavender was on the horse's back, her two small hands clasping the saddle horn. Annie was holding the reins. Lavender couldn't have been more than four, Annie thought, and still looked adorable. Cherubic, if she wanted to be honest. Had she ever actually liked her? Surely, when she was so small, she couldn't have done much to annoy her. She thought back. No, Lavender had been tolerable back then, she decided. It was only when she was old enough to figure out how to manipulate adults that she'd become insufferable.

Annie held out the photo toward Lavender. "Do you remember this?" she asked. "How old were you that summer? Three? Four?"

Lavender couldn't resist sneaking a look at a photo of herself. Her hands snaked around the photo and she held it up close, examining every detail.

"I must have just turned five," she said finally. "I remember this. You'd just gotten your license and we drove out to a big farm. You walked me around on your horse. It was a lot of fun."

Amazing. Once upon a time, long, long ago, she and Lavender had had fun together. Annie suspected that even she'd gotten some enjoyment squiring the young girl around on the handsome gelding that had been hers for a few glorious months.

"The farm wasn't that big," Annie said. "Actually, it was pretty small, compared to mine. But I'm sure it looked big then."

"There was a lady there," Lavender went on. "She had an apron and served us lemonade. I remember it was really hot. Did we go swimming afterward?"

Annie had forgotten that. On the way home, she'd taken Lavender to a lake where she'd persuaded her sister to jump in. Lavender hadn't needed much encouragement. Annie had joined her and the two of them had had an uproariously good time splashing around in the water. Annie's mother was none too pleased when they arrived home, sopping wet, and learned that Lavender had gone swimming without her water wings, but Annie recalled that she didn't make too big of a fuss about it. She was just too tired. Annie's mother did not have the summer off.

"You know, you were a pretty nice big sister back then," Lavender said, as if this was a revelation to her now. "I wish I could have come out more often. But Mummy and Daddy wouldn't let me after that summer."

"Do you know why?"

Lavender made a face. "I guess they wanted me all to themselves."

"Was that a bad thing?"

"They weren't that interesting. I didn't have anyone to play with."

For a moment, Annie felt sorry for her half sister. She was an only child, too—Lavender never really counted, in her mind—but she'd never lacked for friends. They were up and down the street, in school, everywhere. Finding a playmate was never a problem. They were just, well, there, all around her.

"You know, Ashley and you had about the same age difference as we do," Annie said tentatively. "Maybe, by being her friend, you were trying to be a big sister to her."

Lavender swallowed and looked down.

"I think I'm right, Lavender," Annie went on. "I think you realized that Ashley needed someone in her life to look out for her."

Lavender looked up, her face full of tears. "I was just trying to help her," she gasped, the tears now rolling down her face. "She didn't have anyone, not really. Her friends were all stupid and only cared about guys. Her mother was worthless. And Pete—he was a joke."

"How'd you meet her?"

"At the bus stop." Because Lavender's driving privileges were still suspended, Annie suspected that Lavender had made friends at bus stops all over Suwana County. "We took the same route. I'd go to the library some days and she'd go to work. We started to talk every morning on the way into town. We became friends." She gave a loud sniff, and Annie wordlessly handed her a large cotton handkerchief from her purse.

"I hear that she helped find you your job."

Lavender nodded. "It sounded like fun, something I would like to do. Ashley helped me fill out the application and I was hired. We were going to have so much fun working together. And then Mrs. Carr died and everything changed."

"How did it change, Lavender?"

She sighed. "Ashley got fired. They said she took pills from Mrs. Carr, but that never happened." Annie wasn't sure how Lavender could possibly know this but decided not to push the issue.

"I guess some pills were found missing later. Do you know who might possibly have taken them?"

Lavender shook her head back and forth energetically. "I have no idea. Ashley would never let Pete visit her when she was working with Mrs. Carr. She said it was against the rules, and besides, she didn't really trust Pete not to take something."

"Why didn't she trust him?"

Lavender looked straight at Annie. "Promise me you won't tell anyone else if I tell you."

"I promise," Annie lied.

"Pete was dealing drugs. Bad drugs. Ashley had known about it for almost a year. She'd decided to turn him in, but then Mrs. Carr died, and Ashley wasn't sure . . . well, she kind of thought Pete might have had something to do with it. So she decided to hold off until she knew more."

"What was she waiting to find out?"

"I'm not sure. She was going to show me something that day. She said it would explain everything and take care of all her problems. Then Mrs. Carr died, Ashley was fired, and after that she never spoke to me again."

"Why would she not talk to you? You hadn't had a falling out or anything, had you?"

"No, nothing like that. I kept texting her, but she never answered me. And then I found out that she'd died."

"Lavender, why didn't you tell Kim all this? There's nothing you've told me that sounds terribly important to keep secret."

Lavender's face suddenly closed down. *Uh-oh*, Annie thought, *I guess I spoke too soon.*

"What else? I know you're holding something back. It can't be good, Lavender. Ashley is dead. We need to know why she died, and I think you know the answer to that question." She'd almost said "*how* she died." That would have been bad.

"Promise you won't tell anyone?"

Annie nodded again, her fingers crossed under her purse.

Letting out a deep breath, Lavender said in a rush, "I think Ashley thought maybe Pete had come to Mrs. Carr's house and killed her for her drugs. I guess Mrs. Carr took a lot of drugs that were worth a lot of money to addicts. But that's not all. Ashley was seeing someone else—another guy, and he was giving her grief. So now I'm wondering whether her new boyfriend killed her and Ashley killed herself because she felt so guilty."

"What's his name, Lavender? The new boyfriend, I mean?" Annie was ready to shake her.

Lavender looked up, her eyes a blank. "I don't know, Annie, really I don't. Ashley never told me. She was really secretive about him. All I know is, one day when he picked her up from the bus stop I saw his car, but I didn't see him inside. Or, at least, not enough to know him now."

"How long ago was this? And what kind of car did he have?"

"I don't know! Last month, I guess. Maybe sooner. I can't remember."

"And the car, Lavender. What was he driving?" Her voice was rising and she couldn't stop it.

"It was blue. A blue pickup. One of those Japanese models. A Toyota, I think."

The same model and color of the truck that had pulled up in front of the home in the skuzzy neighborhood of Port Chester. Which meant Pete and Ashley's new boyfriend knew each other. And probably were partners in crime.

"But all this could help the police, Lavender. Why not tell them what you've just told me?"

"Because Ashley was afraid of her new boyfriend. I guess Pete beat her up once or twice, but she wasn't scared of him, not like she was scared of the new guy. That's why she told everyone she was moving in with you. She thought she'd be safe at your place."

"Nobody can hurt Ashley now." Annie's patience was rapidly running out. Suddenly, she didn't care if she was divulging confidential information that Kim had shared with her. She had to know the truth.

"You have something of Ashley's, don't you? Something she gave you that you swore you'd never give up."

Lavender's pleading eyes were no match for the gaze Annie now fixed upon her, daring her to deny what she already knew. With a half sob, Lavender rose from the love seat and left the room. She returned a few minutes later with a felt bag in one hand.

"She gave it to me the day before she died. She said it was the key to everything."

As she was speaking, Lavender reached into the bag and pulled out a key, an exact duplicate of what Dan had showed Annie the day Ashley had been found hanging in her barn. But this one would not open Mrs. Carr's front door.

CHAPTER 24

At Annie's insistence, Lavender had called Kim soon after she had brought out the key Ashley had entrusted with her. Actually, if Annie were honest—which she tried to be, whenever possible—Martha played a starring role in convincing her half sister to do the right thing.

"This isn't something you can keep to yourself any longer, dear," Martha had explained with far more patience than Annie would have mustered. "I know you're trying to be loyal to Ashley, and your feelings are commendable. But when Ashley chose to take her life, her privacy died with her. I'm sorry if that seems harsh, Lavender, but Ashley doesn't have the right anymore to hold you to keeping her secrets. It's best that the people investigating her death have all the facts, and you, dear, may be holding an important clue."

Annie had to hand it to Martha—she knew how to

spark her half sister's cooperation. Just drop a hint that what she did would be of vital importance to the world at large and Lavender was putty in one's hands.

After a brief and stilted phone conversation with Kim, during which Lavender repeated the story of when she'd received the key, she turned toward Annie.

"She wants to talk to you," Lavender whispered. Her hand trembled a bit as she passed Annie's cell phone to her.

Annie was aware that Lavender's call to Kim had come at the very tail end of her ten-hour shift, but apparently it made no difference to the deputy.

"Good work, girlfriend. I still say you'd make an excellent member of our police team," Kim began.

"Only if I get to interrogate people."

Kim laughed. "I'm going to swing by now to pick up the key and get Lavender's latest statement on tape. And this time I expect to hear the truth, the whole truth, and nothing but the truth, so help her hide."

"I think that's a reasonable possibility," Annie replied. "Unfortunately, I can't stay to hear it all over again. I've got horses to feed."

"I know. But could you find time to swing by the Sheriff's Office tomorrow morning to show me Clarissa's photo? I realize now that in all the excitement of hauling in Pete and the debacle over Lavender's polygraph, I completely forgot to get your ID of her."

"Sure, Kim. Just be sure to give me the recap of tonight when I get there."

"You got it. See you tomorrow."

"Oh—Kim? One more thing." Annie moved out of the tiny parlor to the kitchen, where she could talk in relative privacy. Martha waved her in; she had guessed what Annie had to say was confidential.

"About those metal balls Tony picked up from my place? Well, Jessica Flynn's just found the same ammo in her necropsy of another animal."

"Yes, we know. Sgt. McCready's already faxed over her report."

"So you know the balls are used as slingshot ammo?"

"I don't know how we could have overlooked that possibility. Unfortunately, we didn't find a slingshot in either of our searches of Pete's cabin or the Port Chester home. Dan's on his way to Pete's parents' place right now, hoping that he can get them to agree to a voluntary search of their home so he doesn't have to disturb Judge Casper on a Friday night."

"Well, I wish him well."

"Pete was arraigned today, you know."

"I'd forgotten. What are the charges?"

"Twelve counts of violating the Controlled Substance Act, including manufacturing and distribution. His bail is set at $300,000. Even for Pete's folks, that's a pretty steep bond to put up. We're hoping it'll be enough to keep Pete in jail for the indefinite future."

"If he turns out to be a killer of small, defenseless animals, I hope he'll stay in jail for the rest of his life."

"I hear you. And I'm glad we've got Pete so tight on the drug ring. With his arrest, I think we'll see a lot of his cellies crumble. But I'd feel a lot better if we could make some headway into Ashley's death. It's driving all of us a bit nuts. If we could just identify the new boyfriend, or even just this odd key. Either might open up a new line of inquiry."

"You'll figure it out, Kim. And I don't think you'll have any more trouble with Lavender. She's so beaten down right now, you probably could get her to clean

your home for life as long as you don't arrest her for all
her previous lies."

"I like that. Thanks for the suggestion."

Driving home, Annie decided it was time to incorpo-
rate some fun into her life. There'd been too much drama
recently, and way too many tears. With a few phone calls,
she devised a plan that perked her right up, and later that
night Annie had gleefully filled in Marcus—on Sunday,
she and her girlfriends were taking an all-day trail ride.
He tried not to show it, but Annie knew Marcus was secretly relieved to learn that only cowgirls, and no cow-
boys, would be saddling up with her. And she made a
point of telling him she'd be riding "a big, beautiful
thoroughbred some wonderful guy gave to me a few
months ago."

What Annie hadn't told Marcus was that she had one
last bit of police work to finish before she hopped on
Trooper's back and took off for a ride with her friends
in the great outdoors.

It isn't my fault I'm still involved, she kept telling herself. *I can't help it if what I told Kim now requires my help.*
Her Good Angel was conspicuously absent from her in-
ternal conversation.

Annie was surprised to see both Dan and Kim's patrol vehicles in the Suwana County parking lot the next
morning. Kim, she knew, worked Saturdays and usually
had Sunday and Monday off—although, she realized,
between working on Ashley's homicide and cracking
Pete's drug business, Kim had recently put in serious
overtime. But Dan considered his weekends sacrosanct.

The fact that he was in his office on a Saturday meant either there had been a break in the homicide cases or he was furiously trying to create one.

She rang the buzzer outside to let Kim know of her arrival. The deputy appeared a minute later dressed in civilian clothes, a Starbucks cup in one hand.

"I've got one back in my office for you," she said as she pulled open the glass entrance door. "I hope you don't mind whipped cream."

"Love it."

The mug shot books already were spread out on Kim's desk. Annie quickly found the book in which she'd seen the photo that most resembled the woman called Clarissa. Sipping thoughtfully on her latte, she turned the pages until she found the right face. Yup, that was Clarissa, all right. She looked younger and healthier than the person Annie had seen running down the street, but it was still the same person—she was sure of it.

She turned the book around and pointed to the photo so Kim could see. Kim nodded, and consulted her computer. When she'd apparently found the entry that matched the photo, she whistled and turned to look at Annie, a pleased smile on her face.

"Clara Ann Waters, AKA Clarissa Waters, AKA Clarissa Smith. DOB 11/17/92. Convictions for minor in possession, taking a motor vehicle without permission, possession of drugs without a prescription . . . and, that's interesting, domestic violence assault 4 and malicious mischief 2. Last known address in Port Chester. Thanks, Annie. Let's see if Esther can locate someone to haul her in."

Kim left her desk and walked down the hall, returning a minute later.

"Bill Stetson is dying to find Clarissa for us," she said.

"He's still chafing from Dan's assessment of his work on Pete Corbett's arrest."

"What? I heard Dan singing his praises afterward."

"Just a show. In fact, Dan's criticisms weren't entirely unfounded. But Bill will learn."

There was a knock on Kim's door, which was slightly ajar. Annie could see Dan behind it. He, too, was dressed in civilian clothes today. It was a bit unsettling to see both officers out of uniform; they somehow didn't seem legit anymore but rather just regular people. Which, Annie realized, they actually were. She so seldom saw them out of their professional roles, she knew little about their real lives, except for the bits and pieces Dan and Kim occasionally revealed to her.

"Come on in." Kim welcomed her boss into her small office. "Annie's just ID'd one of the people with Pete the other day. The one whom Pete asked to be his mule."

"Thanks, Annie. Appreciate it." The words were polite, but Dan sounded dejected. Kim and Annie looked at each other, then Dan. "What's wrong?" they said in unison.

Dan flopped into the remaining empty chair and hung an arm around the back. "Do you want the good news or the bad news first?"

Annie remained quiet. This was not her show, she recognized. Kim leaned forward and said, "How about the good news?"

"The Corbetts gave me access to their home. Pete's slingshot was in the garage, and it's a deadly thing of beauty. Parents knew about its existence—they gave it to Pete a couple of years ago for Christmas—but swear they hadn't noticed it in the garage before now, and they appear credible. So Pete must have stashed it sometime between his last foray into the countryside, which we presume was last Tuesday, and before he was picked up on Thursday. The slingshot's on its way to the lab now. Model fits the ammo Tony found and Jessica uncovered, so I'm confident that we've found our human predator."

"That's great, Dan!" Kim exclaimed. "Congratulations!"

"Oh, and the slingshot had an aluminum alloy wrist brace on it, Annie," Dan added, ignoring Kim's paeans of praise. "That's probably what made you and the little girl—"

"Hannah," Annie prompted him. "Hannah Clare. She's a riding student, and was the first to see Pete in the forest."

"Well, anyway, that's probably what made both of you think it was a gun. From a distance, the glint could easily make it look like a pistol or a handgun."

"Well, I concur with Kim—this is great news," Annie said, wondering why Dan was less than enthusiastic about finding the person who'd been on a small animal rampage, and thankfully was now behind bars on multiple charges, with more to follow.

"Well, it would be, except for just one thing." Dan did like to stretch out his narratives, Annie thought with a twinge of irritation.

"What's that, Dan?" Kim said cautiously.

"Pete bailed out last night at 0200 hours."

"What!" Annie and Kim again spoke as one.

"How could that possibly happen?" Kim asked, incredulous.

Dan sighed. He obviously was not looking forward to sharing the details.

"Someone named Roger Woodstock put up the bond yesterday afternoon. He came in after hours with the paperwork, and out Pete walked. I got the news at 0800. I've already been out to the Corbetts' house. Pete isn't there, and his parents have no idea where their

son might be. Dad swore up and down that he had no
intention of bailing his kid out, and offered to give me
his bank accounts to prove it. Tony and I cleared the
place, just to make sure. Then I sent him over to the
cabin and the house where Pete has last been seen, but
he's nowhere to be found. By the way, the Port Chester
house is now abandoned. Tony's tracking down the
owner now."

"But Dan," Kim said, her incredulity dripping from
every word, "why don't we have Pete's address?"

Dan shifted in his seat, clearly uncomfortable. "It was
Bill's fault," he finally said. "We were short-staffed, and
Bill offered to pull the jail shift last night. Mr. Woodstock, if that's his real name, happened to arrive when
the other two guards were on break. Bill said the paperwork looked in order, but hell, how would he know?
The problem is, Bill didn't know that the bail bondsman delivers the papers, not the person putting them
up, so God only knows what Bill was looking at. And the
kicker is that Bill didn't realize until after Pete was gone
that the so-called paperwork had left with him. So we
have no identifying information about Woodstock, or
anything that might tell us where Pete might be."

Kim moaned and put her head in her hands.

"In fact, Bill's not even certain which bail bondsman
allegedly put up the bond," Dan said bitterly. "It wasn't
the local shop, that's all he knows for sure. Thought it
might have come from up north someplace, around
Cape Disconsolate. Then again, he thought the bail
company's letterhead might have included a Seattle location. I'm wondering if the paperwork was legitimate
at all."

What a disaster, Annie thought. No wonder Bill was so
eager to run in Clarissa. He has to do something right
to make up for this fiasco.

"What are you going to do?" Annie spoke without thinking.

"Before or after I wring his neck?"

Esther's voice came through on his shoulder mike. "Sheriff? Clarissa Waters has been picked up. She'll be here in about twenty minutes. Just wanted you to know."

Dan turned a weary face toward Kim. "You handle this," he said. "I'm going to my office to make some calls."

Kim nodded. Annie slinked out behind Dan and quietly left the building, as easily as Pete Corbett had left the night before.

CHAPTER 25

SUNDAY, MAY 22

Annie felt acutely sorry for poor Bill Stetson, whose error in judgment undoubtedly would be an oft-told tale throughout his career, although its longevity now was somewhat in doubt. She knew Dan had done everything humanly possible to try to rectify Bill's mistake—Kim had privately told her that Dan had been in touch with Judge Casper and Judy Evans, and the Corbetts' home and cabin were under surveillance 24/7. He'd also made sure that every cop in the tri-county area was on the lookout for the defendant, who'd managed to walk out of jail without leaving a current address, all thanks to an unknown benefactor and yet-to-be-identified bail bonds company.

Despite these efforts, Pete had not reappeared by Sunday morning, and frankly Annie didn't give a damn. She was going on a trail ride.

At the last minute, much to Annie's delight, Jessica had decided to join the group. Annie's gooseneck slant trailer comfortably accommodated three horses, but now they were up to five—or four, technically, since Jessica informed Annie she was riding Molly the mule. The only person among them who had a trailer large enough to transport all their mounts was the large-animal vet. Besides, Annie thought as she double-checked her traveling equine first aid kit, there was nothing quite as comforting as having your horse's doctor ride right alongside you.

It was now eight o'clock in the morning. The horses had been served breakfast an hour earlier than usual, and everyone except Trooper was out grazing in the pasture for the day. Her ewes also had been checked and fed. Trooper's saddle, bridle, and blankets were in a neat pile, and his extra gear was stored in a large plastic tub. All Annie had to do was wait for Jessica to arrive.

She was glad she'd thought to invite Lisa Bromwell, who'd accepted her invitation with alacrity.

"It's exactly what Hunter needs," she excitedly told Annie. "He's been doing so well and could use the exercise. You won't believe how happy he'll be when he realizes we're off on a trail ride."

Annie could easily believe it. All of her horses perked up when they realized they were joining a lot of other horses in a big trailer and heading for the open road. The experience of exploring Northwest forests, meadows, and mountains held just as much appeal to the equines as it did to the women astride them.

She glanced impatiently at her watch—8:25. Jessica should be here any minute. She opened the tub for the sixth time that morning and rechecked her supplies— halter, lead, currying equipment, treats, equine first aid kit, GPS, duct tape, rain poncho—all things she seldom used but always packed just in case. She decided to throw in a bottle of fly spray; the horse variety would do for both of them, should any flies or mosquitoes be out this early in the season. But there was something else she was missing that nagged at the back of her mind— what was it? She surveyed her tack room shelves. Nope, nothing there that wasn't already packed. Her view expanded to the saddle posts. Aha—her riding helmet. She was completely hypocritical regarding its use. She insisted that every student rider wear one, of course, and personally supervised its fit. And if she was riding off the ranch, she always wore her own. It was just when she was hopping on Sam or Trooper's back to visit the ewes or check out a pasture that putting it on seemed too much work. She felt a twinge of guilt, then let it pass. She tossed the helmet onto Trooper's saddle blankets. There. She was more than ready to go.

At 8:55, Jessica carefully steered her way down Annie's driveway and in front of her stables. Annie, who'd been sitting on the dirt, flanked by Wolf and Sasha, got up and dusted off the seat of her pants. Judging by the crowd already in the cab, she and Trooper were the last to be picked up. The good news was that they'd also be the first to unload at the end of the day.

"We need your truck!" Jessica yelled as she emerged from the cab. Three more women slowly picked their way out, and Annie watched four rambunctious dogs spill out after them.

"What are you planning—a fox-hunting party?" she yelled back.

"It seemed too nice a day to leave our critters at home." Completely ignoring Annie, Luann ran over to Wolf and Sasha and immediately began ruffling their fur.

"Wolf! Is this your new sister, Sasha? What a good dog! Good boy!"

"Stop or it'll go to his head," Annie said good-naturedly, although in fact she was always inordinately pleased to see other people lavish praise on her cherished dogs.

"Let's get the show on the road," Jill announced firmly. When she wasn't riding one of her three horses, Jill was the operations manager for a manufacturing company in Blackthorn, an industrial community an hour's commute away. She was skilled at directing people, dogs, and horses to do her bidding without their quite realizing how it happened.

"Are you and Trooper all set, Annie?" Jessica asked. Taking a critical look at the vet, Annie thought she'd never seen her look so relaxed or happy. So this was what two days off in a single month could do to an overworked gal.

"We've been ready for hours," Annie mockingly grumbled back, as she attached a lead rope to Trooper's string halter. At first, Trooper had been confused by Annie's command that he stay in the paddock this morning instead of cantering out with the rest of the gang, but instead of racing around—something Baby was still prone to do when left behind—he quickly acclimated to the change in plan and was content to munch on the flake of Timothy hay Annie had tossed in the pen. Now he was well aware that something new was happening, and whatever it was, he was eager to be part of it. As soon as the rig had pulled in and he'd gotten the whiff and the sounds of several new equines, he was on high alert, anxious to meet whoever was in the trailer.

Annie was relieved to see Trooper's enthusiasm. Three months earlier, he had been in a horrific accident when the trailer he was traveling in crashed at a high speed and nearly turned over. Since that time, Annie had spent several hours working with the horse to overcome any lingering hesitation about entering or riding in trailers. She'd always made sure that Trotter or one of her horses loaded before asking him to enter the confined space. But Trooper didn't know any of the horses inside Jessica's trailer. Well, she'd just have to see how well her training would now pay off.

But Trooper was, as his name suggested, a trooper and showed no hesitation as he walked up the ramp and into the open slant space. Jessica was the only one who recognized the significance of Trooper's quiet entry. She walked over to Annie and said in a low voice, "Good job, cowgirl." Annie smiled her thanks. She was enormously proud of the gelding's progress.

Jessica had been correct—the body count in her cab already exceeded the legal limit, so Annie agreed to take her own rig to share the load. Lisa and Jill opted to ride with Annie, along with their two dogs. All the canines were crated in the bed, and thankfully everyone seemed to be getting along.

"This is going to be one wild trail ride," Annie thought with amusement as she followed Jessica's trailer out of her driveway. "Five wild women, four horses, one mule, and six dogs." Judging by the boisterous laughter of her riding companions and the excited barking from the back of her truck, she was counting on the mule to keep order.

Once the trucks had hit Highway 101 and the conversational patter had quieted down, Annie put her cell on speaker so they could keep in close communication with Jessica and her passengers. The trail Jill had chosen—for she was the unspoken director of such things—was twenty-five miles south of Shelby, past a state park, and reached through a short series of dusty forest service roads. Officially, Jill informed them, the trail was part of the wide-sweeping Olympic National Forest and would take them along a picturesque river for several miles before climbing up to a mountain lake.

"According to the park's website, the roads getting there have recently been cleared of debris, fallen logs, and anything else that might impede us." Jill's voice sounded tinny through Annie's small speaker. "But I wouldn't count on that being true for the trails themselves. It's still pretty early in the season, so my suggestion is that we save the heart-stopping gallop we're known for on these rides until we're sure the terrain is clear."

This made sense to everyone in the truck. There was nothing as exciting as racing across a meadow on horseback with your girlfriends, whooping and hollering. It was less exciting if a horse tripped and a rider fell, and a day of fun turned into one of misery, when you had to lead a lame horse or escort a rider out on a makeshift stretcher.

"Maybe up at the lake we'll find a good, flat place to run," Lisa suggested. She'd easily fit into her gang of friends, Annie noticed, despite her relative youth compared to the rest of the women.

"Makes sense to me," Jessica replied from her truck, and for the rest of the trip, the women exchanged tales of trail rides past as well as plans for elaborate overnight excursions they hoped to take during the summer.

They were on the trail by eleven o'clock, an hour after everyone had sworn they'd be, but close enough so that Annie knew their return time would still be in daylight and with plenty of time to enjoy the summit. The plan was to reach the upper meadows by one-thirty, let both horses and riders have lunch and rest, then gallop the horses like banshees and make a sedate retreat downhill, arriving at the trail head by four o'clock. *It sounds like too much fun,* Annie thought.

By popular vote, Jessica and Molly took the lead in the horse train.

"When it comes to sure-footedness and good sense, a molly mule can't be beat," Jessica declared, and no one had the courage—or desire—to dispute her.

Lisa, on Hunter, followed Molly. Jill was next, on her quarter horse, Billy Bob, followed by Luann on her own quarter horse, Gabby. Annie, on Trooper, brought up the rear. Being at the tail end gave Annie a chance to see how well the horse did in a position he seldom took—last. She knew that, given his druthers, he'd rather be at the head of the pack, setting a brisk pace and expecting the others to follow.

Trooper made a few halfhearted attempts to pass his slower compatriots, but after the third time Annie firmly reeled him in, he seemed to get the message. Besides, she whispered into his ear, since he was relegated to such a sedate walk, he might as well enjoy the scenery around him. It was gorgeous, Annie thought, and at this comfortable pace, she was able to take in every detail.

The steady, muted clip-clop of hooves on dirt gradually stilled Annie's mind, and she began to drift to the one topic never far from her thoughts—the strange and unsolved mystery of Ashley Lawton's death. She wondered for the umpteenth time who had killed her, and why.

To be honest, the young woman had had enough problems on her plate to easily justify a verdict of suicide. She'd recently been arrested for possessing drugs that hadn't been prescribed to her, and she'd probably have faced additional charges for the theft of Eloise

Carr's pills, if she were still alive. She was broke and un-
employed. Her ex-boyfriend was a druggie who made
and sold meth on the side and sometimes beat her up.
She appeared to have had many friends, but apparently
was not particularly close to any of them, not enough to
tell them the truth—why else would she lie to them about
Annie giving her a job and a place to crash? Bundle all
these problems and Ashley Lawton had plenty of reasons to consider ending her life. On close inspection,
suicide seemed quite plausible. Sad, but plausible. If
the killer had been smart enough to leave a bale of hay
or small stool by the body, that's unquestionably how
the coroner would have seen it. But the killer wasn't
smart, and now the sheriff was scratching his considerable head and, in Annie's mind, trying too hard to
make Pete the bad guy.

But was Pete really the killer, as Dan kept insisting, or
was it the mysterious new boyfriend? Dan didn't seem
to place half the importance that Annie did on Ashley
telling her friends that she was going to see her new
boyfriend the night before she died. True, without a
name, it was impossible to know whether Ashley had
just been telling another story to please her friends or if
this actually was her plan. If it were, Annie's money was
on the new boyfriend, on the last-person-to-see-her-alive
theory. Besides, Pete had an alibi courtesy of his parents. Again, Dan didn't seem to place much value on it,
and Annie was sure many parents lied for their kids, all
the time. But they hadn't bailed him out—someone
named Woodstock had—which made Annie think it
less likely that they would cover for Pete if they thought
he was actually involved in his ex-girlfriend's death.

And just who was this Woodstock? Who were any of
the sleazy people who tagged along with Pete because

of his drugs? In Annie's opinion, every one of them should be a potential suspect in Ashley's death, and she hoped Dan and Kim were checking their alibis now. She wondered what Ashley's autopsy report might have revealed, and if Kim's interview of Clarissa Waters had shed any light on Ashley's death.

She had too many unanswered questions, but there was too much beautiful scenery around her to waste any more time on the subject. She turned her attention back to the trail in front of her.

The grade grew steeper, and Annie leaned forward as Trooper patiently trudged up a long, sloping hill. At the top was an alpine meadow, filled with tiny white flowers, a precursor to the higher one where the group planned to stop for lunch. Annie was just about to dig into her saddlebag for her camera when she heard Jessica's yell, "Halt! And keep your dogs by your side." Surprised, Annie immediately pulled on Trooper's reins and whistled for Wolf and Sasha, who came bounding toward her. She tried to look ahead to see what the problem was. A fallen log, perhaps? The sight of a mother bear and its young cubs? At least it wasn't a snake—there were no poisonous snakes in the Northwest, for which Annie was very grateful.

"What's going on?" she whispered up to Luann.

"Dunno," was the low reply. "Jessica's got her hand up, so I guess we're all supposed to be quiet. I don't see anything myself."

A few seconds later, they watched Jessica leave the pack and trot off on Molly toward a thicket of trees on the edge of the meadow. She stopped, dismounted, and disappeared among the branches. Thirty seconds later, she emerged again, her face grim. She abruptly mounted Molly and urged her back to the line of riders, all of whom had expressions of frank curiosity on their faces. Jessica walked Molly down the path so she could address everyone on the line.

"There's a man hanging from a tree in that copse. He's dead, although I doubt he's been dead very long. I'm sorry, girls, but this is the end of the trail for today."

CHAPTER 26

Cell phone reception was nonexistent at this altitude, so Annie volunteered to ride back to the trailhead to alert the Sheriff's Office. Lisa offered to go with her. She was looking a bit green around the gills, Annie thought, and she hadn't the heart to say no, although Annie knew she'd get to the base faster without another rider on her tail.

Annie did insist on one thing, and that was looking at the body before she left. It was barely visible from the trail, and Annie gave Jessica high marks for spotting it at all. She pulled the vet aside to explain her wishes.

"I may know who it is," she said in a low voice. "If I'm right, then Dan needs to know that when I call. I don't want everyone to think I'm being voyeuristic—believe me, the last thing I want to see right now is another corpse—but I have to know."

"Of course, Annie. I'll keep mum to the others and make sure no one else goes nearby. This is as good a place as any to eat our lunch. Although I doubt anyone is going to feel like eating now except our horses."

Annie walked into the cluster of trees and steeled herself to look at the figure hanging from a sturdy branch. Her suspicions were correct. Pete Corbett's lifeless body hung from a thick rope looped around his neck and secured to a stout redwood tree. He was dressed in jeans and a ragged T-shirt with the sleeves ripped off; his tattooed arms dangled by his side. And Jessica was correct—he hadn't been there long. It wasn't just because Annie knew when he'd walked out of the Suwana County jail that forced her to this conclusion. It was the fact that his body was unmolested by feral creatures, a fate not spared most of the animals he'd shot with his slingshot. For a moment, Annie thought how pleasurable it would be to let Pete just hang here and let him suffer the same mutilation that had occurred to his prey.

But that wouldn't be right. She sighed, mounted Trooper, and nodded to Lisa, and the two women began their slow descent down the trail. Annie heard Wolf and Sasha's sharp yelps in the background. Their feelings obviously were deeply hurt by their mistress's departure. Luann and Jill had promised to keep them under control and, more important, assure them they would soon be reunited with her.

On the way down, Annie wondered how Pete had even gotten to this secluded site, and realized that she already had classified his death, too, as a homicide and not a suicide. But why wouldn't he kill himself? His drug ring was crushed and his days as a serial animal killer were over. Maybe there really wasn't anything left for Pete to live for. In that case, Annie thought, he'd done everyone a favor.

Yet neither of the previous deaths, both staged as suicides, had turned out to be what they appeared. So perhaps her assumption that Pete's death must also certainly be murder had some merit.

Cell reception at the trailhead proved little better than at the higher altitude, so Annie left the horses in Lisa's care while she drove to find a spot with service. Four miles down the road she saw a small convenience store with a single gas pump. Surely there must be an Internet connection here. The sign on top read PHIL'S PHINE PHOODS. Oh, for pity's sake, thought Annie. She felt like writing him a letter and telling Phil his store name simply was not phunny.

Instead, she parked in the lot and punched in Dan's private cell number. It rang and rang until his voice message came on. Annie hesitated; should she leave a message? Probably not. He'd just have to hear about Pete's murder the old-fashioned way. She punched in 911.

"You've reached the Suwana County emergency response line. If this is a non-emergency, please report your issue on our website at www.suwana.gov forward-slash sheriff's office. An officer will get back to you within forty-eight hours. If this is an emergency, please push pound and wait for an operator."

I could have been shot and bled out by now, Annie thought irritably, but she punched pound and waited once more.

She was disappointed to get an unknown operator and not Esther, but realized belatedly that her relatively remote location had put her in another jurisdiction.

"911. What are you reporting?"

It would have been so much easier explaining it to Esther. Well, here goes, she thought.

"My name is Annie Carson, and I'm reporting a male body found on a trail in the Olympic National Forest."

"Is the person alive?"

"No."

"Have you tried taking his pulse?"

"No. He's hanging from a noose in the woods. Believe me, he's beyond resuscitation."

Annie could hear the *click-click-click* of a computer keyboard in the background.

"Do you know the person?"

Annie hesitated. "I believe his name is Pete Corbett."

"And do you know his date of birth?"

"No. I do know he was recently arrested on a variety of drug charges and bailed out of jail two days ago. Sheriff Dan Stetson is in charge of the case. He'll want to know about this right away."

"Give me the approximate location of the body, please."

"Oh—I'd say four or five miles up a horse trail starting at the cutoff road to Lake Piedmont. His body is in the first meadow you reach, in a small grove of redwoods."

"Will you be there when medics arrive?"

"I'm telling you, this guy doesn't need a medic. He needs a hearse."

"One moment, please."

More *click-click-clicking* in the background.

"Is it possible for a helicopter to land in this area?"

"Probably. But if you plan to do that, you'll have to wait for three horses and three riders and a bunch of dogs to vacate first. If you try to land while we're there, you'll create a stampede."

"Who else is with you?"

"As I said, three horses, three riders, many dogs. We were on a trail ride when one of the riders discovered the body."

"One moment, please."

* * *

Twenty minutes later, Annie finally ended the call. Her phone was hot from use and her battery nearly drained, and she considered her own physical state much the same. Fortunately, a helicopter would not be arriving at the meadow. The operator had ascertained that the cutoff road Annie had mentioned wended its way to the meadow, and both State Patrol and aid cars were on their way via this route.

Annie now suspected that this was the same road Pete had taken, or had been taken by someone, before he died, but she kept her suspicions to herself. There would be time enough to query Dan about this theory, and talking to the 911 operator had been unsatisfying and exhausting. Meanwhile, she had been instructed to stay by the trailhead to give her statement to the police and to provide the names of all her companions. She only hoped the police would let everyone leave before they started their investigation. It wasn't just the gruesome aspect of their jobs she wished to shield her friends from, it also was the time it took to complete it. It was now three o'clock in the afternoon, and she suspected the police would be at the site until at least dusk.

She tried Dan once more before heading back to the trailhead but again got his voice mail. Well, she had tried.

It was a somber group that came down the mountain an hour later. During the wait, Lisa and Annie had unsaddled their horses and had passed the one grooming brush Annie had stowed in her saddlebag back and forth until both Trooper and Hunter gleamed. The police had come and gone and, to Annie's relief, told them that they would prefer that everyone exit the scene ASAP.

They'd also confirmed that the medics, already on-site, had identified the body as Pete's. The news clearly shocked Annie's companion.

After the police had left, Lisa was visibly subdued. She may not have been a close friend, but she had known Pete for years, Annie remembered, and so had to be mourning his loss on some level.

"It must be hard, losing two people you knew in such a short time," Annie ventured.

"I just don't understand it. Why would two people I went to school with take their lives when their lives were just beginning?" Lisa sniffled and drew her arm across her eyes.

This was a tough one. By rights, Annie should be perpetuating the suicide theory, but she found she simply couldn't lie. But what could she say?

"I don't know why Pete died, or Ashley, either. But it's clear that they had a lot more problems than we ever knew about. Maybe we can take this as a lesson for ourselves—to make sure we're aware when our friends are in trouble so we can try to help them."

Lisa turned to her, her grief replaced by sudden anger. "We *did* try, Annie! Honestly! But when someone seems happy and upbeat and then does something like . . . like *hang* themselves, what are you supposed to do? Feel guilty for the rest of your life? Wonder what you should have seen? Might have done? Or might have said?"

She was right. Annie knew it. She realized she, too, had been on the verge of feeling guilt for the rest of her life.

"Lisa, I don't know the answer. I know you were the best friend you could be to Ashley, and you didn't do anything to Pete that forced him into killing himself. Wiser heads than mine should be talking to you right now. I just don't want you to feel sad, that's all. You've got enough going on in your life right now."

And with that, Lisa dissolved into tears and threw her arms around Annie's neck. Fortunately, Trooper and Hunter were too polite to stare.

To Annie's discomfort, her friends insisted on talking on speakerphone about the hanging body on the way back to her stables. There wasn't much she could do about it, and hoped the conversation wasn't too upsetting for Lisa.

"The medics thought he'd been hanging there for only a couple of hours," Jill said, who had made it her business to collect as many facts as possible before the riders were told they could leave. "I'm surprised we didn't see any signs of him on our way up."

"State Patrol thought he'd probably taken the back road," Jessica commented. "Although it's a hell of a long way to walk."

"Especially carrying a noose," added Luann.

It seemed obvious to Annie that Pete had not hiked in, and certainly hadn't lugged a heavy rope with him, but she said nothing to her companions. Let them think it was a suicide. She dreaded the moment when one of them would realize that Pete had chosen a peculiar place to die, especially since he knew full well what the animal kingdom would do to his body in short order. Perhaps that was one of the goals of Pete's killer. Annie wasn't entirely opposed to this form of rough justice.

When the caravan arrived at Annie's ranch, Annie took Luann aside and asked if she minded continuing on in Jessica's rig, crowded or not.

"It's just that Lisa knew the guy who died, and I'd like to get her home sooner rather than later," she told her friend.

Luann readily agreed, and offered to unload Hunter and make sure he was settled.

"I doubt that will be necessary," Annie said. "Hunter's probably the best tonic for her right now. I just don't want her to hear more gory details than necessary."

"Whoops. Sorry about that. We didn't know."

"Not a problem. See you on the next trail ride, and let's hope for fewer bodies next time."

"Amen to that, sister."

On the drive back from Lisa's house, Annie suddenly realized her dogs had been unnaturally quiet, which was never a good sign. Barking and in-your-face behavior was the norm, and when it wasn't happening, Annie got worried. She glanced around her truck to see where they were.

Wolf, she saw with relief, was napping on the floor behind her. But Sasha was crouched in the corner of her extra cab, and Annie could see a predictable scenario unfold in dangerously short order.

Pulling over to the side of the road, she put on her flashers, threw the car in park, and grabbed an old newspaper stuffed between her two front seats.

"Sasha, hold on one sec! Just one sec until I get this under you!"

She started to shove the newsprint under the pup and then stopped, pausing to read a headline. After ripping the page out of the section, she tossed it into her front seat and then shoved the remaining paper under her pup. Ah. She'd made it in time. Her seat covers would be safe. She praised Sasha, gave her a treat, and scooped up the soggy newsprint into a sturdy plastic bag, kept in the car for just this purpose.

Then she turned off her engine and her flashers, picked up the newspaper she'd rescued, and started to read. She'd been smart to save it. What she poured through now was far too interesting to be wasted on puppy potty training.

CHAPTER 27

MONDAY, MAY 23

"He's not in a very good mood," Esther whispered.

"Esther, why are you whispering? Is Dan in the room?" Annie was pacing back and forth in her kitchen, anxious to share the news that Sasha had almost obliterated.

"No, but he's liable to come bursting in here any moment."

"Great! I need to talk to him."

"I wouldn't recommend that right now, Annie. As I said, he's in one of his moods."

Annie knew from experience that when Dan's frustration level had reached its zenith, whoever got in his way would be subject to a raging diatribe on a subject matter that had nothing to do with whatever the person wanted to talk about. All the person would know, when the shouting finally stopped, was that it was all their fault.

"I've lived through enough to talk about them," Annie replied. "I'll take my chances."

"Don't say I didn't warn you. Transferring you now."

Dan picked up on the first ring.

"Stetson," he bellowed into the phone.

She was determined not to lose her temper. "Dan, it's Annie."

"So! You couldn't take my advice, per usual, and had to poke your nose into this fiasco with Pete Corbett."

"Excuse me?"

"I heard all about it from the State Patrol. I swear, a homicide can't happen in this county without your name plastered on the responding officer's report. Why don't you stick to your own business and go ride a horse or something and let us do our job?"

"I *was* riding a horse, Dan. I was on a nice trail ride when Pete Corbett suddenly appeared, swinging from a tree. I guess we should have checked our schedules first."

One remark and already Annie recognized the warning signs of her anger taking over. It started with sarcasm. It seldom ended there.

"Well, why in the Sam Hill didn't you call me first? Why'd you have to get the State Patrol involved?"

Annie took a deep breath. "I did call you, Dan. Twice. On your cell. Both times it went to voice mail."

There was a brief silence. "You should have left a message."

"Even if I had, you know I had a legal obligation to notify law enforcement at my first opportunity. Trooper and I climbed down off that mountain as soon as we could to try to reach you. It's not our fault you didn't pick up. Where were you, anyway?" She might as well try to put him on the defensive.

"Never mind. It isn't important. Talking to my soon-to-be-ex-wife, if you must know. What is important is that you understand that you have an *ethical* obligation to let me know what's happening in *my* case. If I don't pick up, leave a message. Or call Tony. Or Kim. Anyone, so that we don't get our toes stepped on by an outside agency that has no idea of the significance of what they're investigating."

"Really, Dan? You don't think the State Patrol's competent enough to investigate a homicide?"

"Who said it was a homicide?"

"I did. And you know it, too." Her voice was rising, and anger was seeping in.

"You know nothing of the sort. Pete Corbett hung himself because he knew his future was going to be inside a penitentiary for a very long time."

"Dan, doesn't it occur to you that this is the third homicide that was supposed to look like a suicide? Eloise Carr OD'd on pills she'd never taken before. And we know Ashley didn't jump into her noose by herself. Pete was hanging even higher. I didn't see any scuff marks on a tree showing that he climbed up. I didn't see any nearby logs to stand on. Besides, why would Pete choose a place to off himself where he knew he'd be fodder for predators in a few hours? Unless he belongs to some religion that advocates that form of burial, it doesn't make sense!"

"I don't have time to discuss your harebrained ideas, Annie. I'm trying to figure out the best way to wrap up the loose ends of two cases where the prime suspects conveniently die before they can be brought to justice."

"Maybe you should hold off a day or two. Maybe you just haven't found the right killer yet. What do you think of that harebrained idea?" Now she was shouting.

It had been ridiculous to think she could hold her temper when she was insulted at every turn.

Dan ended the conversation the way he did in any difficult encounter. He simply hung up. And Annie, in her fury, completely forgot about the reason she'd wanted to talk to the sheriff in the first place.

She stormed around the stables, rearranging hay bales, cleaning water buckets, doing anything that was physically demanding to keep from imploding. Dan Stetson had often patronized her, and his compliments to her on any topic were few and far between, but he had never, until now, castigated her so thoroughly. He was entirely unreasonable in his criticisms, she knew, but the fact that he could even voice them made her seethe. She understood his frustration—wasn't everyone on the force, as well as she, chafing under the realization that no clue had emerged yet to pinpoint the killer, or killers, of Eloise Carr, Ashley Lawton, and now Pete Corbett? But you didn't see Kim or Tony taking it out on other people. And now she knew she just might have a clue that could help. She picked up her phone to call the one person in the Sheriff's Office she knew was hands down more reasonable than Dan. Not to mention in infinitely better shape.

"I'd be happy to talk to you, Annie," Kim told her a minute later. "I'd like to come over now. Dan is on the warpath, and it's dangerous just to roam the halls. But the pile on my desk is telling me I won't be out of here until probably seven o'clock. Will that work for you?" It would, indeed.

By four o'clock, her stables and tack room were positively glowing. Displaced anger did have its merits, she decided, as she gazed around at the spotless counters, gleaming sinks, and neatly stacked and very clean feed bowls. Every feeder in the stalls had been laboriously removed and scrubbed. Old wall stains had been removed, or removed as much as they ever could be. The dust that had accumulated on Annie's shelves of horse supplements and medical supplies was gone. True, it would appear again within the week, but today everything looked good. She should take photographs, she thought, just to know that once, everything looked like this. If she really wanted to show off, she could forward them to Jessica, who would immediately post them on her Facebook page. Annie didn't do Facebook, despite the frequent urging of her horse friends.

"Social media is a disease without a cure," she'd once told them. Everyone had laughed, but Annie honestly felt that her pronouncement had a ring of truth to it.

She still had two hours before feeding. She could continue her cleaning frenzy in her own farmhouse, or she could take a hot bath. The bath won out.

Marcus called just as she was stepping out of the tub, dripping wet, her skin pink and clean.

"Did I interrupt you?" he said politely. "I know we'll talk later, but I have a question for you now."

"This is fine," she said, trying to dry her hair with a large towel as she talked. For some reason she felt embarrassed to admit to Marcus that she was standing, buck naked, in the middle of her bedroom.

"Great. I know how busy you are but thought I'd ask. Is it possible for you to dig something out of Hilda's boxes in storage for me?"

She sighed inwardly. "Sure."

Marcus's laugh came through the phone.

"I'm not sure I believe that perky reply, but thank you for making the effort."

She sat down on her bed, reasonably dry by now. "What do you need?"

"I'm looking for letters between Hilda and her property insurance agent. I'm trying to wrap up the claim, and apparently there was some correspondence earlier this year about modifying the fire and earthquake policies."

"I hope she wasn't downgrading her coverage."

"On the contrary—she insisted that she have the ultimate package on both contingencies. It would be just like her to demand the best—with no extra premium, of course."

Annie agreed but said nothing. "There are about a hundred boxes in storage," she cautioned him. "Where should I start looking?"

"It should be in a box marked 'Essential Ranch Papers.' The correspondence will be in a manila envelope inside, labeled 'Property insurance.' I asked the movers to keep it and several other boxes of important documents close to the front, in case something like this arose. If you don't find it immediately, don't waste hours searching for it. I'll just put the insurance company on hold and look for it when I'm up for the next board meeting."

Annie was determined to find the papers first. "No problem, Marcus. I've actually got an extra hour and can zip out and try to find it now."

"Could you, Annie? That would be a tremendous help. You don't know how much I appreciate your making this extra effort."

As she backed her truck out of her driveway fifteen minutes later, she thought with immense satisfaction how *some* people didn't have any problem recognizing her for the highly competent, ever helpful person that she was.

* * *

She arrived at the storage unit just as the big electronic door was closing for the day. This was not a problem, as Annie had created a password to punch in at the gate to give her access to the storage rooms any time she wanted. One of the units she'd rented for Marcus contained household furniture and other tangible items, while the other was filled with boxes. The second unit was actually the fuller one; the rancid smell of smoke had permeated most of the furnishings inside Hilda's cavernous home, making them unfit even as donations. Many of the papers Marcus had culled were in similar shape, but because they were affiliated with Hilda's horse business, he'd had no choice but to bundle them up and save them. The ranch computers hadn't survived the fire, and Hilda apparently didn't know about offline storage options or the cloud.

After Annie had rented the two units, she had returned to supervise the move and secure each space with a lock she'd found back home. But she'd never looked inside any of the boxes. It wasn't her business, and she honestly had no interest in Hilda Colbert's affairs. She knew that Marcus was doing only what he had to do to settle his wife's estate, but she felt an irrational twinge of jealousy that Hilda still absorbed his time and thoughts, even from beyond the grave.

She unlocked the unit with the boxes and heaved the sliding aluminum door upward. A wall of neat, white packing boxes greeted her. It was a bit daunting, but Annie was resolved to find the box in record time. Scouring the first row, she saw Marcus's neat handwriting on the side to identify the contents of each one. To her dismay, several boxes held the same label—ESSENTIAL RANCH PAPERS. But at least they all appeared to be in the same area. She pulled down the first box and began to search through it.

Despite Marcus's methodical organization, it took Annie a full hour to locate the manila envelope he had described. Naturally, the precious documents were in the bottom box. She cursed the box and storage units in general, put the envelope in her saddlebag purse, and carefully locked up.

When she emerged into the corridor, she saw a customer fiddling with a lock on a unit a few doors down from Marcus's. The middle-aged woman seemed exasperated and at the end of her patience.

"Can I help?" Annie called out to her.

The woman looked up. "I can't get this stupid lock to open." Her voice reflected her irritation. "It's one of the ones they sell you when you sign up. The owner assured me it was the best there is, and he was selling it to me at a cheaper price than at the hardware store, but I can't get the damn thing to work. If I ever get it off, I'm going to replace it with one of my own."

Annie smiled. "I got the same spiel but decided to pass on the offer. It took long enough just to get the papers signed."

"You too? I swear, I thought we'd never finish the application. You wouldn't think it would be so difficult, would you?"

Annie took the key from the woman's hand and inserted it into the lock. Nothing happened. She jiggled it. The lock still wouldn't open. She pushed the lock firmly forward and jiggled once more. There was a small *click*, and Annie now was able to turn the top clasp to the open position.

"Thank you!" the woman exclaimed. "I don't know how you did it, but thank you!"

"Try pressing the key forward all the way first. That seems to be the trick."

Annie handed the key back to the woman but not before noticing its distinctive markings. They were mirror images of those on the key found on Ashley's body and the one she had given to Lavender for safekeeping.

Now she had two items of importance to tell the most reasonable deputy in the Sheriff's Office. And the fittest.

Dusk had fallen but Annie's ranch was still bathed in the radiance of a setting sun. Kim pulled up just as Annie was exiting the stables.

"Go on in," she shouted to Kim. "The door's open."

Annie had picked up a bottle of chardonnay on her way back from the storage unit. She'd had a feeling that a beverage made of grapes, rather than grain, was more in keeping with Kim's dietary program, and was correct in her assumption. Kim was delighted to open the bottle and pour both of them full glasses.

"I love Oregon whites," Kim said. "How did you know?"

Annie merely smiled. She didn't, until now.

"How's Dan doing?"

Kim gave Annie a sideways grin and shook her head in mock despair. "I think he's worn out and ready for his nap by now. I don't think I've ever seen him on such a tirade as he was today. I hear you got the full brunt of it earlier."

"Did I ever! What a mean, cantankerous boss you have. Frankly, I don't know how you stand it when he gets into one of these fits. He's so unreasonable."

"Actually, he pretty much steers clear of me. The first

time he started ranting at me because things weren't going his way, I read him the riot act and told him if he so much as raised his voice to me again, I'd quit. He seemed to believe me. So now I just shut my door and he never bothers me."

"Smart move. Unfortunately, I seem to sink to his level."

"It's easy to get sucked in, I know. And I'm sorry, Annie. You don't deserve to be treated that way. If you can, try to remember that Dan really is a good cop and a good guy. He's just frustrated with not getting to the bottom of the Carr and Lawton deaths."

"I told him Pete Corbett was a murder victim, too. He heartily denied it."

"Only because he wants the world at large to think that this is just another suicide—although three suicides in as many weeks is a new record for Suwana County. If the public knew we really had three unsolved homicides on our desks right now, the press as well as the commissioners would be all over us."

"True. But I just had an epiphany that I think will interest you."

"Do tell."

"It's the key, the odd key that Lavender just coughed up, the twin to the one found on Ashley's body."

Kim leaned forward. "You've discovered what it goes to?"

"Yup. It opens one of the storage units down the road. The owner of the place sells some kind of special lock to new customers. Claims it's the best and costs peanuts. I got the hard sell a couple of weeks ago when I leased two units on Marcus's behalf, but I declined his offer. It was taking forever just to get the paperwork done. If I'd had a little more patience, I would have realized the significance of Ashley's key back then."

"Hey, you do now, and that's faster than any of us. How'd you figure it out?"

"I was there earlier, getting some papers for Marcus, and the woman at a nearby unit was having trouble with the lock, using that same key. Well, not the same key, but one that looked just like it. She said she'd bought it from the proprietor. So Ashley must have leased a storage unit somewhere on the premises."

"Hot damn! We need to get a search warrant now. This is just the break we've needed, Annie. And if Dan throws a hissy fit when he finds out you're the reason we have it, well, he's going to get one of *my* moods, and look out, Sheriff."

"One more thing, Kim. It may not be significant, but it certainly caught my eye. It's what I had intended to talk to Dan about when I called."

"What's that, Annie? Everything you do seems to turn out golden."

Annie felt a warm glow spread throughout her body. It took so little to make her feel appreciated. All she needed was a small bone thrown to her every now and then. Someday, Dan might be smart enough to realize it.

"Another serendipitous encounter. I nabbed an old newspaper on my way out of a diner up north last week. I was coming back from the equine clinic in Cape Disconsolate. Jessica was with me, and we'd stopped for a quick bite. Today, I glanced at it and noticed a long list of trustee sales with Ronald Carr Junior's name on them. He and his wife are listed as the original grantors in six properties now in foreclosure. I added them up, and he owes close to five million on all of them. I never would have guessed he was in such financial trouble."

Annie pulled out the crumpled newspaper from her bag and handed it to Kim. The deputy quickly perused the listings and nodded.

"I'd say he's in serious trouble. And you don't know how significant this information is. Carr's just filed his mother's will for probate in Suwana County Superior Court. Not surprisingly, he's Eloise's personal representative. Dan sent Tony to the courthouse to find out the extent of the estate. We figured she owned the house in Port Chester and maybe a few blue chip stocks her husband had invested in years ago. You know, nothing for the kids to fight over."

"Don't tell me," Annie said, her eyes on Kim's.

"I'm going to tell you. Yes, she owns the modest little home in town, but she also owns big property in Montana, Florida, and Vermont. Outright. Her stock and cash holdings alone make her a millionaire. With the properties, she died a millionaire several times over."

"While Ron is losing his shirt in the real estate market."

"Uh-huh. And now we're all kicking ourselves for not taking a closer look at him. He was so sympathetic to Ashley, we assumed he was blameless himself. It's our own damn fault, although I can see how it happened. From the beginning, every aspect of Eloise Carr's death pointed to Ashley, and when she died, we figured Pete was the killer. After all, we knew he'd been squatting on your property. But with Pete's death, and what you've just brought to the table, everything's changed."

"Who's the beneficiary of Eloise's estate?"

"Who do you think?"

The two women sat in silence. Annie picked up the bottle of Chardonnay to top off Kim's glass, but Kim put her hand over it.

"I've got to write up a couple of search warrants," she said with a sigh. "I'll call Dan, and we'll get Judge Casper to sign them first thing tomorrow morning."

"For the storage unit company?"

"That, and for anything associated with Eloise Carr's will. I'd like to know the progression of that document, as well, and something tells me Ron Carr is not going to be terribly forthcoming."

Annie pictured Ron in her mind's eye—a dapper man in his midsixties with a ready smile on his face, well dressed, looking every inch the part of a successful real estate agent. She'd seen him only twice, and both times were at events to mourn the loss of lives. Now, she realized, Ron Carr may very well have had a hand in both deaths. Maybe Pete's as well.

She reluctantly put the cork back in the wine bottle. She should have known. Never trust a man who hands out business cards at his mother's memorial service.

CHAPTER 28

At six o'clock, Annie's alarm clock went off with a vengeance. Her right hand came crashing down on the offending item, sending it to the floor. So why did the shrill noise continue? Cursing, she sat up in bed and realized it was her cell phone's harsh ring that now thwarted her ability to sleep.

After stomping over to the dresser where the phone was recharging, she snatched it up without looking at the caller ID.

"This is Annie." She sounded as sleepy as she felt.

"Annie! Thank goodness I got you before you went out to the stables. It's Martha, dear. I can't find Lavender. Is she with you?"

Martha sounded distraught. It was the first time Annie could remember her being anything less than unfailingly calm.

Annie sat down on the edge of her bed and replied,

"No, she's not here, Martha. When did you last see her?"

"Last night, around eight o'clock, and I'm almost out of my mind with worry."

Eight o'clock? That was ten hours ago. Well, Lavender had disappeared before and she'd always shown up like a bad penny. Then again, usually that was after she and Lavender had had a major blowup. Annie couldn't imagine this happening with Martha.

"Was something wrong? Was she upset when she left? Where did you say she was going?"

"Oh my, so many questions. Let me think. No, nothing was wrong. Lavender was catching the bus to go to one of her elder meetings, you know, the classes she takes on Native American symbolism. Or is it spiritualism? I can never quite remember."

Annie put one hand over her brow. "And how were her spirits when she left? No pun intended."

"Oh, fine, dear. Lavender was in a fine mood. She usually gets back around ten or perhaps a little later, depending on whether she takes the bus home or someone gives her a ride. This is all part of her regular routine."

"So what happened?"

"Well, I'm afraid I fell asleep. I tend to go to bed earlier than your sister."

Half sister, Annie wanted to say, but didn't.

"I woke up around two o'clock and assumed that she'd slipped in sometime after I'd turned out my light. But when I got up at five o'clock to let the cat out, I checked her bedroom and she wasn't there. Her bed was still made and she never came home!"

Martha's voice was going up in pitch and she was rapidly working her way into a small fit of hysteria. This had to stop.

"I'm sure Lavender is all right. She probably just spent the night with one of her friends and will be home shortly. I wouldn't worry too much about her. Lavender always lands on her feet."

"Yes, dear, but she knows to call if she's going to be late. She knows how important it is for me to know that she's safe. She wouldn't just decide to do something and not tell me. But she hasn't called and she's not answering her phone. Something must be terribly wrong!"

What was wrong, Annie thought, was Lavender's totally thoughtless behavior. She was sure her half sister was off having fun with her equally wacky chums, with no clue as to how much she'd upset Martha by her unexplained absence. She fully intended to let Lavender have it with both barrels when she decided to reappear. Lying to the police was bad enough, but causing Martha unnecessary stress was even more unacceptable.

"I seriously believe that Lavender's just fine." Annie tried to make her voice sound reassuring. "But if she hasn't shown up by the time I've fed the horses, I'll pick you up and we'll go down to the Sheriff's Office to report her missing. Although I'm not sure there's anything they can do. I think adults have the right to be missing a lot longer than minors before the police do anything about it."

The only way Lavender could be classified as an adult was by the birth date on her driver's license, which happened to be suspended. She searched her brain for something that Martha could do now to ease her agitation.

"Did Lavender leave her address book at home? Do you have the names and phone numbers of any of her friends whom you could call?"

"I've already looked, dear. She must have taken the little spiral notebook where she keeps important numbers with her. I'll call Elder Home Care as soon as the office is open to see if they've heard from her, but I don't think Lavender was supposed to work today."

"It's certainly worth a try," Annie agreed. "Try not to worry, Martha. I'll call you in an hour to see if she's shown up yet."

"Thank you, dear. I knew you'd know exactly what to do."

An hour later, Lavender had yet to resurface. Annie cursed her half sister and quickly showered and dressed. Throwing an apple into her saddlebag purse, she headed out the door. She didn't realize Sasha had sneaked into the cab until she was halfway down the road toward Martha's home.

She was alarmed at the paleness of Martha's face; the stress of the past few hours made her appear more fragile and vulnerable than Annie had ever seen her. Now she was glad her naughty Belgian had decided to hitch a ride. Puppy comfort was exactly what Martha needed. With Sasha on her lap, she was more than content to stay in the truck while Annie scouted out the means by which law enforcement might possibly help find her miscreant sister. She was not looking forward to Dan's response to her plight.

The Sheriff's Office was a flurry of activity; in her haste to help Martha, Annie had forgotten that Kim was in the midst of trying to get search warrants written, approved, signed, and served. Annie found her huddled in her office, her eyes on her computer screen and her hands typing at least eighty words a minute. She realized she couldn't possibly bother Kim now. Dan's office door was locked, a rare occurrence, but Annie could hear Tony and Dan arguing loudly inside, presumably about the new information that had emerged about Ron Carr. The door flung open, and Dan and Tony strode out in the direction of the evidence room. Annie wasn't sure if they'd seen her and decided to ignore her presence or whether she simply was invisible this morning. She quietly returned to the truck to see how Martha was doing.

For a moment, Annie's heart stopped—Martha looked so frail, sitting in her truck, with all the color drained out of her face, that she worried that her friend might have had a heart attack. Her eyes were closed and her hands were neatly folded in her lap. Sasha was sitting by her feet, on the floorboard, looking up and obviously wondering why the nice lady wouldn't pick her up and play with her.

But, no, she could see the small, even rise and fall of her breathing under her sweater. Martha simply was exhausted. She'd done all she could do to find Lavender, and now that the task was in Annie's capable hands, she could sleep.

As well she should, Annie thought. She quietly opened the driver's door and motioned for Sasha to come to her. Snapping on her leash, Annie closed the door with as little motion as possible and returned inside. Someone was going to have to talk to her sooner or later, and she was prepared to wait.

On a whim, she pulled up Lavender's contact info on her phone and selected Call. A bright, cheery voice came on after the fourth ring.

"Hi, this is Lavender. If you've reached this message, I'm off exploring the universe but I'll be happy to talk to you when I'm back. Don't forget to leave your number. Bye!"

A series of beeps followed this uplifting message and then a disembodied voice announced, "Mailbox is full." Probably from all of Martha's messages this morning, Annie thought. She wished she knew how to break into voice mail to see if any of the messages might give a clue as to what was taking Lavender so long to get home. It was now nearly nine o'clock.

She decided to check on Dan again. As she began to walk down the main hallway, several deputies she didn't know walked purposefully toward her. Their gait implied they were on an important mission, but she noticed that everyone stopped to say hello to the beautiful Belgian pup beside her. Sasha was on her best behavior and allowed herself to be petted without jumping up.

Now no one was in their office. Well, Esther would know where they were, she hoped. Tapping on the door of the tiny room that was emergency response central, she peered in and saw Esther doing the *New York Times* crossword puzzle. Annie knew she'd have every blank filled in a matter of minutes; it was only Tuesday, an easy day for cutthroat crossword puzzlers, which Esther certainly was.

She opened the door a few inches. "Where is everyone? I have a missing person report to file."

Esther looked up. "Kim just left for court, and Dan and Tony are holed up in the evidence room, yelling at each other."

"Business as usual?"

"Pretty much. Who are you reporting missing?"

"My crazy half sister. She didn't come home last night, and the angel of a woman who allows her to live with her is convinced she's been abducted by aliens."

Esther put down her pencil. "How long has she been gone?"

"About twenty-four hours."

"Sorry, Annie." Esther shook her head, sadly. "Not much we can do until forty-eight hours have passed. Unless she's been legally declared incompetent and has a formal guardian who can speak for her."

"Legally incompetent, no. Reputation within her own little community, definitely."

"Last place seen?"

"Technically, at home. But she was supposed to take off around eight last night to go to some meeting with Native American elders."

"Well, has anyone checked to see if she showed up?"

"Actually . . . well, no. I don't know the people involved or even the name of the group."

"Let me see what I can find out. This crossword is not sufficiently challenging me. What's your sister's name?"

"Lavender Carson. Thanks. I'll wait outside. And by the way, it's half sister."

Fifteen minutes later, Esther joined Annie and Sasha in the waiting room.

"I think I found the group, Annie. There's one called Native Northwest Spiritualists that meets every Monday night in the Lutheran church basement in Port Chester. It seems to be some kind of New Agey organization. The leader, who calls himself an elder—but, trust me, is second-generation Norwegian—remembers Lavender Carson as a frequent attendee, although he said she wasn't present at last night's meeting."

A small sense of panic began to pour through Annie's body. She'd never considered the possibility that Lavender hadn't gone where she'd said she was going. Maybe her absence was more serious than she'd thought.

But the idea of sharing this knowledge with Martha was anathema to her right now. At least before she talked to Dan or some other person she could trust to give the right advice on how to track down Lavender.

"Thanks, Esther." She hurriedly got up and started jogging down the hall, the pup trotting beside her, happy to be traveling at a speed that usually got her in trouble inside Annie's home.

"Annie! I don't think this is a good time to interrupt Dan." Esther's voice came trailing after her. She ignored it. She'd suddenly remembered what Lavender had told her at the reception following Eloise Carr's memorial service—that she'd told Ron Carr that she had been with Ashley on the day his mother's body was found. He'd told her how brave she was, and she'd thought he was "just the nicest man."

CHAPTER 29

Annie burst into the evidence room. Dan and Tony's backs were to her. Several evidence bags were spread out on a large table, and the men appeared to be examining one specific item. Only when the door slammed behind her did they turn around.

"Annie! What are you doing here?" Tony looked shocked.

"Lavender's missing," she panted. "She told Ron Carr Junior that she'd been with Ashley the day she found Eloise Carr's body."

"So?" Tony seemed utterly confused.

"Dan told him that Lavender lied, that she knew something about the death of his mother and he'd get it out of her. Remember, Dan? You talked to him on the phone, right after Pete's arrest and after she failed the polygraph." It was hard now not to go up to him and slug him in the stomach.

Dan's face went white.

"Where's Ron? Where is he?"

"I didn't know they'd met," Dan said. "I never mentioned her by name."

"Well, she did! She went right up and introduced herself to him at the reception. So he knows who she is, and now I'm worried he has her."

Tony looked at Dan. "Let me find out if anyone's located him yet." He left the room as if being there now was the last place he wanted to be.

"If he's *located* yet? What does that mean? Is he AWOL, too?"

She was practically screaming at the sheriff and didn't care. His careless words had put her sister in danger, and she would make damned sure that he was going to get her out of it. Wherever she might be.

"Hold on, Annie," Dan said, taking both her arms. "Just calm down for a moment until we can sort this all out." He led her to a nearby chair. Annie found herself seated without remembering sitting down, and somehow a glass of water appeared in her hand. She took a long swallow, and her mind felt clearer.

"I assume Kim's filled you in," she started.

"We know Ron's deep in debt but that all his financial problems will be solved once his mother's will passes through probate."

"Oh, no—we know more than that," Annie bitterly responded. "We know that Ron probably killed his mother for her money, then killed Ashley and finally Pete because they knew too much. And now he's probably going to kill Lavender because he thinks *she* knows too much, as well." She was about to cry. It was only the horror of knowing this that kept her from dissolving into a puddle.

"We don't know that, Annie, but that's what we're trying to figure out now."

"Yeah, well, while you figure that out, my sister is in immediate danger. She left home last night at eight, never showed up for her meeting in Port Chester, and has yet to come home. Her cell phone is full and she's not answering. I'd say the odds are pretty good that Ron is involved in her disappearance, wouldn't you?"

Dan sighed. "We've been looking for him since 0600 hours. According to his wife, he left home last night and hasn't been seen since."

"So what more evidence do you need? He has Lavender, damn it, and you're just sitting here. Do something!" Her last sentence ended in a shriek.

Sasha reacted to her mistress's distress by doing the only thing she could think of to relieve her own discomfort. She jumped onto the stainless steel evidence table and grabbed the small toy lamb that Annie had first seen weeks before at Pete's campsite. Clamping it firmly in her teeth, she whirred it back and forth in her mouth until white polyester fiber began to fly around her. As she shredded the animal, she emitted a low growl, daring anyone to take it from her.

Annie stared at her dog, her mouth open. But it wasn't because Sasha was being a bad puppy; Annie knew she'd put her dog under unnecessary stress, and Sasha was reacting the only way she knew how. Something was bothering her mistress, and she was trying to kill the enemy. Frankly, if Sasha had gone after Dan's pant leg, she wasn't sure she would have stopped her. But now she saw something emerge from the remains of the animal that she did not want Sasha to decimate.

She stood up, said, "Sasha, drop," in a firm voice. The dog ignored her and Annie repeated her request. This time, Sasha stopped shaking the toy long enough for Annie to gently take it from her mouth. "Good dog," she told her, and reached into her pocket for the ever-present treats she kept there. There were none. Damn. Well, Sasha was going to have to learn to expect delayed gratification once in a while, anyway. All big dogs had to learn this lesson.

Annie dug her hand into what remained of the sheep toy and pulled out two pieces of paper. The first paper was familiar to her—it was the same lease form that Annie had laboriously filled out at the storage unit the week before. Only this one was in Ron Carr Junior's name. He had rented the unit back in January on a month-to-month basis. He'd chosen the largest storage area, just as Marcus had instructed Annie to, but the number of his new unit was smudged. All Annie could see was an A; the adjoining number was no longer visible on the ink-smudged copy.

The second paper was a handwritten note from Ron to Ashley.

"Darling Ashley," it read. "You know you mean the world to me. But you have to trust me to make sure our future together is financially secure. Please don't meddle in my affairs. Pete and I know what we're doing, and you need to stay on the sidelines. Bad things will happen if you don't understand this. You know I've got your best interests in mind. Trust me to do the right thing." It was signed, "All my love, Ronny."

Wordlessly, she handed the papers over to Dan, who read both in a few seconds, and then spoke into his microphone. But Annie didn't wait to hear what Dan had to say. She rushed out of the evidence room and down the corridor, Sasha running behind her. She reached the glass front entrance door and stopped. She couldn't take Martha with her on her quest to save Lavender. But what could she do?

Tony appeared out of nowhere.

"Come with me."

She turned and ran with him to the back of the
building, where she knew the police vehicles were
parked.

"Get in, put the dog in the back, and do exactly what
I tell you to do."

Normally, Annie would have balked at being told what
to do by Tony or anyone else, but right now she didn't
care. She was just grateful that someone on the police
force was doing something. As he pulled out of the county
parking lot, he glanced in his rearview mirror. Annie
followed his gaze. Several other police vehicles were following closely.

"Dan's filled me in. Only one place Ron could have
taken Lavender," he muttered to Annie. "SWAT team's
on their way, but I don't want to wait that long,"

She silently agreed. Suwana County didn't have a
SWAT team. The closest trained group was thirty miles
away.

She was glad the storage unit was only a few miles
away, and noticed that Tony activated only his overhead
strobes en route, not his siren. He turned into the entrance; the black steel gate in front was closed, inex-
plicably locked at this time of day. Annie gave him her
password and the door soundlessly swung open. It
seemed to take forever. A long line of patrol cars
silently followed them in.

"Down there!" Annie pointed to the building where
Marcus's units were. She was fairly certain that Ron
Carr's unit was in the same structure; every unit she'd
walked by had started with an A. Tony radioed the information to Esther, and Annie watched the other vehicles fan out in a circle, surrounding the enclosure.

"Wait here. Don't move." Tony jumped out of the car
and joined six other deputies already out of their vehicles, waiting for his instructions. It was a brief discus-

sion; Annie watched the group quietly take up positions
on all sides of the building, their weapons drawn. She
noticed that two deputies had eschewed their regula-
tion Glocks and had high-powered rifles trained on the interior. Behind them, she saw the bumper of a blue Toyota
pickup, parked on an angle and nearly out of sight.

Annie hesitated for one moment and then jumped out
of the car. "Stay," she sternly ordered Sasha. Sasha looked
reproachfully at her but stayed put. Annie hoped her dog
would be more obedient than her mistress. As far as she
knew, Sasha had not learned to roll down electric windows—yet.

A few seconds later, Tony emerged from the corridor
on the north side of the building, and Annie jogged toward him.

"I thought I told you to stay put!" he hissed when
she'd reached his side.

"You did! So what? Lavender could be dying right
now."

"And you're going to save her." He put up his hands
as if surrendering the argument. "We don't even know
for a fact that she's here."

"Oh yeah? Look over your shoulder. See that blue
Toyota?"

Tony looked. "Same one you saw in Port Chester?"

"And the same one Lavender said belonged to Ashley's new boyfriend."

Tony groaned. "Let's get moving. Where the hell is
the SWAT team, anyway?"

"Forget the SWAT team. Forget talking. Let's find
out where Carr's taken her."

"Aren't you forgetting something?"

"Like what?"

"Civilians."

"Oh. Are there any?"

"Just checked. Aside from you, none that I can find. Time to see which lock fits this key." He held one of the matching set in his hand.

"Did you bring both?"

Tony stared at her. "If you think for one second that I'm going to . . ."

She snatched the one in his hand and sprinted off.

She realized Tony had no choice but to duplicate her efforts. Starting on the farthest corridor back, she began inserting the key into every lock she saw, whether or not it resembled the one she'd opened for the frustrated woman the day before. She worked fast. If Tony didn't understand that two people could accomplish the job of finding Lavender in half the time, well, that was just his problem.

As each lock steadfastly resisted opening, Annie's hopes began to wane, and her hands began to shake. She wished she'd remembered to tell Tony to push the key in fully before turning it. What if he'd found the right unit but didn't understand the quirks of the lock? On the other hand, if she had taken time to explain, she probably wouldn't be holding a key now, and she was convinced that time was running out. It might be too late; Lavender had been missing for more than twelve hours now, and who knew when Carr had caught up with her—probably early on, since Lavender had never made it to her meeting. She buried her thoughts and moved on to the next corridor.

She could hear Tony on the other side of the hallway, trying locks in succession. They met in the middle; she could tell Tony was seething, but she merely said, "Push it in fully before turning" before escaping to the next corridor.

She passed Marcus's units and paused. Was there any chance Lavender might be in there? None, she decided, as she had both keys and there was no way they could have been duplicated by anyone else. Still, she decided to take ten seconds and give in to her paranoia. Digging into her pocket, she fumbled for the right set. At least these were easy locks to open. She tore open the aluminum roll-up door and stared inside. Nothing. Nothing but boxes and boxes of Hilda's accumulated papers. She sighed and reached up to drag down the aluminum door.

Then she heard somebody hiccup. She was sure of it. She looked around. What direction had it come from? She thought of calling out for Lavender but just as quickly realized this was a bad idea. What if Carr was with her? It might be enough to send him over the edge. So far, any sounds he might have heard would be interpreted as the normal sounds of people accessing their storage units, not seven deputies waiting to pounce. She left the door as it was and slowly walked up and down the corridor, trying not to make any noise. When she heard nothing more, despair started to fill her heart, despite the adrenaline running through her body that told her to keep on going until the right lock made itself known.

She'd been concentrating on her feet, slowly traversing the concrete floor, back and forth, but looked up to see Tony watching her from the end of the corridor. She put a finger to her lips and then pointed around her. He nodded and began to walk toward her. She was at a loss; now she knew Lavender was here, and somewhere close, but how could she and Tony get to her in time, and without precipitating some disastrous outcome?

Another sound came from the interior of a nearby unit. This time, Tony heard it, too. He pointed to the unit two doors left of the one holding Marcus's business files. Both of them froze. Unlike every other door on the aisle, this one was not quite shut. The aluminum siding hung a bare inch above the concrete floor, allowing a small sliver of light to shine through. And no lock was present. Tony gave her the crossed hands sign to freeze and walked quickly out of the corridor. Annie realized that she had not once heard his shoulder mike squawk since he'd been beside her; he must have turned it off, she thought. A minute later, Tony returned with three other deputies, each silently running on their rubber-soled boots down the hall. They took up equidistant positions in front of the aluminum door. Tony motioned Annie to move back to the outside door, which she reluctantly did. Once she was out of the way, Tony gave a short nod. The deputies quietly drew their weapons and trained them on the door. Tony took one quick step forward and ripped it open in a clashing roar.

All three rushed in and Annie ran forward, despite hearing Tony's shouted admonition of "Stand back! Stand back!" Annie looked wildly inside the space for Lavender but saw only rows and rows of cheap shelving piled high with white plastic bags. Finally, in a corner, she saw Lavender slumped on a chair, her head hanging over, her arms tied behind her back. A thick noose hung behind her from the rafters. Next to her stood Ronald Carr. He wore baggy cargo pants and an old sweatshirt, now stained with sweat, looking nothing like the real estate mogul he'd pretended to be when Annie had last seen him. Now he was being handcuffed by one of the deputies as another deputy read him his Miranda rights. Her gaze went back to Lavender. Tony was now on his knees, feeling for Lavender's pulse on her neck. Annie couldn't stop herself. She pushed her way into the crowded space, fell in front of the chair, and shook Lavender by her constrained arms.

"Don't you die on me now, Lavender! Don't you dare die!"

Lavender stirred. She tried to lift her head, but it clearly took too much effort. Annie held her sister's chin and raised it for her. Lavender's face was bruised, and her lips were swollen. She moved her mouth and tried to speak. One word finally emerged.

"Sister."

CHAPTER 30

LATER THAT SAME DAY

It was Lavender who first remembered Martha. "Where is she?" Her lips were so swollen that the words came out sounding more like "Whereisthe?" but everyone knew to whom she referred.

"Not to worry," Annie assured her, "The last I saw Martha, she was napping peacefully in my truck in the county parking lot." Although it occurred to her that Martha may well have awakened by now and might be wondering where she, and Lavender, were.

"Tony, can you ask Esther to check on her?" she asked anxiously. With that, Annie raced off to make sure Sasha was all right in Tony's vehicle. She was. She'd even managed to control her bladder until her mistress took her for a walk. The interior of the patrol car would not have to be scrubbed and fumigated by the jail inmates whose job it was to keep the county vehicles clean.

The six deputies Tony had conscripted were ably

doing their jobs. One had already escorted Ron Carr out of the building and into his waiting vehicle for a free ride to the county jail. The others had quickly sealed off the unit and were photographing and bagging the stockpile of drugs Ron had amassed there. Annie had only taken a quick look at the contents in her haste to get to Lavender, but now that her sister was untied, wrapped in a blanket, and huddling in Annie's arms, she was able to see the extent of the real estate agent's second job. Even Tony had seemed impressed.

"I'll bet you that's the biggest haul Suwana County's ever seen," he muttered to Annie on his way to the main office to inform the proprietor, whom he'd hoped had surfaced by now, that his storage unit would be off-limits for the next several hours.

"What's in here?" she whispered back. To Annie, all white powder looked like confectioners' sugar.

"Crystal meth. Cocaine. Ecstasy. It's a treasure trove of illegal substances," he replied. "Probably enough to supply drug users from here to Olympia."

Lavender was anxious to reassure Martha that she was all right. But Annie, as well as Tony, insisted that she first be taken to the county hospital for an evaluation. No one had asked Lavender what Ron had done to her, and she hadn't volunteered any information, but it was clear that Ron had caused her bodily harm. Annie wondered what kind of mental damage he'd also inflicted. It appeared that Lavender had been held captive for hours.

Kim appeared just as the ambulance to take Lavender to the hospital had arrived. She'd come with the signed subpoena from Judge Casper to search the unit. Technically, it was no longer needed, since the unit obviously had been used in the commission of a crime, but Kim shrugged and delivered it to the main office on the basis that it couldn't hurt. She then climbed into the back of the ambulance with Lavender, who was on a stretcher.

"There's only room for one of us," she said, anticipating Annie's request. "Besides, someone should go back and be with Martha. She's been given the no-frills version of what's happened, but she's still pretty upset. I'll give you a call from the hospital and let you know how things progress there."

Annie didn't bother to argue. Kim was right—Martha did need to hear what portion of the story she could tell, and firm reassurances that her young friend was going to be fine. Besides, Annie knew that Kim would want to interview Lavender privately, and she'd be locked out of the examination room in any case.

"Tell her I *thried* to call," Lavender croaked from her stretcher. Annie nearly burst into tears just hearing her say it.

After conferring with Tony and learning that he and the others would be taking inventory and cataloging evidence long into the afternoon, Annie drove back to the Sheriff's Office. She decided to bring Sasha with her into the county building on the premise that doggy comfort would again be a good thing right now. Anyway, if Sasha was going to be Travis's companion dog, she needed hours of experience being in public buildings amid large groups of people. Sasha was happy to accompany Annie as she walked the corridor down to Esther's office, where Martha was now ensconced, and politely sat whenever a county employee passing by wanted to pet her. Privately, Annie thought the Belgian was beginning to enjoy the nonstop flow of compliments from strangers as much as she did doggy treats.

She found Martha and Esther drinking tea and talking quietly in the small room.

Annie tapped on the glass window on top of the door.

"May I interrupt?"

"Annie!" Martha stood up suddenly and swayed a bit. After using her hand against the wall to regain her balance, she gave Annie a hug. It was surprisingly powerful for such a small woman.

Annie looked at her critically to see if she was all right, but Martha waved her away.

"I'm just a bit sleep deprived, that's all. How's Lavender? Sit down, dear, and tell us everything you know. Would Sasha like one of these Girl Scout cookies?"

Sasha would and did and would have loved many more, but Annie insisted Martha stop at one. She told the women what had happened after she'd left Martha resting in her truck. She omitted the tirade she'd delivered to Dan and her wild dash out of the evidence room; Annie figured Esther probably had heard and seen everything, anyway. And she saw no reason to tell them about snatching the key from Tony's hand. She had merely assisted Tony in his search for Ron Carr's unit, she said, and Tony didn't seem entirely ungrateful, especially after she'd heard the sound of activity within one of them. Esther hid a smile.

Annie also glossed over the scene that she'd encountered when the deputies rushed into the storage unit. She said only that Lavender was seated in a chair with her hands tied behind her, but once freed was able to talk, walk, and seemed perfectly normal, under the circumstances. She was now being checked out at the hospital, but Annie was certain that she would be able to go home later today. She hoped she was right.

Martha was shaking her head by the end of Annie's whitewashed story, but not because she thought Annie had omitted any important details.

"I just can't believe Ron Carr turned into a drug dealer," she said in astonishment. "I knew his mother and father. They were friends of ours. Good, upstanding people."

"I remember Ron Junior as Port Chester's star football quarterback," Esther added, a touch of sadness in her voice. "His father started that real estate business and made a real go of it. I don't understand why Ron Senior's son would decide to embark upon a criminal career, either."

Annie recalled that before becoming Suwana County's primary 911 operator, Esther had been a first-grade school teacher and knew the childhood successes and foibles of most of the county's leading citizens.

"Perhaps he was having a midlife crisis." Martha's tone was thoughtful. "Do you know anything about his marriage, Annie?"

"I don't," Annie replied. "But I do know he was having a midlife financial crisis."

Martha tsk-tsked. "That's no excuse," she said firmly. "Besides, Eloise and her husband were very successful when they had the real estate business. Surely Ron could have asked his parents for help if his finances were in trouble."

But he didn't, thought Annie. Or, if he did, he didn't get the answer he wanted. And now, with luck, they were going to find out exactly how he killed his mother, then his girlfriend, and finally her ex-boyfriend. The question of why he'd taken this path had been asked and answered: first, for money, and then to keep a dirty secret.

Martha was right. It was no excuse.

"Where's Dan?" Annie asked.

Esther informed her that Dan was meeting with the prosecutor, Judy Evans, and then was heading out to the storage unit to check Tony's progress. He planned to talk to Trey, in an hour or so. Unbeknownst to either

Trey or his father, Ron Carr's home would be searched this afternoon. Judge Casper had signed the warrant without bothering to read the fine print.

Suwana County's deputies were being stretched thin today, Annie thought, but then, most of the recent crime in the past month had been committed by just two individuals—Ron Carr and Pete Corbett. With Pete dead and Ron in bright orange jail garb, chances were good that nothing more than a squabble at the local tavern or a missing bicycle would require law enforcement's attention.

Lavender was discharged at four o'clock that afternoon. Since every single Suwana County deputy seemed to be out on missions ordered by Dan, there wasn't much for Annie to do but hang out with Martha and Esther, who gleefully started a game of Scrabble. Esther had unearthed the game from one of the cupboards, although it was missing two Es and one S.

"And I know who took them," she said darkly. "We used to have a deputy who played in the lunch room every day. He was the sorest loser I've ever seen. He probably took all three letters when he retired."

Annie was dragged into the game and proved an unworthy opponent next to the likes of two women whose combined age was almost four times her own. When her cell phone finally rang and Kim told her that Lavender was ready to go home, Annie was immensely relieved—first and foremost for her sister, of course, but also because she wouldn't have to play another humiliating word that netted paltry points.

"How is she?" Annie asked.

"Surprisingly well, considering what she's been

through," Kim told her. "No serious injuries, and in case you're wondering, no signs of sexual assault, which Lavender confirmed. There's nothing wrong with her that time and rest won't heal."

"Thank goodness for that. Did she tell you anything to help the case?"

"She gave us a lot. In fact, I think Lavender gave me the most candid account she's provided in the last week. Ron was to the breaking point when he picked her up—or, I should say, kidnapped her, because that's what he's going to be charged with, among other things. He told her a lot more than he probably expected would ever be repeated in court. He'd planned to hang her, of course, once he'd made sure she'd told him everything she knew about his business. He'd already put the noose around her neck just to scare her into talking."

Annie digested this unpleasant piece of information for a moment, then asked Kim, "Did she? Know much about his drug business, I mean?"

"She was surprisingly innocent of most of the facts. Ashley had told her about Pete's drug usage, but until last night she still thought Ron Carr was just a sweet guy who loved his mother."

Annie was almost sorry she'd asked.

Martha sprang up when Annie told her Lavender was waiting for them at the Port Chester hospital and willingly conceded the game to Esther.

"We should do this more often," she told the operator. "I haven't enjoyed a good game of Scrabble since Fred died. It's been too long. Besides, we've got to keep those brain cells active. That's what I read every time I pick up an AARP magazine."

"I'm all for it," said Esther.

Annie planned on being busy when the invitation came.

At nine o'clock that night, Annie admitted a weary sheriff into her home. Dan had called her a few minutes before, asking if he could stop by. She wondered if he felt guilty about giving Ron Carr information about Lavender that ultimately led to her kidnapping and narrowly averted death by hanging. Or if he now regretted being so slow on the uptake with the information Sasha had literally wrung out of Ashley's toy lamb, which identified Ron as her new lover and the location of his drug stash. Whatever his reason, Annie was feeling rather benevolent at the moment. Her sister was safe, the worst of all the bad guys was in jail, and most important, she was sure that the killings—both animal and human— had stopped.

When she brought down the bottle of Glenlivet from its usual high space, Dan waved it aside.

"Too tired, Annie. If I have a drop, I'll have to sleep on your couch."

Annie hastily replaced it and put on the kettle for tea instead. When they both had mugs in their hands, she thought of the right way to ask her question.

"How far along are you in wrapping up the cases?" This seemed open-ended enough, she thought, and not at all accusatory.

Dan yawned, and Annie looked away. An inside look at the sheriff's molars was not a particularly pretty sight.

"We're getting there," he began, taking a big slurp of tea. "It helps that we now know Ron's motivation for his killing spree. He never recovered from the real estate crash of 2008—just too heavily invested in too many properties to ever see daylight again. Meanwhile, his mother's health was failing, and he needed to find in-home care. Fortunately, Mom had enough money to pay for it, so that wasn't a problem. And for the record, from here on out, I'm merely guessing. But I think the inventory from the searches we performed today will bear me out."

Annie got up and, after searching, found a box of semi-stale oatmeal cookies. She put them on the kitchen table. Dan tended to talk more when dessert was readily accessible.

"Ron probably went to his mother to ask for a bailout. For whatever reason, she wasn't in the mood to help. I've talked with her broker and learned that, while she may have been a bedridden old lady, she still had all her marbles. She talked to her broker several times a week, and he said she often gave him stock suggestions that paid out better than his own. So we have to assume that if Ron asked for a handout, Eloise said no."

"If she did, I'll bet she'd helped him out before and was just tired of bailing him out."

"Probably so. Anyway, by then, Ashley was on the scene, and somehow Ron learned that she was upset over her boyfriend's drug use. We know this because Ron kept a coded log of his meetings with Pete. They start a few months after Ashley began working with Eloise. But Ron also was beginning to meet secretly with Ashley. In short, he was playing both of them. Pete was the perfect foil to run the drug business. I'm guessing Ron fronted the money and Pete and his friends would take all the risks, including manufacturing, procuring, and delivering them down the line. The guy you saw at the county dump was one of the prime distributors."

Dan yawned again, and Annie poured him more tea.

"And Ashley? How'd he play her?"

"Oh, that was purely for pleasure. Ashley probably was crying the blues over her boyfriend and Ron saw a way to, shall we say, comfort her. Only problem was that Ron's a married man. His family's been an established part of the Cape Disconsolate community for three generations, if not longer. He couldn't just up and divorce his wife to marry some chippy."

"I'm surprised that Ashley was with him. Not just because of the age difference. But the letter I found made it obvious that Ashley knew what he and Pete were up to. Why would she break up with one drug dealer just to hook up with another who was twice her age?"

"From what Kim gathered from Lavender, for a long time Ashley really didn't have a clue that her new paramour was involved with drugs or with Pete. She just knew that Pete was dealing and wanted to get as far away from him as possible, especially after she was popped for prescription pills."

"That always seemed incongruous with Ashley's character. What was up with that?"

"She told Lavender that Pete stuffed them in her purse as they were being pulled over on a traffic stop. Pete seemed impaired to the cop, blew a .10, and was arrested on a DUI. When Ashley pulled out her cell phone to get a ride home, the pills fell out in front of the arresting officer."

"Poor thing."

"Definitely. But, to make my point, we found a date on that letter your dog uncovered—May fourth."

"The day she came and talked to me at my ranch."

"And the day before she died. That implies that Ashley had only recently put together the pieces of the puzzle. According to Lavender, Ashley gave her the extra key to the storage unit the day they found Eloise Carr—

she didn't know Ron had made multiple copies. At that point, I think Ashley realized her new boyfriend was no better than the first. She either intended to turn everyone in or to blackmail Carr. We'll never know, although the fact that she told her girlfriends she planned on meeting up with him that night implies that blackmail was on her mind. We do know that she and Pete already feared Ron Carr. Otherwise, why would they have lived in the woods, hiding from the world?"

"Did his family have any idea what Carr was doing—extramaritally and otherwise?"

Dan shook his head. "Apparently Ron's whole family was in the dark, including Trey and his wife. They'll probably bankrupt the business just paying for Ron's defense."

"How about Pete? Can you prove that he killed him, too?"

"We're close. We found several fake IDs in Ron's home office, including one for Roger Woodstock." He took a deep breath. "I shot off my big mouth and told Ron that Pete was in custody. Then Ron bails him out using one of his aliases and kills the sorry son-of-a- . . ."

"Stop." Annie didn't want to hear it. But Dan was determined to continue.

"I killed Pete Corbett," he said simply. "I killed him as much as if I put a gun to his head and pulled the trigger."

Annie shook her head.

"Remember, the person Ron killed was killing innocent animals simply because the woman who broke up with him loved them. Somehow, I think that evens things out."

Dan gave a short laugh. "So Pete needed killing, is that it, Annie? Well, justice doesn't work that way, at least not the way our courts have set it up. But I'll tell you one thing. Ron Carr killed three innocent people, including the one who gave birth to him, and I'm going to make sure he pays for it."

Annie had no doubt the sheriff would follow through on his promise.

EPILOGUE

SUNDAY, JUNE 12

Jessica had agreed to join the board of Alex's Place, and Annie was delighted. When the vet insisted that the next board meeting be held at her large-animal clinic, Annie was a bit surprised but didn't question the request. She assumed that Jessica simply wanted the other board members to know the breadth of her diagnostic tools and medical facilities, and that was fine with her. They weren't on the scale of Running Track Farms, of course, but were still impressive.

On the appointed day, the mercurial weather patterns the Northwest was known for emerged in full force. After a glorious May, in which rainfall had been at an all-time low, June had begun with a steady drip, and on this particular Sunday the drip had turned into a downpour. Local residents with gardens and lawns were delighted; Annie was less so, but she knew to keep her rain ponchos within easy reaching distance year-round. As she turned out her herd into the pasture that morning, she noticed none of her horses seemed to mind the warm rain.

Marcus was flying in that morning by private jet. Annie had offered to pick him up, but he'd nixed the idea, saying the airport was so close to Jessica's clinic that it would be silly for her to make a special trip. So she'd had an entire morning to prepare for the meeting. To her annoyance, she spent far more time on her dress and makeup again than she did prepping for her report on future ranch horses. As she had suspected, Patricia Winters had gently disabused her of the idea that any were suitable as ranch projects, but Annie had located a dozen good candidates among local rescue shelters.

Driving over to Jessica's, she wondered if Dan had managed to take the morning off. In the three weeks since Ron Carr had been taken into custody, he had worked practically nonstop to wrap up the remaining unanswered questions in the case, starting with the death of Eloise Carr. The search of Ron's home had revealed a small pharmacy of psychoactive drugs and narcotics. Some had been prescribed; others had been obtained online. It wasn't difficult to match the drugs found in his mother's body with ones taken into inventory, and Dan was confident that link would ensure Ron's conviction at trial.

Placing Ron at the scenes of Ashley's and Pete's deaths proved more difficult, but not insurmountably so. Both victims had traces of phenobarbital in their system, another drug in Ron's possession, and the crime lab had just reported finding traces of Ron's DNA in the fibers used in both nooses. Ron's wife had supplied an alibi for him on the night and day of both murders, but Dan wasn't too concerned. He'd told Annie that the least believed witnesses in homicide trials generally were family members, and the scientific evidence would trump a wife's story any day.

As Dan had predicted, the Carr family was using all of its financial resources to marshal the best possible defense for their patriarch, but the funds from Eloise Carr's estate were excluded from that pool, at least for now—Judge Casper had seen to that.

"They can throw all the money they want at criminal defense attorneys," Dan scoffed. "The jury's still going to come to the right conclusion."

Ron Carr was unable to contribute any funds to his own defense. Tony had deciphered the coded book and concluded that while Ron had used his last ounce of credit to fund his new drug business, Pete had managed to keep most of the returns. Apparently, Ron's skills in drug dealing were even worse than his skills in the real estate business.

At the moment, Dan and Judy Evans were discussing whether to charge Ron with charges of aggravated murder, which could result in the death penalty. The cost of mounting the trial would be astronomical but, as Judy pointed out, the charges might convince Ron's legal team to try to bargain for life imprisonment, instead. Dan was betting on it.

Annie wasn't much interested in the outcome of the case. It didn't change her day-to-day life, and all she was concerned about at the moment was making sure that Lavender was recovering from the trauma of that night. Surprisingly, for someone whom Annie had always considered the ultimate drama queen, her sister had been remarkably understated about her adventure. Annie knew from experience what it was like to survive a near-death experience, so she understood, in part, why Lavender might wish to put the memory behind her rather than continue to relive it in all its sordid detail.

She couldn't imagine a better place for Lavender to be right now than under the watchful eye of Martha Sanderson.

"I know how you feel about Lavender pulling her weight, dear, but we've decided it's best for her to take a short break from her employment," Martha had told her the day after Lavender returned home. Annie had agreed with this decision. True, she'd jumped back into her horse training business the day after the attempt on her life, but then, she was tougher than most people. Lavender deserved a break.

And she deserved an apology. As soon as Lavender's bruising had subsided and her larynx was no longer sore, Annie invited her out to dinner at the fanciest vegetarian restaurant in Port Chester. Lavender had wanted Martha to come, too, but her friend had insisted on letting the two sisters have their time alone. Privately, Annie wondered if Martha didn't secretly relish the idea of eating a big steak in her sister's absence. Probably not. However, Annie had consumed a double hamburger for lunch just to make sure her protein level wouldn't plummet after a vegetarian meal.

Saying she was sorry never came easy to Annie, but that night she simply spoke from her heart.

"I didn't realize how important you were to me until I thought I'd lost you," she told Lavender. "I know I haven't always been kind to you, or given your needs a lot of thought in the past. I just want you to know that I'll try to do better in the future."

"I've always known you've loved me, sister," was Lavender's placid reply. "Even when you were the most mad at me."

"Really? How?"

"Well, you're always so annoyed with me. If you didn't

care about me, you wouldn't be annoyed. So I figured that you really must like me a lot."

Annie decided not to comment on this. She nodded thoughtfully at her sister as she passed her the hummus.

Annie pulled into Jessica's clinic promptly at 1:45, just as the rain stopped, and saw that the rest of the board already had arrived. Inside, she saw everyone except Marcus sitting around Jessica's conference table. Travis was holding forth. He stopped talking long enough to welcome Sasha to his side, and invited Annie to sit down.

"I was just telling the others about my well-meaning family, whose efforts to run my life are not succeeding," he said.

"Delighted to hear it," Annie said, pulling up a chair. "Did you remind them that you're now the chair of a very important board, and don't need any help?"

"Well, I'm not entirely delusional about the state of my health, Annie," Travis replied. "But I think I still know how to best take care of my needs. They've been after me for years to sell my home and move into a retirement community. Every week, my daughter-in-law leaves brochures on my table extolling the virtues of senior living, and every week I toss them into the recycling bin. I think I've come up with a better idea."

"I'm sure you have. Do you want to share it?"

"I was just about to when you walked in. How about including living quarters for the organization's founder into our new ranch structure? I'd like nothing better than to have hands-on, day-to-day contact with what's going on, and this way I wouldn't have to worry about the commute, since the Department of Licensing doesn't think I should drive anymore. It would be on my dime, and I'd make sure the space would accommodate an old man like me—minimal stairs, walk-in bath, everything that everyone's so concerned about these days to make sure I don't fall and hurt myself."

"I think that's an excellent idea," Annie immediately responded. "Dan? Tony? What do you think?"

"I think it's great," Tony agreed.

"Makes sense to me," was Dan's contribution.

Travis displayed one of his rare broad smiles. "Well, then, we should get this show on the road and make it part of our official discussion. We are a quorum, you know."

"Where's Marcus?" Annie asked anxiously. "Did his jet come in on time?"

"Oh, yes," replied Jessica with a smile on her face. "It came in an hour ago."

"Well, then, where is he?" Annie demanded.

The sound of children's laughter came from somewhere at the back of the clinic, in the area of the outside paddocks.

"Are those children I hear?" she asked incredulously.

"It's the Bruscheau children," Dan explained. "Jessica invited them over to visit with Molly the mule."

"Lovely. How's Molly doing, by the way?"

"Why don't you see for yourself?"

The meeting's agenda was taking a strange turn, Annie thought, but she dutifully got up and walked outside with Jessica. The rest of the board followed in her wake.

To her astonishment, she saw Marcus sitting astride Molly and being led around by three giggling children. He was wearing jeans, a red flannel shirt, and—Annie was amazed to see—Western riding boots. He was desperately trying to look nonchalant in the saddle, she thought, although she noticed that his right hand was clutching the saddle horn. Marcus had always looked incredibly handsome in Armani suits, but now, in Annie's eyes, he looked even better.

"Hey, cowboy," she called over. "Is that your new girlfriend?"

"Not at all!" Marcus shouted back. "I'm just learning how to meet the one I really want halfway."

She didn't care about her pristine silk trousers and she forgot about her age. Without a second's thought, she flew up behind him in the saddle and kissed him.

Acknowledgments

Many thanks to Dr. Cary Hills of Sound Equine, Pegasus Training and Rehabilitation, James Wofford of Fox Covert Farm, Home Instead in Kala Point, ace attorney Ken Kagan, readers Ann Penn, Sandy Dengler, and many others, and horse trainer par excellence Megan Rukkila for reviewing my work and making sure it was accurate and true to life. Megan deserves a double billing, because she, along with Victoria Rose Carter and Gary Johnson, cheerfully took care of Jolie Jeune Femme in the dead of winter, all so that I could finish this mystery. What great friends you are. Many, many thanks to Fern Michaels for her gracious and ongoing support. Last, and as always, thank you, Alan, for being such a sweetheart as I trudged off to my writer's cabin to work all day for so many months. I don't know how you made food magically appear in our kitchen each evening, but please don't stop.

If you enjoyed SADDLE UP FOR MURDER be sure not
to miss Leigh Hearon's

REINING IN MURDER
A Carson Stables Mystery

When horse trainer Annie Carson rescues a beautiful
thoroughbred from a roadside rollover, she knows the
horse is lucky to be alive . . . unlike the driver. After
rehabilitating the injured animal at her Carson Stables
ranch, Annie delivers the horse to Hilda Colbert—the
thoroughbred's neurotic and controlling owner—only
to find she's been permanently put out to pasture.
Two deaths in three days is unheard of in the small
Olympic Peninsula county, and Annie decides to start
sniffing around. She's confident she can track down a
killer . . . but she may not know how ruthless this killer
really is . . .

Turn the page for a special look!

A Kensington mass-market and e-book on sale now.

CHAPTER 1

She awoke suddenly out of a troubled sleep. The silence within her small bedroom felt deafening.

From across the hall in the kitchen, the Seth Thomas clock bonged the quarter hour. Annie Carson looked up. It was 3:15, a time all smart horsewomen should be asleep.

The clock that marked each quarter hour in slow, sonorous tones was a comfort. The vibrate mode on her cell phone was nothing but an irritant.

"Hell's bells." Annie sighed and picked up the offending item. She glanced at the caller ID and swung her legs out of bed. She knew she was going to get dressed, and warmly, too.

"Top o' the morning to you, Annie," came the voice on the other end. "We've got a live one on Highway 3, Milepost 11. Near rollover with a horse trailer."

Annie cringed. "How's the horse, Dan?"

"Scared. But no broken bones or blood—I think. It's a

miracle, but he seems to have survived the crash. Can't say the same for the driver."

"I'll be there as soon as I can throw on some clothes."

"Appreciate that." Dan clicked off.

"And by the way," Annie said to the dead connection, "it's not the top o' the morning. It's the middle of the freakin' night."

Dan Stetson—aptly named, since his head was about as big as a ten-gallon hat—was the local sheriff in Suwana County. Annie was used to getting calls in the middle of the night from Dan, so it didn't take her long to pull on her work clothes, fire up her F-250 with the three-stall horse trailer attached, and gulp down a cup of reheated coffee while she waited for the rig to warm up. She nodded to Wolf, a mangy Blue Heeler who had thoughtfully placed himself in front of the kitchen door in case Annie forgot he existed. He trotted behind her into the frigid air and leapt, in a single graceful bound, onto the back of the truck and into his open crate.

It might have been late February, but on the Olympic Peninsula the thermometer still dropped into the twenties at night, so *layering,* the euphemistic word Northwesterners used to describe heaping on silk underwear, insulated jeans, and a trio of ratty old Scandinavian sweaters, was still the current fashion trend in the dead of night. Annie double-checked her brake lights on the trailer and glanced up at the gun rack behind her. There was her trusty Winchester .30-30, never used on a human—yet.

Annie eased out the clutch, turned on the defroster full blast, and drove slowly to her property gate. She gazed in her rearview mirror for a few brief seconds to imagine her small herd of horses asleep in their stalls. Only Trotter, the donkey, who usually had more sense than the rest of them, was jogging back and forth against the paddock line, plaintively braying his displeasure at her departure.

"Don't worry, you old jackass," she muttered. "I'll be back in time to feed you."

The metal farm gate, as usual, was gaping open at the top of her driveway, and Annie cursed herself for once more failing to secure her property before retiring. At forty-three, she wasn't quite as spry as she'd been at thirty, capable of running an ax murderer off the farm if she'd ever encountered one. But after a lifetime of scrimping and careful saving, she just couldn't convince herself to spend the money on an electric gate, which would have made life immeasurably easier and safer.

Milepost 11 on Highway 3 was only three miles away, but it took Annie a cautious five minutes to navigate it. Fog patches unexpectedly appeared before her, spreading a thick gray spell across the road. Just past Milepost 10, the eeriness vanished. The roadway ahead of her was lit up like the Fourth of July, the whirling strobes and headlights from half of the Sheriff's Office patrol squad staked out in a semicircle in the middle of the highway. Glints of steel shimmered off the berm on the north side of the road. Even with all the traffic, Annie saw in an instant what had occurred.

A long double line of heavy skid marks swerved to the ditch off the right side of the road. At the end sat a Chevy Silverado, its rear end ridiculously suspended in midair. The vehicle apparently had caromed off the road, hit the steel-post fence beyond the ditch, and bounced back to rest. Meanwhile, the horse rig, a gooseneck two-horse slant load, was twisting perilously to the left, held up by only one wheel.

In the center of the semicircle of black-and-whites, Annie noticed an ambulance from the local medical clinic, its back doors ominously gaping open, waiting to receive the body. Two EMTs peered into the Silverado on the driver's side, while another tried to wrench open the battered passenger door, which gave no signs of cooperating. No doubt they were figuring how best to extract the driver, Annie thought. Outside the action sat the prized fire truck from the volunteer unit in nearby Oyster Bay. The two local boys inside the cab looked transparently disappointed that their services would not be needed. Annie had encountered these boys before on similar calls, and unabashedly liked them for their willingness to come out in the dead of night to deal with misery and tragedy on the local highways and farms. She suspected they liked her, too, possibly for the same reasons. That, and the fact that Annie paid one of them handsomely twice a year to shear her sheep.

Annie brought her Ford and trailer to a crawl on the right shoulder of the road. Before she could turn off the engine, Dan Stetson was beside her window, gesturing her to crank it down. Dan looked distraught—not a good sign. He was also eager to talk.

"Don't know what exactly happened here, Annie," he said, slightly out of breath. "It's the damnedest thing. Truck suddenly swerves off to the right, jackknifes, and the trailer almost overturns. Neighbors back there"—Dan pointed somewhere in the distance—"hear the sound of the truck's crashing into their fence line and are on the phone pronto. We get out here, and there's a horse—who seems to be okay," Dan said in response to Annie's panic-stricken look. "I got to tell you, Annie, our in-transit time was one of our personal best, but nothing could have saved this guy. We found him slumped dead over his air bag, which we assume inflated as soon as he hit the Truebloods' fence posts." Dan pointed in the direction of the truck. "Didn't have a chance. Just glad we could save the nag."

Annie's eyes followed Dan's outstretched hand.

"Let me park my rig and join you," she said. Carefully noting where technicians had staked out the road, she eased her truck and trailer onto an unused portion of the shoulder.

She could sense, rather than see, Wolf's excitement from his vantage point in the truck bed.

"Okay, buddy. But don't go messing up any of the accident scene."

She unhooked the carrier, and Wolf obediently bounded out to join his mistress on the ground. They walked over to Dan, who now was scratching his considerable head.

"Interesting that the horse survived, but not the driver," Dan continued. He looked at Annie, as if he expected her to give the definitive answer. Instead, she just stared back at him. The fact was she hadn't the slightest idea why the accident had occurred, although she'd never give him the satisfaction of telling him so.

"Seat belt on?" was her only comment.

"Yup."

"What about the horse?"

"He's out of the trailer, and Tony's handling him, just there, beyond the fence line." Dan pointed again.

Annie inwardly sighed a breath of relief. If Deputy Tony Elizalde had control over the animal, all would be well. Tony had grown up with parents who worked at a local racetrack, and had it not been for a conscientious high-school counselor, chances are Tony would have entered the same trade—grooming, washing, and cleaning stalls. Instead, Tony went to college, took the test to become a deputy in the local county Sheriff's Office, passed with flying colors, and now was one of the steadiest members of the police team. He also knew horses front ways, sideways, and backward. If the horse that had tumbled on its side was now in Tony's care, Annie was content.

She glanced over to the left side of the road and saw Tony trying to calm a strikingly tall bay covered in sweat and skittishly dancing around him. Annie turned her mind to the more immediate problem.

"Who's the owner?"

"Who do you think, Annie?" Dan replied. "You're look-ing at $50,000 worth of horseflesh over there. Who in this godforsaken county can afford the care and feeding that nag requires?"

Annie's shoulders slumped. Who indeed. Hilda Colbert, that's who. Annie hated her. Well, to be honest, she didn't hate her; she just hated the way she treated her horses. Hilda was a relative newcomer to the area, a California transplant who had made millions in the software industry and now fully indulged her passion for raising and riding hunter jumpers and thoroughbreds. Although Annie wasn't sure it was a passion for horses or just a passion for control. She'd seen the way Hilda acted around her champion equines and it wasn't pretty. In fact, the only thing pretty around Hilda was the state-of-the-art riding complex she'd constructed in the val-ley. It truly was a thing of beauty. But inside were housed eighteen neurotic, overwrought horses that didn't know which command to follow any time Hilda was on one of their backs.

"I don't suppose you've called her," Annie said glumly.

Dan snorted. "Hell, no! I'm not waking up the queen. That's your job."

Annie sighed. "Who's the deceased? One of Hilda's under-paid minions?"

"Nope. A guy out of Wyoming. Professional hauler. Can't understand why he swerved, though. You'd think he'd know better than to try to clear a deer."

"So that's what you think?" Annie asked. "Just one of your typical caught-in-the-headlight accidents?"

"Won't know until the State Patrol gets here with the Total Station. But offhand, I can't think of any other reason. It's a straight stretch of road. Unless, of course, he had a heart attack or something."

Annie squinted through the blazing circle of lights and

silently agreed. There was no good reason for anyone to go off the road here. "Odor of intoxicants?" she asked.

"Nope. Unless you count the distinctive odor of Calvin Klein."

Annie laughed. "Maybe he had a hot date with Hilda."

"I hope not. I had to break the news to his wife just a few minutes ago. Doubt she would have been very happy to know hubby was on his way to a dalliance."

Annie realized that to outsiders her banter might have been off-putting, but after working with Dan on a dozen or more accident scenes involving horses, she had picked up the gallows humor so often adopted by law enforcement as a way to cope with sudden death. But Dan's remark brought her back to reality. A man had died, his wife was now a widow, and the valuable horse he'd been transporting needed comfort and a warm stable.

"Keep me posted, will you, Dan?"

"Will do." Just then, Dan's radio squawked, and she heard him revert to his professional parlance.

The thoroughbred was a magnificent creature—sixteen hands or more, Annie guessed, with classic bay markings. Annie walked over to Tony, who stood beside the shuddering horse, stroking its neck and whispering sweet nothings. At least the horse wasn't moving its feet anymore. Annie extended her hand to the bay's nose by way of introduction. The horse nuzzled back, licking the salt and dirt off her hand.

"Aren't you a handsome fellow?" she whispered to him.

"He sure is," said Deputy Elizalde. Tony clearly was in love. It would be hard not to fall in love with this horse; he had pedigree written all over him, and his elegance, despite his nervousness, permeated the air.

"Well, time to get him back in a trailer," Annie said. "This could be tricky." She reluctantly withdrew her now-very-clean hand and walked back to her truck, where Wolf jumped into the driver's seat as soon as Annie cracked the door.

"You're too young to drive," Annie told him, and Wolf agreeably relinquished his spot for the passenger side.

Horses like terra firma, and convincing them to step onto a springy surface that moves can be a hard sell. This thoroughbred, Annie realized, probably had been loaded into a trailer dozens of times and was used to the experience. Nonetheless, it had just survived a terrifying encounter and emerged from a twisted crate of steel that must now be perceived as a claustrophobic nightmare. Horses remember through their senses, particularly visually, and Annie was afraid just the sight of her trailer would turn this proud animal into a quivering beast with one thought: to bolt, rear, strike out, and do anything but get back into the box that an hour ago had threatened its survival.

Annie backed up her trailer fifty feet away from the fence line. She made sure there was hay in the feeder and added a couple of carrots for good measure. With one eye on the bay at all times, she quietly swung open the hinges that unlocked the back doors.

Deputy Elizalde slowly slid his hand up the lead line and started the walk over. Annie watched the bay skitter its way through the blinking lights of the patrol vehicles, its eyes white with fright. Tony was doing a good job, Annie noticed—he had his hand solidly on the lead rope but wasn't gripping it so tightly that the bay felt it had its head in a noose. In her sleep-deprived state, Annie lazily began to think that everything was actually going to go all right.

She was wrong.

Connect with

Visit us online at
KensingtonBooks.com
to read more from your favorite authors, see books
by series, view reading group guides, and more.

for sneak peeks, chances to win books and prize packs,
and to share your thoughts with other readers.

facebook.com/kensingtonpublishing
twitter.com/kensingtonbooks

Tell us what you think!

To share your thoughts, submit a review,
or sign up for our eNewsletters, please visit:
KensingtonBooks.com/TellUs.